DAGGERS OF DARKNESS

ASPEN SHERWOOD

ISBN: 978-1-7382714-2-9

ISBN: 978-1-7382714-3-6

Book Cover by MiblArt

Map by Cartographybird

aspensherwood.com

For my brother - I will always fight by your side, regardless of the odds.

LUNENSOR MOUNTAINS

THE
MUMBLING
FJORDS

NORTHHOLD ⊙

GRAYTHORN

FAIRGUARD ○

THE
BONE
PASS

⊙ EBONWELL

NEWTIDE ⊙

LEMNORA
FOREST

○ HAZELPEAK

COBALT
LOCH

○ DIRT TOWN

GOLDHELM

◉ CAPITAL CITY
⊙ MAJOR SETTLEMENTS
○ MINOR SETTLEMENTS
◈ KNOWN RUINS

THE ISLAND NATION OF

DRYSDEN

MAPPED

IN THE PRESENT AGE

THE AGATE SEA

ALSO BY ASPEN SHERWOOD

NIGHTMARES OF NIGHTFALL SERIES

ASPEN SHERWOOD

DAGGERS OF DARKNESS

CHAPTER
ONE
BRYN

S creams echoed around me—some rocks around us were taller than I was, bouncing the noises around the space until they blurred into one sound.

Skolli spiralled from the skies, their wings flared. The monstrous forms were almost completely hidden in the darkness, the moonlight casting harsh shadows on their descent.

We were careful not to travel in the dark, but we didn't have a choice, given a delay earlier in the trip and the tight deadline.

The caravan wagons banged together as they stopped, no doubt using the rocks as a natural defence from the Skolli. The merchants and their families ran around, corralling their horses and children to get them to safety.

I leapt from my saddle, already drawing a dagger.

"Get behind us!" I screamed as I spun to face a Skolli. The monster was just as terrifying as they always were, with powerful legs and long, strong arms that ended with viciously sharp talons. Its mouth was full of fangs, with a necklace of glass bobbles around its throat. Its immense wings were tipped with claws, and it stood over a foot taller than me.

The glass bobbles around his throat were empty, which meant one of two things: it had just started hunting for souls to harvest, or that wasn't the point of their attack. Either way, I wouldn't let the Skolli lay a single claw on the people of the caravan or their goods.

I pushed a woman from the caravan behind me with one hand while the other threw the dagger through the Skolli's eye. It crashed to the ground, its body skidding across the snow-covered road.

Two men from the caravan stood near me as their weapons shook in their hands. I raced towards them as thuds echoed around us—the Skolli had landed.

We were out of time.

I had seconds to determine whether to allow them to join the defence. They would be a weakness if they weren't up for the fight. I would be distracted trying to help them rather than focused on the battle.

And I had only a moment to make the call.

"Have you fought Skolli before?" I asked, my eyes darting around us, trying to track down the Skolli in the darkness. They would be on us in moments. I couldn't linger with them.

The younger one answered. "N-no."

They would be of no use in this fight. I had seen the state of their weapons as we travelled with their caravan. Specks of rust had lingered behind, the blades not entirely dull but not fully sharp either. No well-trained warrior would ever have blades that looked like that.

They would be dead in moments.

"I need you to light fires along the edges of the caravan. We can't fight what we can't see. Then, get to safety behind the wagons. Leave the rest to us," I said before I charged back towards where Óskar fought.

He was firing rapidly, keeping the Skolli at a distance. But he had missed one, no doubt not seeing it.

And now it was going to attack him from his blind spot.

I sprinted towards them, tearing across the remaining distance between us.

It swung down towards Óskar, but I leapt in between them, catching its claws with my crossed daggers and deflecting the blow to the side. I spun, my feet sliding on the packed snow. The Skolli knocked me aside with a giant wing. I landed roughly on the ground, my hip barking in pain. I grunted, getting my hands under me and pushing up from the ground, as a familiar burn started in my veins.

I welcomed the burn as it pooled in my legs, my body shifting as I stood. My feet burst through my boots as I grew a foot in height.

I launched myself at the monster, fuelled by the powerful Skolli legs I had shifted into, and sliced cleanly through its neck. Its black blood sprayed around us, the warm splatter on my skin causing unease to settle in the pit of my stomach.

"I need a better vantage point," Óskar panted from my side as he fired another shot.

"Go," I said, palming two daggers. "I'll hold here until you find a spot." My eyes scanned the monsters before me and picked out my next target.

There.

I spun one of the blades in my fist and punched it through the neck of my marked Skolli. It fell forward, taking my weapon with it, as it slumped to the ground. Dead.

I flipped my other dagger, firing it at the next monster. It stuck into the hilt in its throat.

I allowed the burning in my veins to spread to my hands and mouth. Claws curved out from my nail beds as my fangs pressed into my lips.

Who needed blades when you could shift your very body into a weapon? I could become stronger and faster. I could even the battlefield, even slightly, between me and the monsters before me.

I jumped atop the next Skolli, fuelled by my stronger legs, and ripped out its throat with my fangs before leaping to the next.

"Bryn!" Óskar called. I risked a look, turning back towards his voice to find him atop one of the caravan wagons. The sky was starting to lighten behind him.

A Skolli jostled me from the side, knocking me off balance while I was distracted. Before I even had the chance to regain my footing, Óskar had fired an arrow. It fell to the ground before me, but I paid it no mind as I climbed over its body and continued towards Óskar.

I worked my way back towards the caravan wagon. I didn't bother climbing to the top beside Óskar; I would be no help there. Instead, I placed my back to it and settled into a fighting crouch. Children were crying behind the wagon, the adults' comforting words almost completely drowned out by the sound of battle.

I would not allow a single Skolli to get past me to them.

I didn't think as I jumped from one Skolli to the next, never stopping longer than a few moments. Blood sprayed from my claws with every swipe as it dripped from my fangs. It painted the snow around us and covered my body. The warm feeling of blood on my skin was becoming familiar—I didn't know what concerned me more lately. Worrying about the fact that I might freeze again at the sight of blood, even though I hadn't for weeks, or that I would become used to being covered in it.

But I would gladly paint myself in it, the black blood of the Skolli or my own ruby red blood, if it meant someone else wouldn't have to. If it meant that I could shield people from the monsters that could not protect themselves.

Those monsters would not lay a single talon on the people behind the wagons.

"Bryn! Get up here!" Óskar called.

I didn't hesitate as I jumped up to join him.

"What's wrong?" I asked between breaths, my words slurred from my fangs. I spat to the side of us, trying to rid myself of the metallic tang of Skolli blood.

"Georg needs help." Óskar fired at another Skolli.

I turned, searching for him in the chaos. He was protecting the centre of the caravan, alone without a comrade by his side. The Skolli, as if sensing our weakness, had focused more of their attack on the centre of the line. Georg held them at bay due to his speed and strength bloodrites, but that would only work for so long.

Eventually, he would leave an opening, and the monsters wouldn't hesitate to capitalize on it. Regardless of how fast or strong he was, he still had blind spots. He could only sustain his bloodrites for so long before recovering. And the second that he showed that weakness, the second that he left his back open or his speed lagged, the Skolli would take advantage of it. No doubt wounding him or worse.

He needed support, and he needed it soon.

The warriors of the caravan weren't strong enough fighters to face the Skolli. Which only left the five of us. The Verndari.

"If I go, you'll be left open," I panted.

"With my arrows, I have a better chance of keeping them at a distance." Óskar shot again. "Go, he'll get overrun with just his axes."

I jumped off the caravan wagon directly onto the shoulders of a Skolli. I crouched down, using its head for balance, and punched my claws clean through its eye.

I kept my eyes averted as the warm blood splattered on my skin.

I freed my claws, pushed off the Skolli's body, and sprinted towards Georg.

My Skolli legs were faster and more powerful than my own, allowing me to cover the ground between us in just a few moments.

The sky continued to lighten, but still not enough to drive the remaining Skolli back to their dark hidey holes. They had to find places to hide that completely shaded them from the sun during the day, or they would die.

We just had to last long enough for the rising sun to become too threatening to them.

I attacked from outside the crowd of monsters around Georg, not wanting him to mistake me for an enemy within the masses.

The Skolli surged, trying to surround me as well.

I kept moving—the second I stopped moving, I was dead. I punched, swiped, kicked, and bit my way through the Skolli one by one trying to make my way towards Georg.

I could finally see the flash of his axe with only a few Skolli between us.

I took out three more of the monsters before one viciously backhanded me. My head snapped to the side, and I fell hard to the ground from the momentum. My mouth and cheek throbbed. Cursing, I rolled to the side as it stabbed down at me with the claws on the tips of its wings. An axe pierced the Skolli, forcing me to close my eyes as its blood painted my skin.

"It's dawn," Georg said. I blinked open my eyes to find his hand held down before me. I reached out, my body burning as it returned to normal, and allowed him to help me to my feet.

We stood within a ring of Skolli corpses.

Georg studied me for a moment. "You're covered in Skolli blood."

"I know," I grimaced, the motion pulling at the blood on my skin. "It feels like drying mud. Not to mention, I can taste it." I gestured to my mouth before spitting again. Regardless of how effective the fangs were in combat, I couldn't get used to the metallic taste of the blood.

And, honestly, I didn't think I should ever get used to it.

Georg wrinkled his nose. "I didn't need to know that." He surveyed the grounds around us with a sigh. "We'll need to devise a strategy for being down a man. We can't be leaving holes like we did tonight. That's how someone dies."

I nodded; my throat tight. Georg rested a hand on my shoulder.

"Come on, let's go check on the others," he suggested with a gentle squeeze. Georg pulled his arm back with a wince, his hand wrapping around his bicep.

"Are you hurt?" I asked, already reaching for him. After battle, there was always soreness—in your throat from yelling orders, in your muscles from using your weapons. But his wince didn't seem like soreness. It seemed like pain.

And pain came from injuries.

Blood dripped off the tips of Georg's fingers, my stomach churning at the sight.

I bit down on the anxiety building in my chest and gently pulled his hand from his arm.

"It's just a scratch," he said. I pushed up his sleeve, thankful to see that it wasn't anything worrisome.

"I still need to clean it, but it won't need any stitches," I said as Óskar joined us. I quickly scanned him for any injuries that needed my immediate attention. Nothing major. "Would you mind surveying the people from the caravan and sending anyone that needs healing to me?"

"Bryn!" Gil called as he wove his way through the caravan of people. Runa followed behind him, my saddlebags in her hands. He reached for me, barely hesitating, before his hand gently cupped my cheek. "Are you okay?" He tilted my head to the side to see where my cheek and lip were surely already swollen and bruised. More than likely bleeding under the layer of black Skolli blood that covered me.

I rested my hand atop his. "I'm fine. You're not hurt, are you?"

"It should just be bruises."

"Should be?" I gently squeezed his hand, trusting that he was not downplaying any severe injuries. "I'll check you out after I finish with everyone else. Are you able to help me?"

His vibrant green eyes softened. "Of course." He took my saddlebags from Rúna and helped me set up a makeshift healing station. Our movements well-oiled from plenty of practice as the Skolli attacks had increased. We flowed around each other, not just familiar with our task but aware of where the other was at all times.

I opened one of the jars and scooped some of the cream with my fingers. I covered Georg's cut with it, allowing it to bubble as it cleaned. When it was done, I wiped away any access cream before tightly wrapping a bandage around his arm. I checked him for any other injuries before moving on to Runa.

8

I cleaned out the cut across her eyebrow before wiping the dirt, sweat, and dried blood with a wet cloth that Gil passed me.

Luckily, no one had severe injuries. Two of the people from the caravan needed stitches, but no one was in any serious danger. It didn't take me long to heal everyone with Gil a silent companion by my side. It wasn't the first time he had assisted me in the field, and it was certainly not going to be his last. The attacks had only gotten worse in the past month. Gil had even taken to carrying some extras of my most important supplies in his saddlebags in case I ever ran out. I often saw him also packing a pair of boots for me when I inevitably tore through my own when I shifted. I packed my own extras, but sometimes it wasn't enough.

Once I had finally given Óskar a formal check, Gil silently nodded toward my tent that had been set up by some caravan members after the fight.

I followed him inside. He leaned across me, the heat of him warming my body, and tugged the flap closed.

"Where are you hurt?" I asked softly, not wanting to disturb the peaceful silence surrounding us as I was already reaching for the tin of bruise paste.

"My ribs." He unbuckled the armour covering his torso and set it to the side of the tent.

"Let me see," I said as my fingers tugged at the bottom of his shirt. He watched me for a moment before laying on his side, facing me and lifting his shirt to reveal his ribs.

I gasped. "Oh, Gil." It was hard to appreciate the muscled lines of his body with the dark bruise that had spread the entire length of his rib cage. I scooped some cream from the jar and rubbed it into his skin. Once I had covered his ribs, I gently pushed him onto his back to cover the bruise that had spread to his stomach. My fingers gently drifted across his skin—down his ribs, across his stomach, just above the waistband of his pants. I alternated circling my hands across his skin and gentle brush-strokes of my fingers as I ensured that the cream was rubbed in.

Gil groaned, his eyes falling closed as his hand fisted by his side.

"I'm sorry!" I froze my movements, my hand lingering on his skin just above his waistband. "Did I hurt you?"

He was silent for a moment. "No." He shifted beneath me. "It feels...fine."

"Then what—" His cheeks flamed, his eyes opening just long enough to glance down just below my hand.

I followed his line of sight and could see how much my hands on him like this affected him. "*Oh.*"

Oh.

My cheeks burned. When I healed people, I didn't focus on the other person's body like that—I had to concentrate on what I was doing.

Had I taken extra time and effort rubbing in the cream, enjoying the moment with Gil? Basking in the relief that we had both made it through yet another fight relatively unscathed?

Yes.

Had I expected his reaction?

No, but I really should have.

While we had continued to grow closer together during the month since my official appointment to the Verndari, we hadn't explored too much with each other yet.

I finished rubbing the bruise paste into his skin. Gil sat up and pulled his shirt down. His hands lingered at the hem for a moment before reaching for me. "Come here."

I scooted forward and let Gil drape my legs over his lap.

He wet a cloth with his waterskin and wiped my face clean. "What happened?" He moved on to my arms, carefully cleaning every last drop of Skolli blood from my skin. So that I didn't have to do it myself—so that I wasn't exposing myself to the risk of a trigger.

Protecting me.

"I got clipped by a wing," I said as I passed him the jar of bruise paste. "I got lucky."

The bruise paste was cool as his fingers, rough from hours spent holding his swords, rubbed it into my skin. "You are right, but it is hard to remember that when you are sitting here with a split lip and a bruise covering half of your face." He ran his thumb along my bottom lip.

"I'm okay," I whispered, resting my forehead against his as I gently kissed the pad of his thumb.

He swallowed. "I'm glad."

He kissed me, his lips hesitant against mine. Not wanting to hurt me. I pressed closer to him and wrapped my arms around his neck. He tangled his hand in my hair and kissed me harder.

"Verndari," Georg called. "This caravan will be leaving within the hour!"

Gil groaned, his head dropping down to the crook of my neck. I giggled softly, running my fingers through his hair. He mumbled unintelligibly against me momentarily before finally lifting his head from my shoulder. His eyes drifted down my body, his lips pressed into a thin line.

"You are covered in blood," he finally said.

"It's not mine."

"I could tell that much, considering it is black as night." Gil was quiet for a moment. "Pass me your armour. I will clean it while you change."

I pressed another gentle kiss to his lips. "Thank you."

"I will wait outside while you...undress."

"You don't have to go," I said quietly.

Gil gently lifted my legs from his lap and eased his way to the tent flap. "Yes, I do. For now."

CHAPTER

TWO

BRYN

With the barrier weakened, the attacks had only grown. In size and number.

We alerted every city, village, or town to prepare their defences every nightfall, regardless of how rudimentary they were.

But with the settlements on high alert, the Skolli and the exiled commanding family that controlled them decided to attack the more vulnerable. The caravans and merchants had become the favoured target. We couldn't protect all the travellers on the roads, and the shipments couldn't stop.

They were easy prey.

There hadn't been many reports of the Ógn, but those monsters could hide much easier. The shapeshifters could take on any persona to hide their true form, making it incredibly difficult to track them. The only leads we had were reports of nightmares. Still, with the increase in attacks, it was hard to sort out what were nightmares and what were memories being relived in people's subconscious.

Needing all the alliances we could get, Ragna advised that

we shouldn't participate in the limited protection afforded to the caravans. However, this shipment of metal and weaponry from the north was too valuable to warrant anything other than the Verndari's protection.

So we rode out to meet them, guiding them during the day and guarding them through the night.

We had been less than a day's ride from the fortress when we were attacked.

It was lucky that no one was seriously hurt and that the caravan's merchandise wasn't damaged.

Pétur's absence didn't just hurt us because he betrayed us —it continued to hurt us every time we had to fight. Since I had awakened my bloodrite and joined the Verndari, our plans and tactics revolved around a team of six. We tried using the strategies from before I was found, but those didn't work when we had to face an actual Skolli. Our best chance at surviving a fight was fighting the monsters in pairs.

And right now, we were only a group of five.

Someone was always the odd one out.

Someone was always at more risk of injury, if not death.

So far, we had been lucky. We had been battered, bruised, cut, and stitched back up. But no one had died due to our gaps in strategy.

But our luck was bound to run out.

The sun was just threatening to sink behind the horizon as we guided the caravan safely through the walls of the fortress. The gate shut behind us, a solid wooden bar sliding into place to secure it further. Warriors were tightening the last pieces of their armour at the base of the walls. They nodded in greeting as they went about their final tasks before the sun set—filling waterskins, sharpening their weapons, and checking their armour.

Someone rang the bell by the gate three times to alert the fortress of our arrival as the stable hands came out to take charge of our horses. Some of the fortress staff guided the drivers of the caravan wagons to where they would park, while others led the rest inside.

Baldur appeared next as he always did. He was always the last person to see Rúna off and the first one to welcome her back. To the people who lived in the fortress, it had to seem like the acts of a man in love.

But we knew better.

He was watching her, controlling her for as long as he possibly could.

Rúna dismounted her horse, her shoulders rolled back as she turned to face him. I dismounted my horse, unable to watch the display I knew Baldur would put on as he welcomed her home. To everyone else, it surely seemed as though the Commanding Son was overjoyed to see his partner's safe return, but to us, it was nothing more than a reminder of the role that Rúna played for us.

"Well?" Baldur hissed, the pleasant smile on his face completely contrasting with the tone he used. A mask to disguise his intentions.

"Well, what?" Rúna snarked as she grabbed her saddlebags.

Baldur's hand whipped out, gripping her wrist with white knuckles. "Is that how you should speak to the Commanding Son?" he threatened, his voice no louder than a rasp. Gil tensed by my side. I intertwined my fingers with his and gave him a soft squeeze.

We couldn't jump in. Not unless Rúna asked us to.

"My apologies, Commanding Son," Rúna said with a false

smile. "Thank you for being here to welcome the Verndari and me home."

Georg rolled his eyes from where he stood beside Óskar and tilted his head towards the fortress.

"I will always be here to welcome you home, Rúna," Baldur said, brushing her blonde hair behind her ear.

I stepped forward, taking Rúna's saddlebags from her. Baldur didn't bother to acknowledge me.

Gil and I followed Georg and Óskar towards our wing.

"Come, have dinner with me and tell me of your travels," Baldur suggested from behind us. Gil hesitated momentarily before walking by my side more stiffly than before.

"We'll check in on her later," I whispered to him. "She has to be close to him. Otherwise, her whole plan to discover if he is the traitor won't work. Then everything she is going through will all be for nothing."

We knew that Pétur had been the traitor within the Verndari—he had left a month ago to join the exiled commanding family at their fortress behind the barrier in the mountains. But a traitor remained within the Commanding Family, and all our money was on Baldur.

Rúna was the only one close enough to him to find proof before he lowered the barrier completely. He had something on her, blackmailing her to ensure that she was in a relationship with him. She had been determined to turn the situation into an opportunity to help us. As painful as it was to watch her go through it, Rúna was our best option to find proof of his actions.

Gil swore under his breath. "I know, but it is hard to have her around him when we know how he treats her."

"When this is all over, we'll make sure that Rúna makes

him pay for every second of pain that he has caused her," I promised. "Every second."

THREE

BRYN

Georg cancelled training the next morning.

Even though none of us had been seriously hurt, with the way my bruises were smarting, I knew that it would have been miserable.

I let myself sleep longer than I was usually able to, waking once the sun had already risen in the sky. My eyes were still heavy, but I was less tired than I had been.

Sleeping on the road was never restful. Sleeping on the road while you are actively anticipating an attack? That was even less so.

With Pétur gone, the watches at night were much longer, which didn't help.

With Pétur gone, a lot of things became harder.

I rose from my bunk with a sigh. The floorboards made my toes curl, my body desperately wishing to return to the warmth of the furs on my bunk.

I dressed for the day, throwing a cloak over my shoulders to ward off the winter chill that seemed to have sunk into the walls of the fortress.

The common rooms were empty, only glowing coals left behind to show that someone had used the rooms at all that morning. Gil and Óskar had decided to spend their days with their sisters, and Georg was most likely holed up in his office getting caught up on the tasks he couldn't do while we were on the road. Rúna was inevitably by Baldur's side, wherever that was, leaving me alone to grab a muffin from the breakfast table.

As far as I knew, Fannar was not currently on an assignment and was surely wrapping up his training with the Royal Regiment for the day.

I grabbed an extra muffin for him and entered the main part of the fortress.

If I thought the stares and whispers were bad when competing for my role as Verndari, they were nothing compared to the stares we all have now. Emilía still got looks, too, I had seen them, but they were nowhere near as prevalent as ours were. She seemed to thrive under the attention anyway; I only wanted to avoid it.

I supposed it made sense. Emilía had tried to take my position as a Verndari and the power that came with it while I had simply wanted to do my duty. She had competed for power and status. I had competed to honour a promise to my father and do what I thought was right.

The driving force of our competition was starkly different; it made sense that our reactions to the attention were also different.

I kept my shoulders back and my head high as I strode through the fortress. My overdress and cloak billowed around me as I walked.

A man spat at my feet as I passed. I allowed my bloodrite to flow to my mouth, the burning only lasting for a moment. When I smiled at him, it was full of fangs.

The action made my bruised face shriek in pain, but it was worth it to see the man's reaction.

The man flinched. "I didn't see you there, Jarl Brynja. My apologies."

"I'm sure you didn't," I said, my mouth burning again as it returned to normal. "I accept your apology."

It was hard to remember at times that I may have to lead these people in battle, that they might fight beside me. Bleed beside me. Die beside me.

But they were scared and needed someone to blame. And some of them had determined that it was our fault that the Skolli had returned.

Well, some of them were scared. Others were biding their time. Undoubtedly, some people in the fortress would not be by my side should we be on a battlefield together. No, some of them would be across from me, doing their best to kill me.

Some saw me as an enemy they knew they had to face, while for others, I was the villain they could blame for what was happening. I understood that—I expected that.

But it didn't make the hate, the fact we got *spat at,* any easier to bear.

It was hard to tell the difference between someone who blamed you and someone who hated you, so each time I fell victim to the looks, the anxiety in me grew. Who was blaming me for someone's death, and who was wishing for my own?

Sometimes, I couldn't tell which was which.

A little girl, no older than six or seven, ran up to me with a single flower. She hurried away just as quickly once I had taken it without speaking.

"Thank you!" I called after her.

She spun back towards me. Her face was red, but her eyes were sparkling. I smiled back at her just before she ran out of sight down the hallway.

And those interactions were almost worse than the ones that blamed me. Because if I failed, all I would see were the people who thought we were their last hope.

As I turned the corner, Fannar was laughing with Lúdvík, the sergeant of his line.

"Bryn!" he called out, grinning. "You're back!"

I threw my arms around his shoulders, laughing as he spun us in a circle.

He placed me back on the ground, his eyes briefly scanning me. His eyes landed on my cheek; on the bruise I knew spanned halfway across my face. "Run into some trouble?"

"Nothing we couldn't handle," I said. Fannar crossed his arms. "I was clipped by a wing. It's just a bad bruise."

"And the others? They're alright as well?" Lúdvík asked. The Verndari and the Royal Regiment had had to work closely in the weeks since Pétur left and weakened the barrier, allowing more monsters to flood the land. Of course, we were closer with some lines than others, but we were closest with Fannar's line.

I nodded. "Bumps and bruises, nothing serious."

"Good. I'm glad to hear it." He clapped Fannar on the shoulder. "I promised the wife I would have lunch with her before the sergeants' meeting. If I don't go now, she'll have my head."

I laughed, waving goodbye to him before looping my arm around Fannar's. "I have the morning off and was wondering if you wanted to visit Ma with me."

"I have a couple of hours before I'm needed anywhere."

I held out the extra muffin I had taken from the breakfast table. "I brought food."

"Well, you know I never say no to food." Fannar ate half of the muffin in a single bite as we set off toward Ma's rooms. "Another one?" he asked, nodding towards the flower I carried.

"Yeah," I said. "She was younger than the last one."

"We'll do everything that we can. That's all we can do."

I sighed. "I'll give everything that I have to give."

Fannar said nothing, but I knew he was thinking the same thing.

Ma was walking around the rooms, her eyes bright and aware. She still hadn't spoken, and I don't know if she ever would again, but she was fully present.

And that was a big enough gift on its own.

"I'm back, Ma," I said. "No serious injuries to report."

She gently cupped my cheek briefly before moving to the teapot.

"Bryn's got another flower for you. Where would you like it?" Fannar asked.

He had been the one to suggest that I give Ma the flowers that people had taken to giving me. I didn't want to keep them in my rooms, to have the reminder of their desperate hopes for us so close. But I didn't want to throw them away either. That felt even worse as if I were throwing away their hopes and well wishes. It felt too close to tempting the gods when I knew I would face the monsters again sooner rather than later.

Whether Ma knew what the flowers meant or not, I didn't know. But she loved having them throughout her rooms. The flowers have brought more life to her rooms and more colour to her life. With Fannar and I becoming increasingly occupied with our duties, it was a relief that she had something to brighten her days.

I had even seen Gil and Óskar sneaking her flowers whenever they visited with me.

Fannar tucked the flower into one of the vases before making himself comfortable in a chair. I laid back across the bench, a pillow tucked under my head.

Ma placed a tray full of tea on the table in front of us, taking her own tankard and setting it down on the little table beside her favourite chair. She took a sip before draping a blanket over her legs and focusing on us.

"Gil and Óskar both wanted to say hi but had commitments with their families today," I said.

Ma brushed away my words with her remaining hand, a small smile on her face.

"Training is going well," Fannar jumped in. "All the weapons I pick up come easily, but the war axe is still my favourite."

"Why?" It had always surprised me that Fannar seemed to lean towards the war axe. I had never pictured him with the large weapon when he started training with the Royal Regiment.

"You're going to say that I'm crazy."

I grinned. "Does that sound like something I would do?"

"Yes. Yes, it does," Fannar deadpanned. But his eyes lit up with excitement as he kept going. "There's just something about it. I barely notice its weight when I'm fighting with the war axe. It's like it's an extension of my arm. It's almost like it's singing in my hand when I fight with it."

He had taken to training and fighting with an ease that I was almost envious of. I took to the endurance well, my stamina built up by years of running daily with my dad. But it had been a battle to gain expertise with my daggers and even more effort to gain control of my bloodrite.

But I hadn't realized that the war axe had come that easily to him. Almost effortlessly. Something so right that he compared it to music.

"That's a rather poetic way to describe a weapon," I teased.

Fannar rolled his eyes. "I've only used it on Skolli, so it's more of a defence mechanism. It's not like I'm on one of the raiding ships launching attacks on the neighbouring islands."

"Oh, I'm sure," I agreed with a snort. "Is that how you would describe my shifting too? Defence?"

"No. That's simply your inner self revealing itself to the world."

I threw the pillow at Fannar's face, his laughter ringing through the room. My giggles joined him as he easily caught the pillow and aimed it back at me.

Ma shook her head with a small smile, her body relaxing into her chair. With her room filled with flowers, her basket of sewing on the ground by her chair, and a tankard of tea in her hand, Ma was the picture of serenity. A calmness had settled over her since she had begun interacting with the world again, no longer a shell of herself like when Da had died.

When I visited her, whether alone or with Gil, Fannar or someone else, I could almost feel myself melting into the bench. My muscles released the stress I had been carrying, and my mind slowed and focused on the moment.

A little bit of peace in the chaos.

CHAPTER
FOUR
BRYN

My cheek and eye had taken on a lovely green hue when I woke the next morning. I winced at the sight, already reaching for the bruise paste. If it looked this bad with me reapplying it multiple times, I could only imagine how it would have looked without it.

I rubbed the cream on gently, the bruise smarting at my touch. I pulled on my typical training clothes before heading towards the common rooms. Georg would have given us more time off after a fight to allow our bodies to heal before Pétur left. Or to mostly heal at the very least.

Before we were short a man, leaving us vulnerable in a fight.

Before we were being sent out to fight the Skolli more than ever before.

Before we spent more time bruised than fully healed.

We had learned to fight through soreness and how to train through pain. We had no other choice. Not if we hoped to ensure we all made it out of our next tangle with the Skolli alive. And with the barrier as low as it could be and the monsters not worrying about the need to stay hidden, it was not a question of whether we would face the Skolli again, but *when*. And the odds were that it was much more likely to happen sooner than later.

A welcoming fire was crackling in the fireplace of the common rooms, the dining table already laid with various foods for breakfast, the fortress staff well aware of our routine.

Rúna was the only one at the table, her golden hair neatly pulled back in a horsetail and dressed very similarly to me. It was a rare morning when both of us beat the guys to the table —we valued our sleep more than the average person, more likely to bite someone than smile at them if they woke us up too early.

Especially when we had recently returned from being in the field where we were constantly on edge, expecting an attack.

Rúna reached for the fruit bowl with a barely concealed wince as I joined her at the table.

"Are you alright?" I asked her. "Did he—?" I left the question open. I wouldn't put Rúna at risk by openly asking if Baldur had hurt her. Even in our wing, there was a chance that we could be overheard, and we couldn't risk it, especially now.

Everyone had seen their sparring match in the Crepuscule Tournament last year when he had beaten her so brutally with his staff that she had to be carried out of the ring. That alone should have shown what type of person he was, but in Drysden, where military prowess meant more than anything else, many people overlooked it. Baldur's actions are seen as a display of power rather than cruelty.

As far as everyone knew, it was a one-time thing, and I wasn't about to put Rúna at risk by starting those kinds of rumours. Especially when we still didn't know what he had on her. Whatever it was, was important enough to her that she was putting up with his treatment before she even knew of the possibility of the traitor. And anything that meant that much to her meant that much to the rest of us.

I hadn't seen him hurt her since he beat her needlessly during their sparring match at the Crepuscule. But just because I hadn't seen it didn't mean it didn't happen. I knew he was not gentle with her, but I didn't know if it was worse. If there were bruises beneath her clothes, or long since healed by Hákon, that we couldn't see.

She gave me a sad smile, dark circles under her brown eyes before her gaze slid to the table. "He was a little *enthusiastic*," her lips twisted on the word, "when I arrived back in the fortress. I just returned to my own rooms early this morning."

"Rúna," I breathed, my chest tightening. The fact that she was going through this because we had no better choice, because the Commanding Son had something on her, weighed like a weight in my stomach. "Did he—?"

"No," she scoffed before taking a bite of her food. "I didn't say no. It's just—" She paused, shrugging her shoulders. "I didn't, I *couldn't* risk anything, so I just went along with it."

I swallowed thickly, reaching for my own food. The thought of eating after what Rúna revealed made me nauseous, but I wouldn't make it through the training session if I didn't eat. I forced a forkful of food into my mouth. "Does Gil know?" I asked quietly.

"No. None of the others do. And I don't want them to know, not until it's over," Rúna stumbled over her words, her vulnerability lacing every one. The fact that she opened up to me about what she was going through meant that she trusted me or needed someone to talk to. Or both. And I wasn't going to betray her confidence.

"Then they won't know. They will not learn it from me." I reached for her, giving her hand a squeeze. "And I am here for whatever you need. Anything, Rúna."

Rúna just smiled at me as Gil and Georg finally joined us. Gil sat beside me, briefly checking that Rúna and I had some food in front of us before filling his own plate. Georg sat beside Rúna, ruffling her hair gently, before plating his breakfast.

"Anything?" Gil asked, his focus fixed on Rúna.

Any hint that Baldur was the traitor among the Commanding Family?

Any hint that Baldur was working with Pétur to dismantle the barrier that barely separated us from the exiled royal family and their monsters?

Anything that would give him the ability to protect her from Baldur?

"Nothing," Rúna said, her words resigned. "Nothing at all."

The conversation shifted to lighter topics, especially once Óskar entered with Yugar, his dog, by his side. Yugar immediately started his typical routine of begging for any food he could possibly get. His black fur shone in the sunlight that streamed through the windows, illuminating his best puppy dog eyes.

I concealed a grin as everyone snuck Yugar bits of food under the table, as though he wouldn't get a full plate after everyone had eaten.

Once we were done eating and Yugar had his breakfast, we gathered in the centre of the training hall. I spent more time in the training hall than every other room in the fortress except for my personal and common rooms. The high wooden rafters were as familiar as the roof of my rooms, the wooden floorboards with their white-painted sparring circles as familiar as the path I used to run with my Da.

Along one wall stood six weapons racks—one for each of us, Pétur's still standing there. Empty. Pulling my weapons belt from my rack, I fastened it around my hips as I took my spot beside Óskar. The four of us, Rúna, Gil, Óskar, and I, stood in a half circle facing Georg.

"We all know that we are at a significant disadvantage with Pétur gone," Georg said. "There have been a few close calls in the field, and we cannot allow that to happen again."

"Well, considering there used to be six of us and now five, there will always be an odd man out," Óskar contributed.

Georg sighed. "In thanks for that you and I are going to drill on hand-to-hand combat when we're done here."

Óskar groaned.

I chuckled, drawing Georg's attention. "Would you like to join us, Bryn?"

"No, I'm alright, thank you," I said, regretting getting involved. Georg was the best hand-to-hand combat fighter out of all of us; Gil was the only one of us close to him in skill. And while Georg wouldn't hurt us, he would put us through our paces. With the bruises I already had, that was the last thing I wanted to do after training for the day.

"Then we're going to return to the matter at hand. We need to see if there is a way to mitigate the danger of being down a man."

"There is a reason our pairings are the way they are. We can always flex if needed, but the pairings are designed for the best effectiveness of our fighting styles and bloodrites," Rúna said.

Georg sighed. "You're right. We have to evaluate what risk is worse—changing the pairs or having a hole where Pétur used to be."

"I need to stay with Rúna," Gil said. "I need her bloodrite

when I have to use mine. The only person that could take her spot would be Óskar, but his arrows would not be able to do the same as her light."

Whenever he used his bloodrite, the darkness he wielded threatened to overwhelm him, and sometimes it did. It required every ounce of his attention to try and keep it under control, so he often lost sight of the fight around him. I had been helping him learn to maintain control, just as he had been helping me with my fear of blood, but it still took a lot of effort on his part to ensure that the darkness didn't sink its hooks into him.

"You need a close combat fighter by your side, Georg," Rúna added. "That leaves Gil or Bryn. Gil needs a mid-range fighter, if not a distance fighter, paired with him when he uses his bloodrite, so that leaves Bryn."

No one spoke for a moment. There was no good answer here.

Gil and Rúna had been fighting by each other's sides since they were children first learning how to spar. Óskar and I had been working for months to hone our fighting styles with each other. There was one odd man out here without Pétur—Georg.

"We're going to try Bryn and Rúna together against Gil and Óskar," Georg said, gesturing to the sparring ring.

"That doesn't solve the problem of you being alone," Rúna pointed out as she unravelled her whip and stepped into the circle. I took my place by her side.

Georg nodded. "You're right, but it will show us our options."

He started the spar, and I immediately set my sights on Gil. He was the close combat fighter of the two of them, making him my responsibility. He had a sword in each hand, and I quickly palmed a pair of daggers. We circled each other, both waiting for the other to make the first move.

Gil lunged towards me, his blade flashing through the air. I knocked it aside with one of my daggers before slashing at him. He spun out of the way and out of my reach.

We circled each other again; this time, I was the first to make a move. He blocked it easily, launching his counterattack. I went to move out of the way but stepped on something, rolling my ankle slightly and knocking me off balance. Gil quickly dropped one of his swords, his fingers wrapping around my waist.

He spun me around, my back flush to his chest and placed his blade against my throat. Gil dipped his head down to the crook of my neck, his lips against my skin. "I win."

"That was good. Bryn stepped on the end of Rúna's whip, but she is not accustomed to watching for that like Gil is," Georg said. Gil sheathed his sword, but I stayed where I was, leaning against his chest. His hand rested on my waist.

"You have all trained to fight with whoever is around you in whatever scenario arises. I'm getting there myself. I knew about Rúna's whip but forgot about it during the spar. When everything is going to shit, and we have to fall back on established patterns and teams to make it through, can we honestly say that these teams would work?" I asked.

No one said a word.

Because every one of us already knew the answer.

No—they wouldn't work.

FIVE

BRYN

I pulled the herbs from my satchel and placed them on the tabletop. I had taken a quick trip to Goldhelm, the capital city of Drysden and where the fortress was located, to replenish some of my supplies. It felt weird stepping away from the fortress and my responsibilities inside of it to go shopping.

But we were burning through my healing supplies at a disturbing rate, and I wouldn't let us be caught short in the field when needed.

The Verndari turned to me as their healer when we were in the field. I would not let one of them die just because I was unprepared.

It was why Gil carried extra supplies in his own saddlebags.

I grabbed my wooden cutting board and knife from my shelf and began to finely chop the first set of herbs. They were one of the three herbs needed in the cream that helped slow bleeding.

I finished the chopping, scrapped it into my mortar and

reached for the next set of herbs. I began to peel the prickly outer layer to reveal the soft inner heart of the plant that I needed.

A knock sounded at my door.

"Come in!" I called as I sliced the plant in two. I grabbed one of the halves and squeezed it into the mortar. I glanced over my shoulder to see Gil, a softness in his eyes. "Hi there," I said before finely chopping the other half of the plant.

Gil closed the door with a soft click and made his way over to me. The warmth from his body seeped into my back as he peeked over my shoulder at the tabletop. "The cream to slow bleeding?" he asked, his breath causing a rogue curl to dance across my cheek.

I nodded. "I figured we would need it before long. Especially with how our training went this morning."

Gil gently tucked my curl behind my ear before heading towards the shelf where I kept my prepared supplies. He grabbed a fresh tin of cream and brought it back to the table. I started chopping the final herb. "Shit," I muttered, realizing that more of my supplies were running low.

Gil rested a hip on the table, his arms crossed over his chest, as he watched me work. "We will find a way to get through this. There is a solution."

"Will we find it in time?" I asked, my voice soft. My hand started to shake. "Will we find it before one of us is seriously injured? Or worse?"

Gil gently took the knife from me to finish the chopping. "We will do everything we can."

He scraped the chopped herb into the mortar and began to crush it with the pestle. I didn't speak as he worked, allowing the rhythmic scrape of the pestle to try and soothe me. Once everything was ground into a fine paste, I combined it with the cream and marked the top with a dollop of black wax.

I set it aside and turned to find Gil already watching me.

"Sometimes everything isn't enough." My voice cracked.

Gil slowly drew me closer until my body was flush with his. I tilted my head back to look into his eyes. He gently pressed his lips to my forehead. "Everything is all that we have. We cannot expect ourselves to give more than that."

"We've been lucky so far. Our injuries have been minor—a few bruises here or a couple stitches there. But our luck is bound to run out, and someone will be seriously hurt, Gil. What if *I'm* not enough to heal them?"

Gil's hands rested on my waist momentarily before lifting me onto the table before him. He braced his hands on the wood on either side of my hips. "It does not need to fall entirely on your shoulders, Bryn. Let me help. Let me bear some of it."

I swallowed against the thickness in my throat. "I'm trying."

"It does not matter who we are paired with in a fight. Whether you are with Óskar or I am with Rúna. Whether you are with Georg or you and I are fighting side by side. We will all have each other's backs. We will always guard each other through whatever we may face." He pressed his forehead to mine. "I will give everything I have to keep you safe, whether you are fighting by my side or someone else's."

My tongue darted across my lip, Gil's eyes following the movement before locking on mine again.

"And I will do whatever it takes to ensure *you* walk off the battlefield."

To ensure that Gil, *my Gil*, walked off the battlefield, not the darkness that tried to overtake him whenever he used his bloodrite.

Gil opened his mouth to speak, but I lay a finger gently over it. "You've gotten even better at comforting speeches," I teased.

"I do my best." His lip quirked as he stepped closer to me.

Right up against my knees.

His eyes locked on mine as I slowly opened my legs, placing my knees on either side of his hips.

Inviting him to step even closer.

Gil lingered where he was for a moment, his hands leaving the tabletop to rest on my thighs. The heat of his palms seeped through my clothes as he flexed his fingers.

Then, he finally stepped closer. Right up against me.

One of his hands brushed up my body to rest on my cheek, his fingers trembling. I reached up to loop my own arms around his neck. His fingers tangled in my hair, his thumb gently tipping my head back before he pressed his lips to mine.

I leaned further into him, pulling him even closer to me.

His lips seemed to sear through me as the kiss became fiercer.

As though we were starving and the only sustenance could be found in each other's lips.

Gil's hand tightened in my hair, curling strands around his fist.

I nipped at his lip.

A growl rumbled through his chest and into my fingers. "*Bryn,*" he breathed as though my name were both an answer and a curse.

His lips trailed across my cheek, down to my throat. Every press of his mouth to my skin burned through me. My hands dropped down to his shoulders, my nails digging into him.

Gil found the crook of my neck, my collarbone, left bare from where my loose shirt had slipped down my shoulder a bit.

He lingered there. His lips, his tongue, his *teeth* practically branding me.

His fingers gripped my hip before he finally lifted his head, his eyes alight.

Gil swallowed, his fingers flexing. "Bryn," he rasped. His hand dropped from my hair to wrap around my shoulders. He tucked his forehead into my shoulder, his skin warming my neck. He pressed one last kiss to my throat before wrapping me in his arms.

"I know," I whispered, kissing his hair, not needing to voice the rest of my thoughts. I know that he's trying. I know it's still hard for him to be so close to me after years of keeping himself at a distance.

I closed my eyes and rested my head against his, allowing the comfort of being wrapped in his arms to seep into my very bones. To soothe me from the inside out.

THE WAR CHAMBER was my least favourite room in the fortress.

Well, besides the sets of rooms, the prisons, set aside in the bowels of the fortress for Gil's family. For when the darkness took complete control of their bodies. I hated that place with every fibre of my being. Luckily, I had only had to see it once.

I spent far too much time in the War Chamber.

The windowless room was lit by lanterns on the walls and candles on the table, casting harsh shadows across the walls and faces of everyone.

The King Commander and his family took up a portion of the table with Rúna in a chair between Baldur and his brother Hákon. Kier, with his hair tied back from his face in a braid, and two others represented the Striking Shadows—the elite warrior intelligence force commanded by Ragna, the King Commander's oldest daughter.

A handful of powerful Jarls, either in money, bloodrite, or both, sat around the table, including Jarl Ottó. He had pushed to have his daughter Emilía take my place on the Verndari, forcing me to compete to earn my rightful place.

I had won.

Ottó and Emilía had been alarmingly quiet in the month since I had been officially named a member of the Verndari. Especially considering their family backed the exiled royal family in the Dark War.

Then there was us. The Verndari.

What remained of us, that is.

As usual, I sat between Óskar and Gil with my shoulders back. I refused to show an ounce of weakness in this room. These walls were filled with some of the most powerful across Drysden and surely riddled with people who would turn on us as soon as the barrier fully dissolved.

"Hákon. Report," the King Commander demanded.

"The Royal Regiment has successfully filled all of the positions that were open after the attack on the fortress a month ago," Hákon said. "Every line has faced the Skolli in the field and are becoming more adept at fighting them. We are ready to depart on a moment's notice."

"And the healers?"

Hákon leaned forward, bracing his forearms on the table before him. A bruise was fading on his temple. "I have been working with every healer in the fortress to ensure that they have the supplies and training needed to face the growing threat. I have instructed Regiment members to offer my training to any healers willing to travel to the fortress."

The King Commander nodded, his face grave. Drysden

didn't have a large fighting force commanded by the King Commander. The only troops under the King Commander's control were the Royal Regiment and the Striking Shadows. Every Warlord and Jarl maintained their own forces, and it was up to them to determine whether they would support the King Commander. That meant a lot of pressure fell on Hákon and Ragna's shoulders, especially when we were still unsure of where the support of the realm would fall.

"Ragna," the King Commander nodded to her. "Report."

"Some of the Warlords and Jarls have declared their support, both in forces and supplies, to us in the past month," she said. The dark circles that lingered under Ragna's eyes were the only sign of the long hours she was putting in to gather information for the King Commander. "However, many have yet to declare their support." Her eyes briefly landed on Ottó and a few others in the room before she continued. "No one has outright denied us, but it is not enough for my Shadows to visit and ask them. Some need more encouragement."

I knew she meant exactly that—encouragement. It was one of the most sacred laws in Drysden that the Warlords and Jarls were to maintain their own forces that could not be forced or manipulated into doing the King Commander's bidding. To force them to serve against their will was a one-way trip to a coup.

We couldn't risk fighting a war on two fronts. We had to ensure that we did everything by the letter of the law, not that it would matter to the Jarls and Warlords planning on joining the exiled commanding family. It would matter to the people sitting in the middle not yet decided which way they would fall.

Especially when we needed them to choose our side.

"What do you suggest?"

"We need to send out the Verndari to key players. They need to know that the threat is serious and that we need them. Sending the Verndari shows the true need for their support and shows each Jarl and Warlord a high respect."

The King Commander was silent for a moment. "Where would you suggest they start?"

"Jarl Einar. Not only does he command one of the largest military forces in the realm, he is also rich in supplies. We need him. And to send anyone other than the Verndari would insult him."

No one spoke, allowing the King Commander to evaluate her suggestion.

He finally turned towards Georg. "Are the Verndari ready to ride?"

"We can be ready for such a journey in two days." Georg ran a hand over his head. "King Commander, Jarl Einar's stronghold is in Wolfmire, correct?"

"Yes, it is. What does that matter?"

Georg hesitated momentarily, surveying us before returning to the King Commander. "We are vulnerable being down a warrior. And with Wolfmire in the north, there will be fighting we will face. We are at a disadvantage."

Baldur scoffed, his fingers drumming on the tabletop while his other hand rested on Rúna's arm. "Just do your job. You had five before the girl was found. You have five now."

"It is only a matter of time until our vulnerability catches up to us, King Commander." Georg continued, ignoring Baldur's statement. "We need a solution."

"What would you propose?" the Queen asked, leaning forward in her chair. She was perfectly put together, not a hair out of place or a shred of anxiety on her face. A facade of a

queen designed to assure her people that there was no immediate danger.

But her eyes were sharp on Georg as she awaited his
response. The Queen was well aware of the threat we faced and
knew the brunt of it would be borne by the Verndari, the Royal
Regiment, and the Striking Shadows. She knew that she
needed us at our strongest if we stood a chance of winning
what lay ahead.

If her children who led those forces had a chance of
walking off the battlefield alive instead of being carried to their
pyre.

"We need to fill the hole left by Pétur," Georg finally said.

Only the snapping of logs in the fireplace filled the room
around us.

I barely dared to breathe—terrified for the King Commander's reaction and braced for the response of the others.

My fingers fiddled with my pants, unable to stay still as I
awaited what came next. Gil pressed his leg into mine to give
me something to ground myself with. In return, I gave him a
small smile, his eyes softening the smallest amount.

"Are you saying the Verndari are unfit to complete their
duties?" The King Commander's voice was ice.

"No. I am saying that having us down a man has us at a
disadvantage. That has not affected our work, but we have to
be realistic. It will eventually catch up with us. We need to
address it now while we have the chance," Georg said, his voice
steady. "We have only sustained minimal injuries, but that will
change if we do not replace what we have lost."

The Queen nodded. "We shouldn't put you at additional
risk if we can avoid it. The question is who to put in the open
place."

"My daughter, Emilía, would be more than happy to serve

the King Commander and his family as a member of the Verndari." My chest tightened in response to Ottó's words. Not only was Emilía a dark and slimy person to her core, but her family also supported the exiled royal family. She wouldn't be joining us to help us.

She would be trying to cut us down at the knees.

"She did almost earn the title of the Verndari," Sigrún, the King Commander's youngest daughter, pointed out.

"Emilía took Bryn down in the combat with very little effort," Baldur added.

Óskar leaned forward. "Emilía won because of an underhanded trick. The whole reason she is not a Verndari is because Bryn is more skilled than she is."

"My daughter is more than qualified—"

"I would have thought, Jarl Ottó, that after her last failure, you would have spent more time licking your wounds before entering the fight again." The King Commander glared. "Your daughter was not good enough to be considered a Verndari a month ago and is still not good enough today." A vein in Ottó's head bulged, his face going red. "Who else is there?"

The war council descended into chaos.

"There's Lúdvík. He would—" one of the advisors suggested.

"—No, he's too important to the Royal Regiment for me to lose him to the Verndari," Hákon interrupted.

"Then one of the newer members, they can't have been too ingrained yet," Baldur said.

Hákon shook his head. "No. The ones that haven't quite found their place yet don't have the skills needed by the Verndari. They are good, don't get me wrong, but they need more time to become great. And to join the Verndari, they need to be phenomenal."

"Then may I suggest my other daughter, Svanna?" Ottó suggested, his scheming voice scratching down my spine. Svanna wasn't anything like her sister Emilía, and I didn't think she would betray us if she were to join us. But the very idea of doing anything Ottó suggested filled me with doubt.

He had tried to oust me from the Verndari the moment I arrived in the fortress to advance his plans; there was no doubt in my mind that he was acting from the same place now.

We could not allow him to have his way.

There were many different views in the chamber, different agendas, and it seemed as though everyone had decided this was just the opportunity, they needed to get their hooks into the Verndari. They had never been able to gain access to us before, and now they were desperate.

Like sharks with blood in the water.

They had seen how Ottó's efforts had played out. They saw the same possibilities that he had and would do their best to get the person they wanted on the Verndari. To help us or cut us down, it didn't matter—they wanted to manipulate the situation, and that meant that they couldn't be trusted.

"No." Gier crossed his arms over his chest. Svanna sat quietly by his side, showing no emotion as the debate about her continued around the table. A carefully blank face, revealing nothing about what she truly thought.

"No?" Ottó's face started to turn a concerning shade of red. "Who are you to tell me no?"

"While the Striking Shadows hold a higher position than you, Jarl Ottó, I understand that Gier doesn't personally outrank you. But I do." Ragna said, forcing me to hide a smirk from her words. "Svanna has a very important role with the Striking Shadows. I cannot place her with the Verndari without severely weakening my team. She stays there."

Ottó's hands closed into fists on the table. "Just because my daughter may be warming your bed does not entitle you to control her actions."

"Watch how you speak to my sister," Baldur growled. I exchanged a wide-eyed look with Rúna; I had never seen Baldur defend Ragna like that.

I hadn't seen him stand up for a single person before; he had always been the one to kick them while they were down.

Ottó let out a humourless laugh. "Are these elite fighting groups, or are they simply match-making services? My own daughter with Ragna, not to mention the two Verndari courting or fucking or whatever they are doing." He flung an arm out towards Gil and me.

"Until you fight alongside us on the front lines, you can keep your tongue between your teeth," Gil hissed, his body tensed beside mine.

"And even then, you can take your thoughts and fuck right off because we don't give a damn what you think of us," Óskar added with a cold grin. "You might outrank some people in this room, but you don't outrank us, so I suggest you speak to your superiors more respectfully."

I squeezed Óskar's hand in thanks as Ottó's face reddened further. Rúna's eyes sparkled as she watched the scene unfold in front of her from her spot beside Baldur instead of beside Gil as she should be.

She may be unable to speak up in the war chamber, having to fulfil the role of quiet, dutiful partner to Baldur, but that didn't mean she didn't feel the same way we did.

Especially when it came to defending Gil from the hateful opinions of Ottó.

"Enough." The King Commander barely raised his voice, but it still cut through the room like a knife. "Ragna. Hákon.

You two have the most experience with the warriors in the realm. Who would you propose?"

Ragna drummed her fingers on the table for a moment.

"Aron. He's led various groupings of warships during the raiding season for three years, and he's deadly with any weapon. Many anticipate that he inherited his father's skills and suspected bloodrite."

"Who was his father?" I asked.

"The Spirit Sword of Greythorn."

CHAPTER

SIX

GIL

I waited for Bryn in the courtyard, my cloak blocking the coldness of the stone against my back, where I leaned against the wall. She had mentioned her plans to run with Fannar and Yugar the night before, and I was hoping to catch her when she returned.

Her laughter reached me first, carrying through the gates. My head lifted towards the gates, a smile pulling at the corner of my lips from the sound.

Yugar entered the courtyard first, Bryn shortly behind him, beautiful with rosy cheeks, sparkling eyes, and a wind-tussled braid. Fannar followed after—he had yet to best her in a race. I pushed off the wall, making my way over to them as he began to pace with his hands on his head.

"I see that Yugar won again," I teased Bryn gently as I reached them.

She turned towards me, a smile brightening her face even further. My heart stuttered in my chest, still in awe of the woman before me. That someone as bright, purely good, could care for someone like me. A person with a monster simmering just under the surface.

"He has four legs. I only have two," she joked.

"He has four very short legs. Your two can cover much more ground in a single step," Fannar said as he finally regained his breath.

Bryn spun on her heel; her eyes narrowed. "And you have the longest legs of the three of us. By your logic, you should have beaten both of us rather than coming last."

"I have long since made my peace with the fact that I will never beat you in a run," Fannar joked before wrapping her in a hug. "I'm off. I promised Lúdvík that I would meet him before our training session." Fannar clasped my shoulder on his way towards the fortress.

It still surprised me, sometimes, the ease with which Bryn and Fannar shared that they cared. They didn't hesitate before approaching me, and they didn't remain out of arms' reach.

At times, I was envious that she grew up outside the fortress without the weight of being a Verndari on her shoulders when she was just a child. But another part of me was incredibly grateful that she was spared the childhood that we all had.

"I wasn't expecting to see you out here," Bryn said with a smile.

"I noticed that you needed to replenish your herbs, and I was going to go down into Goldhelm to purchase some more if you wanted to join me."

Bryn rose up on the balls of her feet to press her lips to my cheek before looping her arm through mine. "Lead the way." She rested her head against my shoulder as I led her towards the gates.

The guards at the gate still gave me a wide berth, but they

didn't show outright hostility towards me. They had seen me fight; they had seen me use my bloodrite. But they had also seen me helping Bryn with the healing. Slowly, the warriors were recognizing that I was more than my darkness.

The hard part was convincing everyone else.

I passed Bryn a pair of gloves from my pocket. She often went without on her runs, warm enough from the exertion. But the walk to Goldhelm would surely be much cooler. She took them with a grateful smile and pulled them on.

A light snowfall started, snowflakes clinging to her bright red locks and eyelashes.

"Are you warm enough?" I asked her, gently easing my arm from her grip, wrapping it around her shoulders, and tucking her close to my side.

"I'm perfectly warm," she said, looking up at me. "I'm surprised that you suggested the trip into Goldhelm. It's not something that you enjoy."

"You needed more supplies," I stated. I didn't love the crowds in Goldhelm or the stares we received whenever we walked through the streets. But that judgement carried through to the fortress, and I had slowly discovered areas that I enjoyed within the city. "And I enjoy spending time by your side."

Bryn rested her head against me again as we continued to the city. As we entered Goldhelm, a boy crossed our path. Bryn's steps faltered as he passed, his head tilted toward the ground.

Long leather gloves stretched over his elbows with long straps buckled over his shoulders. A matching mask covered the bottom half of his face. Only the skin around his eyes was visible with the hat he wore.

Every person he passed backed away from him even though the boy did his best to avoid them.

People resumed their movements through the streets once he was gone, like a shark parting a school of fish before they continued their journeys.

"What was that boy wearing?" Bryn asked, her voice hushed so it wouldn't carry to the people around us. "And why were they giving him such a wide berth?"

"He has the Hunger," I told her, my voice just as quiet. "He was born without a bloodrite, leaving the power inside him restless. He can steal someone's bloodrite with a single touch and use it as though it's his own."

"Hence the gloves and mask."

I swallowed, my heart aching for the young boy. Ostracised for something that he had no control over, no say. "Exactly."

Bryn was quiet for a moment. "I have never seen someone with the Hunger before. Is it rare?"

"It is not uncommon," I told her as I guided her towards the shop. "His parents must love him very much. Most people with the Hunger are killed when they first show the signs."

Bryn looked back over her shoulder as though she could see the boy. Her heart, her pure soul, was probably aching for him, for every person with the Hunger that died suspiciously as a child.

I pushed open the door to the shop, and a rush of warm air poured out to meet us. The shopkeeper, an elderly man with deep wrinkles and a kind smile, looked up from his ledger at the front counter.

"If it isn't my favourite customers." His voice crackled with age as he slowly stood from his stool.

"I'm sure that you say that to all of us." Bryn smiled as she stepped forward to clasp hands with him. "Please, do not stand on our account."

He patted her hand gently before retaking his seat and turning towards me. "It is a pleasure to see you both. Do you know what you are needing?"

Bryn nodded, grabbing a woven basket from the stack by the counter. I stepped forward, taking it from her, and contently followed her around the store.

She went from shelf to shelf, methodically navigating the space. Her shoulders loosened as she studied each herb she picked up. Bryn evaluated the flowers on some and the colour of others. She held a few close to her nose, her eyes fluttering close as she inhaled their scent.

Each herb that passed her inspection was passed to me. I carefully placed each piece in the basket, ensuring that nothing was bent, torn, or damaged. By the time we finished the store circuit, the basket was full, with various shades of greens and vibrant petals overlapping one another.

I placed it down on the counter for the shopkeeper to tally up.

"It has barely been two weeks since you were last in here to restock," the shopkeeper pointed out as he delicately made his way through each plant in the basket. "And now you're back with another purchase just as large as the last."

"I'm sorry if it's affecting your business. I can spread out my shopping to a few other stores to ease your burden," Bryn offered.

The shopkeeper brushed away her words with a hand. "Nonsense, Bryn. You will come here as you usually do. I have no concerns about my business. I was worried about you both. The number of medical ointments and creams this could make is substantial, and you are already back for more."

"We have seen a greater need for the supplies in the field," I said, carefully choosing my words.

"And I have been making large batches and sending what I don't need to the healers' stores," Bryn added.

The shopkeeper carefully bagged each of the items. "Very well." He collected the money and passed me the bag. "Both of you stay safe, and I will see you next time you need to replenish."

CHAPTER
SEVEN
BRYN

I pulled my fur-lined cloak tighter to my body as the cold winter wind whistled down the road. I had been warm enough earlier in the day with Gil, but I had been careful to dress in layers for this trip, especially since we were heading toward the water.

Georg was equally bundled up by my side, a thick hat covering his ears. He had glared at me when I asked if the lack of hair on his head made the cold more miserable.

The snow crunched under our boots as we descended towards the docks at Goldhelm. When we finally decided that Aron would join the Verndari, we knew we had to let him know immediately. With our departure into the field, we had no time to waste.

While Aron lived in the fortress and often trained with various groups and warriors there, he went to the shipmaker's shop weekly to monitor the development of warships for the coming Raiding Season. He led a small contingent of ships each season and personally oversaw the care and development of each one.

Although, if he fit in with us, I doubted that he would be leading the ships again. He would have too many duties tied to him at the fortress to be gone for weeks or months at a time.

The docks were almost deserted; the shipmaker's shop was the only building showing life.

A rush of warm air met us when Georg pushed open the door to the shop. Shop felt like too small of a word to describe the place. Hulls of ships were lined up inside in various stages of repair and construction. One end of the large room was dedicated entirely to sails, countless different designs hanging from the wall, and a table covered with another that was in progress. The opposite end had many long oars lined up, each set boasting a uniqueness to the one beside it.

It wasn't hard to spot Aron. He was taller than anyone else in the shop, and his broad shoulders made him take up more space than anyone else. His hair was tied back in a messy knot on the back of his head.

I pulled my cloak from my shoulders as we walked through the shop towards Aron.

He turned to face us as we got close, his eyebrows raising briefly in surprise before he schooled his face into a more neutral expression. He bowed his head in respect. "Jarl Georg, Jarl Brynja, what brings you here?"

"It's just Bryn," I said.

Aron smiled at me and nodded his acceptance. "Bryn, my apologies."

"As you know, the Verndari are down a man since Pétur has...left." Georg hesitated. Aron would need to know the whole story eventually, but not now. Not surrounded by people like this. It was a story to be told when no other ears were around to overhear us. "With the Verndari being sent into the field more often, we cannot afford to be down a man."

Aron crossed his arms across his chest. "I'm guessing that you are either here to ask for my recommendation or to ask for me. Which one is it?"

"We've been sent for you," Georg said. "There was a War Council this morning. Multiple names were considered, but we finally settled on you."

"Who suggested me?" Aron's words weren't hesitant, but they weren't sure either. His fingers drummed a steady rhythm against his arm.

We had caught him off guard. He hadn't been expecting this.

I shifted the weight on my feet. "Ragna was the one that put your name forward, but the King Commander who officially decided it."

In other terms, he had no choice but to join us.

"And you?" Aron's eyes drifted between Georg and me. "Do you and all of the Verndari believe that I should be that person?"

"You're a born warrior, Aron. You're also a leader both on and off of the battlefield," Georg said. "Your father was incredibly gifted with several weapons. People even speculated that it was a unique bloodrite. You have that same gift."

Aron swallowed. "I've spent the last years leading Raiding Ships. That's completely different than what the Verndari do."

I stepped forward. "You've faced the Skolli before. You fought alongside us a month ago and had my back when you didn't even know me. That's the type of person I would want on the Verndari," I said, swallowing back the unease at the fact that I would have died without him. "I was the new girl —I know exactly what you're feeling. But trust me when I say that if I can make it through as a Verndari, you certainly can.

Aron ran a hand over his hair. "And the others feel this way, too?"

"Most of us haven't fought with you, but we have heard about you. Both from the Raiders you have led and from talk around the fortress." Georg paused for a moment. "I'm not going to lie to you and say this decision was entirely ours." His words were quiet, his eyes darting around the room to ensure no one was close enough to hear what he was saying. "But we are happy with it. You are a strong warrior, fierce with any weapon, cunning in your tactics, and you care for the people you lead. That's the type of person that we want to join us."

Aron nodded, hesitating before guiding us to a small room in the back of the shop. It was a small office, the entire space occupied by a desk and a shelf. But once he shut the door behind us, it became private.

"How do I fit in? I may have more advanced fighting skills than Pétur, but I won't replace his bloodrite on your team."

"Our team," Georg corrected. "I don't think anyone can replace Pétur's bloodrite. And honestly? I don't know how we will plan to face it in the field."

I draped my cloak over the back of the chair, freeing my hands. "We don't want you to be a replacement Pétur. We need you to take his place, but we need to find how the six of us work together instead of trying to mould you into Pétur's image."

Aron's shoulders sagged, just for a moment. Vulnerability shone clear in his eyes before he blinked it away and straightened his back. "I'm guessing that some key players had their own suggestions for who should take the place. Did Jarl Ottó suggest one of his daughters?"

Georg nodded. "Both of them were brought up."

"I've heard whispers in fortress hallways and in the shipyards," Aron's voice was quiet even though no one was in the room with them. "Seems like someone is polling the intentions of the warriors. Discreetly, of course, but asking around where certain players may fall should something change."

"I haven't seen Ottó doing it," I said, equally as quiet.

"Ottó would be noticeable. A young lady cozying up to a warrior here or there, her lips close to his ear so that her sweet nothings aren't overheard? That happens all the time in the fortress. You'll dismiss it in the same moment you witness it."

"Emilía."

Aron winked before his face turned grave. "Right in one. I've been sharing everything I can with Ragna, probably why she suggested me."

"She knows that you don't agree with Ottó."

Aron nodded before opening the door. I scooped up my cloak and fastened it around my shoulders as he led us toward the entrance of the building. "When do I start?" he asked.

"We'll move you into your new rooms tomorrow. We leave the next morning on an assignment," Georg said. "We will help you get settled and gather everything that you need today to be ready for you tomorrow."

"Strike hard, strike fast, eh?" Aron said with a wry smile. The formal words that were used to send the Verndari into the field.

Georg chuckled. "Welcome to the team."

EIGHT

BRYN

When we returned from our search to find Aron, Georg gathered Gil, Óskar and I in one of the meeting rooms in our wing. I sat beside Óskar at one side of the table with Gil across from me. The seat beside him was open—Rúna's spot. Georg sat at the head of the table, as he always did. The place to my right, at the foot of the table, was open. Empty.

But not for long. As of tomorrow, it will be filled once again.

"We will do a full briefing once Aron joins us in the morning. However, I want to ensure that we all understand how this will all play out so that we can support him," Georg said.

Rúna slipped into the room and took her seat next to Gil.

"Ragna will brief us on the details of our task on the morning of our departure. Specifically, the things that she didn't want to share with the War Council as a whole. We likely won't have time to train with Aron before we leave, so that must be a priority when we arrive at Wolfmire."

"And if we encounter any Skolli on our journey?" Gil asked.

Georg's face was grim. "He must fit in with us as best as possible."

I shifted in my chair. "He fit in just fine when the Skolli attacked the fortress. He'll have a bigger role now, but I don't think he will shy away from it."

Gil's eyes simmered at the reminder of just how dead I would have been without Aron. We both knew the risks we had accepted when we swore our oaths as Verndari, but it was different when it was a person you cared for. The very thought of Gil at risk was enough to churn my stomach; I could only imagine how he felt when he realized that I had almost died.

"The training matters as we try to figure out where he will fit best with us. I want to try different combinations and see what works best."

"Aron isn't going to be your partner?" Rúna asked.

"He very well might be. But it would be stupid to pair him with me because it's easy. We want to ensure our best on the battlefield, so we must find the most effective combinations."

I brushed a curl out of my face. "I thought we already tried that."

"We've started to. Just because the pairings we tried didn't work the best doesn't mean that another one won't," Georg sighed. "He's more than likely going to end up my partner. It's the most logical thing to do. But we can't disregard the other options simply because it's what we assume is best."

Óskar reached a hand down to scratch Yugar's head. "Some of the members of the merchant caravan came up to me on me and Yugar's walk this morning asking whether we would be protecting them when they left. Obviously, we're not, but I wasn't about to trigger a panic by speaking out of turn."

"For once," Rúna added quietly.

I snickered as Óskar threw a crumpled-up parchment at her head.

"We all know that some of the caravans, and the supplies in them, are too important to risk sending them without a guard. So Hákon has decided that he will assign a line of the Royal Regiment to all of the protection details we were taking before," Georg said. "Lúdvík's line is being briefed on the duties now."

My chest tightened to a point of almost pain.

That was Fannar's line.

Fannar's line was responsible for our protection details— the most important and *dangerous* assignments.

My leg started to bounce, my body practically vibrating with anxious energy.

I looked up to find Gil's eyes already on me. He scanned my face quickly, his lips pursing as he read what was undoubtedly written clearly across my face.

"I haven't had very many interactions with Jarl Einar, and I don't have a plan for how we should approach this," Georg said. He ran a dark-skinned hand over his bald head. "I know that he's respected and that his fighting forces are some of the strongest in Drysden. Wolfmire, his city, is one of the largest in the realm, and I have only heard good things about it. All of that suggests to me that he is a strong leader. A good leader. But other than that, I have nothing." He sighed. "You have the rest of the day to yourselves. Prepare whatever you need, and see whoever you need to see before we leave. Hopefully, Ragna will have some insights that we can use tomorrow."

I tuned out Óskar and Rúna's playful bickering as I jumped out of my chair. I couldn't sit still. I needed to move; I needed to plan.

I strode for the door, heading straight for my rooms. I

didn't wait for Gil; I knew that his steady footsteps were the ones that followed me through the hall. I burst into my room, unable to stop moving as I paced in front of the fireplace.

Gil gently shut the door.

"Fannar is going to be taking over our details," the words tumbled out of my mouth, my fingers clutching at my curls. "Fannar is going to be out there in the worst situations—"

Gil gently caught my shoulders, stopping my movement. "Fannar is on one of the most skilled and trusted lines in the Royal Regiment. He has strong warriors to watch his back."

He didn't try to tell me that he would be fine or that he was sure that everything would work out.

Gil would never give me generic platitudes or tell me something he didn't know was true. He and I both knew that Fannar would see combat and that there was every chance he could be hurt. No one left the battlefield the same as they entered it. They would leave injured or grieving for their fallen friends and comrades.

Or perhaps their wounds would be invisible, hidden deep within their psyche. They could be war scarred just like I was. Like I still was at times.

Instead of telling me pointless platitudes, Gil would focus on what could reassure me. Of the quality of warriors in Fannar's line, of the incredible Sergeant who led them.

"He has fought the Skulli before," Gil continued, his fingers gently untangling my own from my hair. He brought my hands up to his face and kissed the palms of each one. "He knows what to expect and how to prepare for it."

I nodded before resting my forehead on his chest. His soothing scent filled my nose as he wrapped his arms around me.

We stood silently for a moment, the crackle of the fire and Gil's heartbeat the only sounds surrounding me.

"Ma was getting better," I whispered, tilting my head to look at Gil. "I don't know what will happen to her progress with both Fannar and I away at the same time."

Gil kissed my forehead, his lips lingering there as he spoke. "Hákon and Ragna will spend more time in the fortress than any of us. Talk to them."

Hákon had seen Ma at her worst, had seen her shortly after the attack on Ebonwell. He had examined the healing that I had done on her stump after she lost her arm to one of the Skolli that attacked our village. He had been one of the people that came running when Ma started screaming when she awoke. He was there when she withdrew within herself, not speaking, not moving, completely disassociating with the world around her.

Besides Fannar and I, Hákon knew both Ma and the situation the best.

It was a good idea.

I stretched to my tiptoes, wrapping my arms around Gil's neck.

"Thank you," I breathed before pressing my lips to his. He pulled me closer, one of his hands snaking up to coil in my hair. The lingering anxiety that was running through my veins turned into liquid heat as he gently nipped at my lip.

His fingers trembled against me, so I pulled back slightly to look up at him; his eyes were alight with heat.

"Would you come with me to talk to him?" I asked breathlessly.

"Of course," he said with a soft smile.

Gil and I walked side by side through the fortress, his hand on my back as he gently led me toward Hákon's office. I had never visited Hákon in his official office before; I had never had a need to.

It was on the bottom floor of the fortress near the entrance closest to the Royal Regiment barracks. The wooden door was quite simple in its design, built for function rather than beauty, but it was wonderfully taken care of and stained a rich, dark colour. Gil knocked on the door, and Hákon called for us to enter just a few moments later.

His office was a bright room, with a wall filled with windows allowing the winter sunlight to stream in. One wall held a large chalkboard with formations drawn on it, while another held nothing but bookcases. A cabinet full of medical supplies and a rack holding some armour decorated the space.

Hákon leaned on the front of his sturdy wooden desk, his arms crossed. He nodded to us in greeting.

And in one of the two chairs in front of the desk sat Fannar. He turned to us with a smile.

"I was just talking to Hákon about our options regarding Ma whenever you and I are both gone from the castle," Fannar said.

I let out a small laugh. "I came here to do the same thing. Gil suggested it." I sat beside Fannar, Gil taking residence behind my chair, his hand on my shoulder.

"I was just about to reassure Fannar that I will personally check in on your mother," Hákon said with a smile. "She has come a long way, and I don't want to see her slip back to where she was any more than you. And, if I'm ever away or unable to visit her, Ragna has already told me she will do so."

A weight lifted from my shoulders. "Thank you."

"If it is alright with you, I would like to introduce some of Ragna and my trusted friends and servants to her. In the rare event that all four of us are called away from the fortress, I would like to know there is still someone we can trust to look in on her."

Gil's hand drifted to rest on my neck, his thumb brushing the skin. I shared a quick look with Fannar before tilting my head subtly to Hákon. I was fine with it, so I would let Fannar make the final call. After all, as well as I thought I knew Hákon, Fannar knew him better. Since Hákon was the Hersir of the Royal Regiment, their commander, he was around him far more than I was. He had probably seen sides to him that I never have.

And Fannar loved Ma just as much as I did. He would only choose what was best for her.

"We trust you," Fannar said. "If you trust them to check into her, we will too."

Hákon nodded. "Of course. I know both your positions in the realm and what comes with it. I will ensure that the people I introduce can be trusted."

"Thank you," Fannar said. He stood from his spot, turning towards me. "You leave soon."

I nodded. "The day after next. Will you be there to see us off?" We didn't usually have the time or the ability to see each other off recently. But this wasn't our typical deployment, and we didn't know when we would return.

"If I'm in the fortress, I will be there."

I stood to join him and threw my arms around him in a tight hug. "Promise me that you will be as safe as you can."

"As long as you promise to do the same."

"Deal."

NINE

BRYN

The next morning, Gil walked me to Ma's rooms before he left to find his sisters.

To say goodbye like I was.

I let myself in, the rooms now bright and welcoming, knowing that Ma was doing better. That she was up and moving around. That she wasn't still curled up, absent and unresponsive. While she still didn't talk, that was still much better than it was.

And if that was all I got of her back, if she never spoke to me again, that was enough.

Ma was in her room arranging some winter flowers in a vase. She was in a casual dress much nicer than she had back in Ebonwell, thanks to the handsome salaries that both Fannar and I made. The sleeve was neatly pinned under the stump of her arm.

"Hi, Ma," I said, stepping up beside her. "Those look lovely."

Ma smiled and added one more flower before stepping back.

"Did Fannar bring you those flowers?" I could see that one or two of the blooms were ones I had been given by people in the fortress, but most were not.

Ma shook her head and gently tapped over my heart. I paused for a moment, considering what she meant.

"Gil did?"

Ma nodded with a smile. My chest filled with warmth—with gratitude. I had no idea Gil had visited my mom alone to give her flowers. He had brought them with him when we had visited her, and the fact that he did it on his own and thought of her meant more to me than I could explain.

I would have to find a way to thank him for it.

Ma led the way to the two chairs in front of a large window. She used her hand to draw a blanket over her lap as I sat in the other chair.

She tilted her head, her eyes trained on me.

"I wanted to come by to say goodbye," I said. "I will leave with the Verndari tomorrow. We will probably be gone for a while."

Ma just watched me.

"Fannar will still stop by but may have to leave. If we aren't here, Hákon will visit you. You remember him, right?"

Ma nodded.

"His sister may visit too, or some other people from the fortress. And I will stop in to say hello when I get back as soon as I can."

I couldn't tell her I would visit her when I returned. There was no way of knowing when I would be able to visit when I returned. And even though visiting her would be one of my priorities, there was no way of guaranteeing that there wasn't something more urgent that had to happen first.

When I stood to leave, Ma stood as well, her hand landing

on my forearm to make me pause. When she had my attention, she let go, raising her hand to gesture for me to wait. She pulled something from a cabinet before returning to me. She pressed a container into my hand, the top marked with blue ink.

Ma had made some healing supplies.

It would be the first batch that she had made since Ebonwell. Since Da had died and she had lost her arm. I never thought that she would make any again. I had assumed that part of her was lost, just like her voice seemed to be.

I wrapped my fingers around the container, my throat tight. "Thank you." I cleared my throat. "I hope that I won't have to use it."

I met up with Óskar and Yugar partway through the fortress and joined them for the walk back. Like me, Óskar kept his shoulders back and chin high, ignoring the vitriol spewed at us as we passed and acknowledging the well wishes and prayers to the gods for our success.

We slipped into the Verndari wing, and I closed the doors behind us with a sigh, slumping against them.

Aron stood in the entry to the wing, two chests and a handful of bags by his feet. He peered down the hallway into the wing and then up the stairs to the second floor, hesitating.

"You new around here?" Óskar joked as Yugar ran up to Aron, his tail wagging.

Aron knelt down to scratch between Yugar's ears. "New, a little lost, and pretty overwhelmed," he said.

"We can't help with the new bit, but we can guide you to your rooms. Then we can show you around and try to ease the overwhelming part for you."

Aron nodded, his shoulders loosening. "I would appreciate it. I've never been in the Verndari wing before."

"Not many have. We try to let only the people we like past the doors," Óskar said. He slung a bag over his shoulder and grabbed one of the trunks. Aron did the same. I picked up the last two bags and followed them up the stairs. "All of our personal rooms are up here. The common areas, training hall, and important spaces are downstairs."

Óskar opened the door to Pétur's rooms—Aron's space now.

The maids in our wing had done a good job of preparing it for his arrival. The wooden furniture was polished until it shone, not a speck of dust anywhere to be seen. Not a single hair to show that Pétur had once lived there. A clean slate for Aron.

"You have a living area here, with some additional space for you to add whatever you want to make this feel like home," I explained. "Through the curtain is your bedroom and a bathing room."

"Great," Aron said. He spun in a circle, surveying the space. His eyes landed on a tapestry that hung on the wall with his family symbol. An intricately embroidered purple stem with elaborate thorns on a rich green background. "How long until this room feels less strange?"

I gave him a small smile. "Not as long as you think. It didn't take me too long to feel at home once I started to bond with the others."

"Aw shucks, Talon." Óskar playfully bumped me with his hip. "I didn't know you cared so much."

I rolled my eyes before smacking him with one of the cushions from the bench in front of us. "You're ridiculous."

Aron laughed. "I've never seen the Verndari so relaxed. I always thought you were all rather formal."

"Well, Talon is still new. You'll need to give her a little more time to get a stick up her ass." I hit him with the pillow again. "Hey!"

I ignored Óskar, turning back to Aron. "We have to be formal, or at the least composed, whenever we are in the fortress or in front of the public. But when we are in our wing? Or somewhere where it is just us? Then we are free to be ourselves and not worry about how we are being perceived."

"You're all very close, aren't you?" Aron asked. I nodded. "That must have made it even harder when Pétur left."

Óskar sobered at his words. "It did." He clapped his hands together. "We'll leave the unpacking to you, but how about a tour before you start?"

We led Aron back towards the stairs, pointing out each person's room as we passed. We showed him the training hall and armoury on the main floor before taking him into the common rooms. "We eat dinner here together almost every night," I explained. "You can miss one or two before Georg will hunt you down and drag you down to dinner by your ear."

Aron laughed. "I'll make sure that I'm at dinner tonight. I would hate to make a bad impression on my first day."

ARON DID EXACTLY what he said he would do and joined us for dinner. Óskar and I had waited for him in front of the door to his rooms. The shock and the smile that followed when he saw us waiting brightened my day.

Surprisingly, Baldur hadn't demanded that Rúna eat with him for her last night in the fortress, so all of us were together for dinner.

The first time as the new Verndari.

"Hello everyone, I'm Aron. I don't bother using my title, and I hope you won't either."

Rúna snorted as she began to fill her plate from the dishes in the middle of the table. "Trust me, we try to avoid ours most of the time."

"And you may end up with a new title yourself," Georg added. Aron wasn't officially a Verndari and had sworn no oaths. But if he were to fit in well, it would only be a matter of time before he earned the title himself and became one of us. But just because he didn't have the official title didn't make him any less than us. If he was willing to bear the weight of being one of us, accept the risks, and fight alongside us, then he was a Verndari. Title or no.

"How about we share some things that are essential for him to know so that he can fit in with us," Óskar suggested before taking a drink from his tankard. "I'll start. Rúna gets nasty if she's hungry, and if you wake her up early without a good reason, there is a good chance she will hurt you."

Rúna threw a roll at Óskar, who caught it with a grin. "You are making me sound like some kind of crazy person. I promise I'm not as bad as he is making it seem. Don't believe a word he says."

Aron laughed. "I won't, I promise." He smirked. "Not until I see it for myself, at least."

She threw another roll at him as I giggled.

"I'll go next then," Rúna straightened up in her seat, acting like the proper lady she was taught to be, not some hooligan who threw bread at the table. "Don't sass Georg—he finds the punishment that annoys you the most. Óskar usually does hand-to-hand combat with Gil when he gets on Georg's nerves. And he will make you have dinner with us almost every night."

"I have been warned about the second one, but I will keep the first one in mind."

"It seems like it's my turn then," Georg said. His eyes darted between Gil, Óskar, and I before returning to Gil. "Gil may not be the most vocal of us, but don't let that fool you. He is probably the most observant of all of us. And if his darkness is ever winning the battle, get Bryn or Rúna. They have the best chance of getting through to him."

Aron nodded as Óskar scoffed. "Yeah, that's because one's practically his sister who won't put up with his shit, while the other is the girl he likes, and he wants to get inside her—"

"I dare you to finish that sentence," Gil growled, not looking up from the meat he cut. "I will make you pay for every word next time we spar."

Óskar stammered. "He wants to get inside her heart, is what I was going to say."

Rúna laughed so hard that water almost came out her nose. Aron hid his gaping mouth quickly, no doubt getting whiplash from the stark contrast of who we were versus the sides of us he had seen in the fortress.

"Bryn can outrun any of us. Yugar is the only one that can keep up with her for a prolonged amount of time," Gil said. I smiled at him, relieved that he was the one who was doing the two facts about me. He wouldn't say anything too bad. His eyes took on a playful sparkle. "She also snores."

I gasped. "I do not!"

"Perhaps you do, perhaps you do not." He shrugged, popping the bite of meat into his mouth.

Óskar snorted, and Rúna's laugh echoed through the room.

I rolled my eyes, a smile tugging at the corner of my lips. "Óskar, I'm sure you've noticed, is the jokester among us, and no one is safe from his antics." Óskar sat up in his chair, no doubt proud of my statement. "And there will be times that you will probably prefer Yugar's presence over Óskar's."

"Now that was uncalled for," Óskar said, narrowing his eyes at me.

"Yugar is quieter."

Aron laughed, shaking his head. "Well, this certainly won't be boring, will it?"

"Boring is the last word I'd use," Georg agreed with a grin. "Unfortunately, since no one here can share facts about you just yet, you will have to be the one to do so."

Aron was quiet for a moment. "You're not going to let me just be nice about myself, are you?"

"If you wanted to lose all of my respect, sure," Óskar nodded sagely as he took another bite of his dinner.

"He's being dramatic," Rúna said. "But if you want to be one of us, then you should really share at least one remotely embarrassing thing."

"And she says that Óskar is the dramatic one," I whispered to Gil, causing his lips to quirk.

Aron thought for a moment. "I love being in motion— running, sailing, riding."

"Oh, gods, another runner," Óskar muttered.

I smirked as Aron continued. "In terms of embarrassing, my mother says that I might as well settle down and marry my weapons since I've yet to bring home a girl to meet her."

Georg chuckled, raising his tankard in a toast. "Welcome to the team, Heartbreaker."

TEN

BRYN

Thee was an anticipation, a constant thrum of energy, through my veins when I knew we were being sent into the field. When we were unexpectedly sent to Hazelpeak, my veins had pulsed with anxiety, and nerves rushed throughout my entire body.

But now, with my saddlebags and trunk packed, my body was itching to get on the road. To get to where I had to go and do what needed to be done.

The faster we left, the sooner we accomplished what we had to do, and the quicker we could return. Which meant being back in the fortress with Ma and relieving Fannar and Lúdvík of our assignments.

Freeing them from the risks and duties that we bore on our shoulders.

Planned departures were different from emergency deployments, including a pre-departure briefing. Which is why we sat around our meeting room table, dressed in our leather armour, our belongings already given to the stable hands to take care of until we were ready.

I couldn't sit still. Every nerve and vein in my body pulsed, ready to get on the road. My leg bounced beneath the table, the only outlet for my buzzing energy.

Ragna took Georg's typical place at the head of the table and passed out a packet of parchments to each of us.

"As you know, we are sending you to Wolfmire. Wolfmire and the surrounding lands are governed by Jarl Einar," Ragna explained as I began to flip through the parchments in front of me. "Jarl Einar and his forces are renowned in battle, and we need to be certain that they will be fighting by our side should this escalate further. Not to mention that his coffers and store-houses are deep and would be an incredible boon to us if he is willing to open them."

The information in the parchment was robust, but not in the way that I expected. Less of it was focused on Jarl Einar himself; instead, it focused more on the things under his control. Pages were dedicated to his military forces and others to his city, Wolfmire. The section outlining who he was, was quite limited, and most of the information on Jarl Einar regarded his past. His accomplishments, past allies and deci-sions, and things he had been a part of.

"Where do his loyalties currently lie?" Georg asked, thumbing through the parchments himself.

"We don't know. Jarl Einar not only keeps his cards close to his chest but also doesn't have a pattern of who he supports. He does what he believes is right, not what his friends tell him to do."

Rúna shifted in her chair, placing her packet in front of her. "You're sending us there to gauge what he will do."

"I'm sending you there to win his support." Ragna sighed, her gaze landing on each of us. "I cannot stress how important Jarl Einar's support is. If the other pieces fall, as I suspect, then we need him. If he remains neutral, we are in trouble. If he sides against us, we won't survive."

"How long do we have?" Georg asked as he studied the final page. "Is there anything for us to go on? An angle for us to take with this?"

"We will recall you to the fortress if needed, but you are to do whatever you can to convince him regardless of how long it takes. I have no guidance to give you on how you should approach him. He supports what he believes is right and who he believes earns it. You—" Ragna looked to all of us. "You all need to convince him that you deserve it—that we deserve it."

Nerves began to overwhelm the energy pumping through me just minutes ago. In the last few weeks, we had been needed in multiple places at once, forcing us to pick and prioritize where we went. We had to determine where our support was essential, not just important or wanted. Ragna assigning us to Wolfmire *indefinitely* highlighted the importance of Jarl Einar's alliance.

Important enough to remove us from the fortress that was rapidly being divided by alliances. Important enough that any protection details that may be needed were being handed off to the Royal Regiment.

We could not fail.

Ragna led us out of the room as we naturally settled into our typical pairings.

Georg and Aron in the front.

Óskar and I behind them.

And Gil and Rúna watching our backs.

Our horses were ready in the courtyard as we arrived with a small wagon attached to a pack horse. So were the crowds.

Fortress staff, residents, and warriors were crowded in the courtyard. This wasn't an emergency departure; there was no imminent threat for them to worry about. Just plenty of time for word to spread that we were leaving.

The crowd parted as we made our way closer to our horses.

Some shouted well wishes while another spat at us.

I didn't flinch, smiling at the crowd around us as I kept my fingers from shaking with every scrap of willpower I had. Óskar settled Yugar in a special carrier on the packhorse as Baldur joined us, a stable hand scrambling to keep up with him as he led his horse through the crowd. Another servant followed behind, carrying a trunk.

Rúna tensed as he came closer. Gil shifted closer to her side.

"Put my trunk in the wagon," Baldur ordered the servant.

Rúna wiped her face clean of any emotion. There was only one reason that Baldur would issue that order.

He was coming with us.

"What is going on, Baldur?" Ragna asked carefully. We couldn't afford to show any discord, any disconnect, especially within the Commanding Family.

"I'm joining the Verndari on their assignment."

No.

If Jarl Einar was as important as Ragna made him out to be, and I had no reason to doubt her, we had to ensure that he aligned with us. But if Baldur was indeed the traitor as we thought—he would do everything he could to ensure that didn't happen.

"I didn't realize that you were joining them," Ragna said, her face carefully blank.

"It was a new decision—it was made just this morning."

Rúna's face lost what little colour she had, her fingers freezing on the straps of her saddlebags.

Georg had no option but to dip his head in agreement. "Of course. We would be happy to have you join us."

"The Verndari were just preparing to leave. They depart in just a few moments," Ragna said as she turned for the gates with a sigh. "I will take my place for the departure."

Fannar pushed through the crowd, and the people started to shift easily once they saw the Royal Regiment insignia he wore.

He nodded at the others when he reached us. Óskar clasped his shoulder before mounting his horse.

"I wasn't sure if you were going to be able to make it," I said, wrapping my arms around Fannar's shoulders.

"I almost didn't, but I'm happy I did." Fannar gave me a gentle squeeze. "Be careful out there, yeah?"

The stable hands cleared the path to the gate as Georg and Aron mounted their horses.

I nodded and stepped towards my horse. "You too. You better be in one piece when I get back."

"I'll see what I can do," Fannar teased before stepping away from our horses with a wave to the others, his eyes lingering on Aron, curiosity flickering. I had forgotten that he still hadn't met him. I would have to introduce them when we got back.

Before mounting, I checked my saddlebags and straps and buckles one last time. Óskar positioned his horse beside mine as we took our places behind Georg and Aron.

Baldur headed straight for Rúna.

"Happy to see me?" he asked, his words neutral, but his eyes alight with malice.

Rúna's throat bobbed. "Of course, Commanding Son. We are happy to have you join us."

My eyes landed on Gil. His body was stock still, like a predator ready to pounce.

He didn't move for a moment before he forced himself into the saddle. Not getting involved with the situation, regardless of how much his protective instincts were probably begging him to.

Screaming at him to.

Baldur smirked, his thumb brushing Rúna's cheek, lingering on her bottom lip. "That's just what I was hoping you would say."

He left to mount his horse, taking his place at the head of our caravan as he was entitled to as Commanding Son.

I didn't look back to Rúna; Gil would ensure she was okay. For me to get involved would be suspicious as no one in the fortress knew that she was forced into this situation.

They all thought that she had chosen it.

Ragna blew the horn and provided our official departure; the traditional words were again issued across the courtyard. Strike hard, strike fast.

Once outside the gates, we settled into an easy pace to account for the pack horse and wagon.

Just us and Baldur for days on the road.

What could go wrong?

ELEVEN

BRYN

Whenever we were on the road, outside the fortress walls, a weight always seemed to lift off Rúna's shoulders. She smiled easier and laughed like she used to. Our trips were her escape—her chance to regain her strength before she was back in the fortress.

Before she was back with Baldur.

As hard as it was to be in the field and in danger, she craved those moments because she was free. I don't think I will ever forget the look on her face when she realized that Baldur was joining us.

Baldur led our caravan down the road. He had left Rúna alone so far, probably because her position was in the rear, and he couldn't bring himself to lower himself from the place of importance that allowed him to lead the caravan.

Instead, he had a small conversation with Georg and Aron, his voice louder than I am sure any of us liked, but no one would tell him to be quiet. Not until the sun began to sink below the horizon and noise could spell our deaths. Besides, if he was talking to Georg and Aron, he was leaving Rúna alone, which was enough for me.

"Are you okay?" Gil asked Rúna, his voice barely loud enough to reach me.

"I'm fine." Rúna's voice was equally as soft. "I don't have any other choice other than to be fine. I don't want to let it consume me. I still want a choice. So, I choose to be fine. Maybe if I say it enough, it will be true."

The road curved to the left, hugging the base of a hill on the right. A small game path crested the hill, but it was largely overgrown.

"I wonder what animals use that path," Baldur mused, his voice carrying down the caravan. "Rúna, do you have any idea?"

"I wouldn't presume to know," Rúna said, her voice quivering slightly. Her horse's ears twitched towards the path. "Óskar would probably know better than I do."

"Odds are that any of the local wildlife would use it." Óskar's head was tilted to the side as he studied the path. "It almost looks like a small travelling route, but that makes no sense. It would have to be a game trail of some kind. I'm not seeing any initial signs that it is a path for a specific animal."

Baldur scoffed. "Of course you don't." He dismissed Óskar easily, as he usually did. As too many people did.

"What's that supposed to mean?" I hissed. I knew very well what he meant. He meant the same thing that he always did, that Ottó did, that other people in the fortress did.

They thought that Óskar wasn't worthy of his position as a Verndari. That his bloodrite was weak. But they didn't realize that regardless of his bloodrite, animals had free will.

At times, they pushed back and didn't listen to him, but

that didn't mean that he wasn't deserving of his position on the Verndari. He was an elite archer, and his bloodrite saved us more than it cost us.

But it was an easy thing for people to criticize.

I wouldn't stand for their criticisms any more than I would stand for them treating Gil like he's a monster.

"There's nowhere great for us to set up for the night," Georg said, diverting the conversation away from the dangerous waters it was drifting into. "We must get off the road early and get all set up. Otherwise, we will be at risk."

"Where are you thinking?" Aron asked. "We probably won't reach the forest in time."

"There's a semi-sheltered area before the forest. We will aim for that."

The conversation that flowed afterwards was stilted. Awkward. No one quite knew how to behave now that Baldur was here. It threw off the typical camaraderie amongst us, which was already feeling a little odd with the addition of Aron. I chatted quietly with Óskar, the soft murmur of the other duo's conversation floating around us.

Georg finally directed us off the road when the sun was getting low on the horizon. We journeyed around a hill; it wasn't as covered as I would have preferred, but it was better than being in view of the road.

"It's cold rations tonight. I don't want to risk any lingering smoke from a fire," Georg said. "Let's get the tents set up. Baldur, is your tent in the wagon?"

"I didn't bring one, I'll just share with Rúna," Baldur said as he dismounted his horse.

"Rúna shares with Bryn." Georg ran a hand over his head with a sigh.

Baldur shook his head. "No. That won't work." He slung an arm around Rúna's shoulder once she had finished tending to her horse. "I will be with Rúna."

Rúna didn't say a word.

"That's alright," I said lightly. It was the very opposite of alright, but I couldn't say that. "I will sleep in another tent." Being kicked out of my tent was not worth the argument that was sure to arise if I pushed back against Baldur. It wasn't worth the effort.

"With only three tents, we will have to have a tent of three," Georg explained.

"I can join Gil and Óskar's tent. If it's okay with them."

Gil nodded. "Of course."

"Tent buddies!" Óskar cheered as he picked me up and spun me around. He placed me back down and turned towards Gil. "Three people in a tent is going to be tight. If anyone has to snuggle Bryn to save space, I want it to be me."

"I would like to see you try," Gil said, the corner of his mouth quirking up in a smirk. He gently pulled me back against his chest, his hand resting on my waist.

I smacked Óskar's shoulder. "You can't just claim me like that!"

Óskar laughed. "We'll put her in the middle to both snuggle her."

"Bryn can sleep in the middle if she likes, but if you think she will be cuddling both of us, then you will be surprised," Gil said as he and I began to put up the tent. Óskar lifted Yugar down from his carrier. "Not to mention you will have your dog to cuddle with."

Once the tents were set up, we gathered in the centre where the fire pit would usually be. We ate bread, cheese, and cold meats before relaxing until sunset.

Rúna sat between Baldur's legs, her back to his chest. His arm was wrapped around her chest, his hand holding her shoulder. Rúna was the picture of ease if I ignored her tensed shoulders. I sat between Gil and Óskar, resting my head on Gil as I scratched between Yugar's ears.

"How did this happen?" Aron asked, gesturing to Rúna and Baldur. "When the rumours started going around the fortress, I didn't put much weight on them, but it seems the rumours are true."

"I have always known that I needed to marry someone powerful," Baldur explained. "The King Commander can't have any weaknesses, which includes having someone weak by their side."

"Not all of the Queens have had bloodrites," Gil said.

Baldur nodded. "Correct. But they have all been powerful in some form. If not their bloodrite, it is in military prowess, money, or connections. I can hold my own on a battlefield, and I do not need money or connections, so I knew I wanted someone with a strong bloodrite."

"So that led you to Rúna?" Aron asked.

"There were a few different potential options that I was debating between." His eyes swung to mine for a moment before focusing back on Aron. My stomach rolled, a coldness pulsing through my veins. Why would he have considered me? I couldn't even control my bloodrite when he focused on Rúna.

Was it just because I was in the process of earning my title as a Verndari?

Baldur made it sound so cold. Like he had a check list of all the women in the realm with strong bloodrites and he had been crossing them off one by one.

"A few months ago, I learned that Rúna's intentions might

be aligned with mine," Baldur continued. "And now we are here."

He didn't learn anything besides whatever information he now held over her. Rúna's intentions had never aligned with Baldur's, where their facade of a relationship was concerned.

Aron didn't seem convinced by Baldur's story. Whether it was the tension that seemed to have settled over us like a blanket or Rúna's complete lack of contribution to the conversation, something had him hesitating over accepting Baldur's story. But he eventually nodded, acknowledging what he had said.

I would have to fill him in as soon as I knew he would have our back and keep our secrets. He had given me every reason to trust him so far, but with something this important, I needed to be sure.

The sun sank lower over the horizon. There were only a few moments left before we were in complete darkness.

"We will rotate watch as we always do," Georg said, standing from his spot. "Rúna will take the first rotation."

"I think someone else should take the first watch," Baldur disagreed.

Georg pursed his lips, his fingers rubbing at his forehead. "Óskar will take the first watch, followed by Rúna. Then, we will rotate through the rest of us. Aron, myself, Bryn, and Gil."

He didn't bother assigning Baldur to watch. I doubt he would be willing to take his turn, but I wouldn't want him to anyway. The last time one of the traitors took a watch, we were ambushed, and I almost died.

I would be happy to avoid that this time.

I led the way to our tent, Gil close behind me. It was a tight squeeze with three people. We had the bedrolls pressed right up against each other and our saddle bags pushed above the heads of the rolls.

"I can take the middle if you prefer," Gil said as he closed the tent flap behind us.

"It makes more sense for me to be in the middle. I'm the smallest of the three of us." I removed my boots, placing them at the foot of my bedroll before starting on my armour. "Besides, I don't mind, it doesn't make me uncomfortable."

Gil did the same, removing his layers until he was left with his loose shirt and pants. He knelt on his bedroll, untucking the blankets and furs and overlapping them with mine.

Making one large bedroll.

"Is this alright?" he asked.

I climbed onto my side, facing him. "Yes, it is. I would have suggested it myself if I thought you would be okay with it."

"It is becoming easier, more...natural." He joined me, his forehead resting against mine.

Easier to trust himself around me. Easier to let himself touch me, to let down the walls he had spent his whole life building.

My tongue darted out, wetting my lips. His eyes traced the movement.

"I'm happy to hear that," I said softly.

I gently pressed my lips to his, fighting every desire to push my body closer and deepen the kiss. In the field, in a spot exposed with little cover from the Skolli, was not the place to give in to the needs coursing through my veins and pooling low in my stomach. I rolled over to my other side and got comfortable.

Gil snaked a hand around my waist and pulled me close so my back was pressed to his chest. So that every part of our bodies touched. His hand snuck under my shirt, pushing to the bare skin of my stomach, his thumb brushing across me gently, leaving a line of fire in its wake.

"Trust me," Gil whispered as he kissed the crook of my neck, his breath fanning across my skin. "I am more than happy to say that."

TWELVE

BRYN

A few days later, we reached Wolfmire.

And what a city it was.

Sturdy, reinforced stone walls completely encircled the city, standing as tall as three houses. Some buildings were taller than the walls, the towers spiralling high into the sky. Some were perfectly straight, some lopsided as though they had been added throughout the years. The walls were guarded well, with warriors spaced evenly throughout. A team of four were stationed by the open gates.

One flagged down a young boy no older than ten. They whispered into the boy's ear, who nodded and took off at a run, quickly disappearing amongst the people on the street.

Baldur was stopped by one of the guards. "Commanding Son Baldur and the Verndari. We are here to see Jarl Einar."

The guard dipped her head in respect. "He will be up at the castle. Follow the road to the left, on top of the hill. You can't miss it."

Baldur just led his horse into Wolfmire, not acknowledging the woman. Georg nodded his head in respect as he passed.

Wolfmire was unlike any city I had seen before.

It was densely packed since the entire city was contained within the walls. Some buildings and towers reached four or five stories into the air. The streets were filled with people going about their days, wagons transporting goods and warriors. Plenty of warriors.

The mountains in the distance made the city hilly in areas, and the castle was on top of the tallest. A massive stone structure with numerous towers and large outer buildings.

The main roads were wide and easy to navigate, but the smaller side streets and alleys were small and twisty, as though they had had to fit around the buildings. It was as though the city had long since outgrown the ground inside the walls and had been forced to become creative to house everyone.

It took us a little while to navigate our way to the castle, which was even more intimidating up close.

Five large barracks ringed the castle, with various training areas, paddocks, and stables between them.

Some stable hands came forward to take our horses.

I dismounted, discreetly stretching my muscles that ached from days in the saddle.

"Good tidings. Would you be able to point us towards Jarl Einar?" Georg asked one of the many warriors nearby. Everywhere I looked, I could see one. Training, walking through the grounds, laughing.

"This time of day? He's probably in his study. First floor, west wing," he said gruffly.

Georg and Baldur led the way to the study, with the rest of us following behind. They occasionally stopped other warriors or castle staff to be pointed in the right direction.

Eventually, we reached a shut, dark-stained wooden door.

Georg knocked.

My fingers fidgeted with the edge of my furs, anxious about what lay behind the door.

Gil's fingers brushed mine, resting against them until they finally stilled. Centering me—comforting me.

"Come in," a gruff voice called from inside the room. Georg opened the door, allowing Baldur to enter before following him in. The rest of us filed in one by one, Gil closing the door behind us.

A man close to Georg's age sat behind the desk. His closely cropped blonde hair matched his neatly trimmed beard. He had faint lines by his eyes and bracketing his mouth. Jarl Einar was dressed in nicely made but utterly practical clothing. When he stood to greet us, he was just taller than Rúna. His hands were covered in small silver scars, the result of countless cuts and scrapes from various blades.

"Jarl Einar," Baldur said, clasping hands with him. "Well met."

"Good tidings, Commanding Son," Jarl Einar bowed his head. "Verndari. To what pleasure do I owe this visit?"

"I don't know if you have heard, but the Skolli have returned to torture Drysden."

Jarl Einar scoffed and rested his weight on the front of the desk. "You don't know if I've heard? My forces have been fighting them, boy."

Georg stepped forward. "They've attacked Wolfmire?"

"No. But they have been attacking the smaller settlements and caravans around us in the north. So have the Ógn," Jarl Einar said, crossing his arms over his chest. "Wolfmire is a stronghold—the northernmost stronghold. We must help protect the people around us even if, *especially if*, the fortress has not deemed us worthy of support."

"We have had to prioritize other things. We can't risk

spreading our forces too thin." Baldur straightened his shoulders, preparing to counter anything that Jarl Einar may say.

"Oh yes—are you talking about the attack on the fortress? The battle where the Verndari and Hákon fought, and you were nowhere to be found?" Jarl Einar asked, his brow arched. "Or are you referring to the fact that right after the attack, one of the Verndari left the fortress alone? Later to be followed by the others who returned without him?"

Jarl Einar was more informed than I had thought he would be. The news about Pétur leaving after the attack wasn't widely known, which meant that Jarl Einar had his own sources of information in the fortress.

Observant sources of information.

"You forget that I, like many other Jarls, send rotations of my forces to the fortress every month to support the country. They notice things while there and inform me when they return." Jarl Einar straightened and crossed his shoulders over his chest. "Or, perhaps, you don't even notice that they are there."

Georg stepped forward. "Then you know what we currently face, what may await us in the future. Will you support us? Can we rely on you?"

"Not yet," Jarl Einar said. His words caused my stomach to tighten into knots. "Viciously beating your opponent when they have already lost earns you no favour with me." Baldur's face reddened. Rúna kept her shoulders back, giving no sign that his words affected her, but her eyes wouldn't lift from the floor. Either she was ashamed, or she knew that she couldn't hide the anger that swirled within them. "Naming a Warlord to the Verndari for his skill and accomplishments rather than a high-ranking Jarl for their title is a good step." Jarl Einar nodded to Aron before turning towards me. "So is a village girl agreeing to, and succeeding in, competing for her title even though it should be hers by birthright."

"How do we earn your support?" Aron asked, stepping forward. I joined him. Jarl Einar had respect for us, no matter how small, and it seemed like he had absolutely none for Baldur.

Perhaps Aron and I were our best chance.

"Convince me that you deserve it. Otherwise, regardless of how bad it gets, you will not see a single coin, warrior, or weapon from me."

He gestured to the doors before turning back to his work. Clearly dismissing us.

Gil led the way out to find a servant waiting for us, who quickly dipped into a curtsy.

"I have five bunks available throughout the barracks and two rooms for the girls," she said.

"I will stay with Rúna. Only four bunks will be needed," Baldur sneered.

She curtsied again. "Of course, Commanding Son, forgive me. If you follow me, I will show you where you will all stay during your time in Wolfmire."

My room was directly across from Rúna's. Well, Rúna and Baldur's.

It was a small room, but it had everything that I needed. A large bunk took up most of the space, while a desk occupied one of the walls. A storage chest was tucked in the corner, and a small window looked over the towers and buildings of Wolfmire.

My trunk and saddlebags were already at the base of my

bunk, so I draped my heavy furs over the covers and followed the others to their bunks.

While the furs were warm and formal, they were a nightmare when navigating busy hallways and crowded areas.

"Unfortunately, we do not have four bunks together in one barrack," the servant explained as she led us back into the courtyard. "You will be split up."

"That's no problem. We appreciate your work in getting us situated," Georg said as we entered the first barracks.

The barracks were rowdy, filled with rows of bunks stacked two high. Most of the bunks were neatly made and empty, but there were warriors throughout, lounging or chatting with each other.

The servant led us to a set of empty bunks, neatly folded blankets and furs.

"Two of you can sleep here," she said. "The other two will be in another barracks."

"Are the other bunks closer to the door?" Óskar asked.

She nodded. "They are."

"Then I will stay in the other barracks. It will be better for Yugar."

Gil gestured to the bunk. "I will stay here."

"So will I," Aron said.

"Then I will show the others to their beds," she said.

Aron and Gil began making their bunks, Aron on the bottom and Gil on the top. The other warriors around us watched us, assessing us.

One stepped forward, a small smile on his handsome face. He reached out to clasp hands with me. "Good tidings. Welcome to Wolfmire. The name's Luck."

"Bryn," I said before gesturing to the others. "And this is Gil and Aron."

"You're new to the team then, Aron?" he joked, bumping Aron's shoulder.

Aron laughed. "Brand new and thrown into the thick of it." He turned towards Gil and me. "Luck and I sailed together yearly on the warships. We fought side by side, and our hammocks on the ships were directly beside each other. I think he knows me better than anyone else at this point."

"You're lucky to have him. He's wicked fast with a blade." Luck grinned as he continued, "Not to mention my Ma loves him. That also has to count for something."

"I know how good of a fighter he is. He has already saved my life once," I said.

Luck sauntered towards me. "Let me save you from boredom while you're here. I can take you into the city."

Aron laughed so hard he bent over, his hand on his stomach. "That is the worst thing you have ever said to a girl."

"I thought it was pretty clever, playing off of what she said."

I giggled, leaning into Gil. "It was pretty bad."

"Not to mention she's already with someone. You wouldn't want to tangle with him," Aron said, his eyes darting past his friend to land on Gil and me.

"I'm sure I could take him," Luck said, chuckling. "Who is it anyways?"

"Me." Gil wrapped an arm around me, his hand curling around my hip.

Luck spun on his heel, his mouth gaping like a fish. He shut it with a snap, a smile spreading across his face. "I had no idea."

"Now you know."

Luck chuckled. "Well, my offer stands to both of you. I

would happily show you the ropes or take you into the city if you would like."

Aron wrapped an arm around Luck's shoulders. "Show me around—let me in on the who's who of Wolfmire while we let the other two get situated."

Luck waved with a small grin before leading Aron to a group of warriors. I laid down in Gil's bunk as he continued unpacking. The warriors around us glanced over, curious, but none were actively judging us—*him*—like they did at the fortress.

That was enough to let me relax even further into his bunk, still aware but not fully on guard.

"Luck seems friendly. A bit forward, maybe, but nice. It will be good to have at least one person who knows us here," I said.

Gil looked at me from where he was organizing the chest, one eyebrow arched. "Planning to take him up on his offer of exploring Wolfmire then?" he joked, a small smile threatening at the corner of his mouth.

I threw the pillow at him, which he easily caught. He set it on the foot of his bunk as he finished what he was doing. "Not in the way he meant it. For all of us, though, it might be fun to explore the city one afternoon."

"I agree," Gil said as he closed and locked the chest. He picked up the pillow and turned towards where I lay on the bunk.

He tucked the pillow under my head before placing his hands on either side of me. He leaned down so close the warmth of his body seeped into my own. Gil tucked his head beside mine, his breath dancing across my ear and neck. "We should do it."

"Do what?" I breathed, wrapping my hand around the back of his neck. "There's plenty of things we should do."

"Go down into Wolfmire together. Explore the shops before finding a dining house or a tavern."

I smiled at him. "Would we have the time for it?"

"We will make the time for it," he said, pressing a kiss to my ear, the crook of my neck, my cheek.

I turned my head, catching his lips on my own. "We'll make the time," I agreed before kissing him again.

THIRTEEN

GIL

The people I passed didn't acknowledge me, but it didn't feel like it was because of my darkness. They were preoccupied with their schedules, so used to being surrounded by warriors, that I didn't receive more than a cursory glance.

I had dressed carefully, comfortably yet presentable, without a single Verndari symbol or family crest. More than happy to blend into the masses of people around me, to be one of the many instead of one of the few for a few moments.

After a few wrong turns, I found myself outside Bryn's door.

I knocked before tucking my hands into the pockets of my trousers.

A bang sounded within the room, followed by a muffled curse before the door swung open to reveal Bryn.

She was dressed like I was, her white shirt oversized, the neck slouching down her arm, leaving her shoulder bare. Her curls hung freely around her head, some strands falling over her face.

Bryn blew her hair out of her face as she rubbed at one of her knees.

"Was that the crash that I heard?" I asked, nodding towards her leg.

"Yes," Bryn hissed, brushing her fingers over her knee one last time before straightening. She held the door open wider and stepped back to let me in. "I wasn't expecting to see you tonight."

I draped my cloak over her desk chair as she shut the door. "I was not planning on it either. But I was lying on my bunk when I realized I did not want to sleep yet. The bunks were so loud, with so much going on, and I—" I paused, trying to find my words.

"And you wanted some peace," Bryn finished for me with a small smile on her face.

"And I wanted to see you," I added softly.

Bryn's smile lit up her eyes as she held a hand to me. I stepped forward, interlacing my fingers with hers.

"Were you already in bed?" I asked, noticing the disturbed furs on her bunk and the dimmed lighting in the room as I pulled her closer to me.

"I was just reading." She moved closer to her bunk, our fingers still interlocked, our arms stretching between us. "You can join me if you want."

"I would love to."

I climbed into her bunk, resting my back against the headboard. I gently pulled her to me, her back against my chest. Wrapping one arm around her body, I used the other to pull the furs over us.

Bryn picked up the book and carefully flipped through the pages to find her spot.

"What are you reading?" I asked, my fingers tracing mindless shapes on her.

"It's a story about a girl who is an archaeologist and a boy who translates texts into different languages and their journey."

"Sounds interesting. Have you gotten very far into it yet?"

Bryn twisted, looking up at me with a smile. "I was still in the first chapter, but I'm going to start from the beginning because I think you might like it."

"You do not have to do that," I told her, brushing some of her hair behind her ear. "I am sure I will be able to follow along wherever you left off."

"I want to," she said, returning to the book.

Her soft voice filled the room, the crackling of the fire accompanying her words. My body loosened, and my muscles finally released the tension that had been growing in them. Her voice soothed every agitated, anxious part of my soul, leaving calmness in its wake.

I allowed my eyes to fall shut as I pressed my forehead to the crook of her shoulder, pressing a lingering kiss to her throat. My lips drifted lazily across her skin as she continued to read.

She finished the chapter and shifted in my arms. I lifted my head to find her setting aside the book before turning to face me. Bryn's eyes were as soft as her smile.

"That's a little distracting when I'm trying to focus on the words on the page," she teased me.

"I did not know that anything had that kind of power."

"If anyone could do that it would be you." Her eyes drifted to my lips. "It would be that."

She laid down in her bed, my body naturally following her

lead. Mirroring her movements as though it were powerless to resist her pull.

We shared the same pillow, our breath twirling between our faces.

"Would you like to stay here tonight?" Bryn asked. "It would be quieter than the barracks."

I swallowed thickly. "As much as I would love to stay here, I can't. Not yet."

"You've stayed the night before." Bryn's eyebrows were furrowed, but her words weren't accusatory. She was simply trying to put the pieces together, not pushing my boundaries. Always aware of the walls I was slowly working to tear down. "We shared a tent on the way here."

"I was there to comfort you or share a tent with others. This would be different."

Bryn smiled softly. "This would be different," she agreed.

"I would want to kiss you, and if I did that, I would not want to stop," I said gravely. "I cannot stay here. Not yet."

FOURTEEN

BRYN

With no separate dining area for us to use, we had to eat in the main hall with everyone else. Our only private room was mine; it wouldn't be good for appearances if we hid away all day. Unfortunately, all the indoor training rooms had been reserved before we arrived, leaving us with one option—training outside. Luck recommended one of the outdoor rings, claiming it was the warmest option, and Georg quickly reserved it for the next few weeks.

The next morning, I dressed in my warmest training clothes and went to the main hall to find something to eat. Gil and Aron were already there, sitting with Luck and some other warriors at a table. I slid into the open spot across from Gil.

The main hall consisted of several tables with benches on each side. Jarl Einar's banner hung from the wall behind the table on the raised platform. Several servants walked through the hall with pitchers of various drinks while the food was already set out on platters on the tables.

"Good morning," I said, reaching for a food platter. I

speared some pieces with my fork, placing them on my plate. "Did we really beat Georg down?"

"Georg is bunking with Óskar," Gil reminded me, sipping his drink.

"Does Óskar sleep in longer than the others?" Aron asked.

I shook my head with a smile. "No, that's Rúna, but Óskar is a close second." Gil raised an eyebrow at me, clearly hinting that I should include myself in that statement.

Georg entered the hall at that moment, a bleary-eyed Óskar beside him. Yugar trotted happily at their side, his nose working overtime with all the food around him.

They joined us, and Aron introduced Luck to them. Yugar sat beside Luck, no doubt sensing a new target for his puppy dog eyes. When he went to scratch his head, Yugar simply raised his paw, knocking it against Luck's hand.

Óskar chuckled. "Now you have to give him a bit of food."

"Why?" Luck was already reaching for a piece of meat to give to him.

"He does that whenever he gets his food, but sometimes he senses opportunity or weakness and will do it when he wants something," Óskar explained as he filled his plate.

"It's his form of begging."

Óskar nodded. "Yes, exactly. Much more civilized than the dogs that bark to get what they want."

Rúna and Baldur entered next. Baldur immediately headed for the raised dais, where Jarl Einar and his family sat while Rúna joined us.

She took a seat by my side. I found her hand under the table and gave it a squeeze. *I'm here.* It said. *We're all here.*

Rúna smiled sadly at me for a moment before she straightened her shoulders and sank into the comfort of her typical behaviour. Gil watched every interaction between us, focusing on Rúna for a moment, his eyes sad, before turning towards me. I gave him a small, barely noticeable shake of my head.

Leave it for now.

"What's the plan for today?" Rúna asked.

"Sparring," Georg said, finishing a bite of his food. "We'll try different combinations with Aron to see what works best."

Óskar leaned forward so that he could see Aron around Georg. "You can't have Talon—she's mine."

"I thought she was with him?" Luck gestured between Gil and me.

"I am," I said simultaneously as Gil said, "She is."

I pushed my plate away from myself, full. "Óskar and I are partners, same as Gil and Rúna. We fight together and train together. We know how each other fights and thinks in a battle."

"I'm also the only one with a giant eagle for when she throws herself off of walls," Óskar said.

"That was one time!"

"One time is all it takes."

Gil nodded. "He is right." His face said everything that he didn't. It takes one moment on the battlefield for me to get injured. For me to get killed. And the fact that I didn't hesitate, didn't think before I pushed myself off that wall terrified him. What could have happened.

What might still happen whenever we stepped foot on the battlefield.

I knew how he felt because I felt the same way about him.

Georg sighed, shaking his head. "Children, children." He stood from the bench. "Time to get to work."

He led us to a smaller training area outside that was tucked into a crook of the castle. It was empty; only a handful of warriors walked by. Covered in a thin layer of snow, the ground was certainly frozen. Luckily, it was hidden from the wind, protecting us from the cold.

I would hate to see the others if this was the warmest option.

Georg hopped the wooden fence into the centre of the ring. "The only way to know what may work for our pairings would be to try them out. We will start with Bryn and Óskar against Aron and me."

I climbed on the lowest rung of the fence, swinging my leg over the top and dropping down on the other side. Óskar joined me after wrapping a blanket around Yugar. For a dog, he got very cold very fast in the winter. Not to mention that he was spoiled, and that dog knew it. He just had to give us a look, and he would get anything he wanted.

I swung my arms back and forth to try and warm them up in the cold. "Bloodrites or weapons?"

"Weapons only for now," Georg said, swinging his war axe to warm up his muscles.

I pulled a couple of daggers from their sheaths while Óskar checked that his arrows were properly padded so that no one got hurt. "So, how do you want to play this?" I asked him quietly. We kept our backs on the others so they wouldn't see what we said. Not that they wouldn't be able to deduce it on their own. We were well-versed in each other's fighting styles, strengths, and weaknesses. "What's the plan here?"

"I'll take Georg. If we were to fight with our bloodrites, I'd be our best bet at keeping his speed and strength at a distance. You'll need to take Aron," Óskar said as he tucked his arrows back in his quiver. "If you can even reach him. His arm span is probably longer than your whole body."

"Shut your mouth. You forget that I have some pull with the one of the people you hate to spar against," I teased.

Óskar grumbled, swinging his quiver over his shoulder. "Let's just talk about something else?"

"That's what I thought," I snickered.

I turned my attention to the other side of the circle where Aron and Georg stood with their weapons in their hands. A war axe in Georg's and a pair of slightly smaller ones in Aron's.

"Standard rules," Georg said as we took our spots in the circle. "The first person to be incapacitated or knocked out of the circle loses. Gil, count us in."

Gil was leaning against the fence surrounding the ring, his foot on the bottom rung and his arms resting on the top. "Set," he paused. I bounced slightly on the balls of my feet as I waited for him to start the spar. "Begin."

Óskar immediately fired a shot between the two men, separating them. He followed it up with a second arrow straight at Georg.

I surged towards Aron while Georg was distracted. I didn't stand a chance if they came at me together. Not without my bloodrite, at the very least. They were taller and stronger than me; I was done if they were to face me together.

Aron shifted, balancing his weight easily, and swung one of his axes over his head.

I blocked it with my crossed daggers, the strength of the blow ringing through my arms. I twisted my daggers, attempting to lock the axe between them, but he slid it through them easily and slashed at me in the same movement.

Talented with his weapons was an understatement.

I spun out of the way, throwing my daggers at his feet, forcing him towards the thrum of Óskar's bow. I lunged back in, two fresh blades in my hands.

Aron knocked them away, spinning and countering with his own swipe.

I ducked under the swing and snapped out a kick at his stomach. Aron jumped back to avoid it, bumping into Georg, causing him to stumble the slightest bit.

I leapt forward, resting the blade of my dagger against his throat.

Aron swallowed. "I yield."

"That wasn't perfect, but it has promise," Georg said. "We were a fresh pairing against a more seasoned one. There will be some growing pains. But I think it is a base that we can build off of."

"It will take time for us to anticipate each other's moves the way the others probably do," Aron agreed. "And it will take me some time to figure out where exactly I fit into this group."

A slow clap carried over to us as Jarl Einar joined Gil and Rúna at the fence. "Well done, you flowed very smoothly around each other." His words were threaded with sarcasm and judgment.

"It was our first-time training together since Aron joined us," Georg said as we joined the others.

"I can tell."

"It will take time for us to be as conditioned as a unit as we were with Pétur."

Jarl Einar scoffed. "The Verndari are supposed to be the most talented and lethal unit of warriors in the realm. The fact that you look like that—" he gestured towards the circle "—at the time that we need you most is concerning."

"We are talented. We are not perfect," Gil said. "The lethality doesn't come overnight—it is honed."

"I understand that more than anyone. I do. But how can I

have faith that you can lead my men if I am not there when you look like that when you are sparring?"

I tucked my daggers back into their sheaths. "You trust in us because of who we are and our actions. You say you respect us for adding Aron to the Verndari, but that means you'll also need to respect us for the work it will take. You don't get one without the other."

Jarl Einar surveyed me for a moment. "Fair enough. But you'll need to show me more than that to convince me to provide my support."

"We will prove it to you," I said, straightening my shoulders. "It's not the first time I've had to prove something to others."

"I suppose it isn't."

Jarl Einar left without another word.

"I'd say that we're doing a great job so far, everyone," Óskar joked, scratching Yugar's ears. "Stellar work."

Georg went to track down some of the leaders of the warriors while Rúna disappeared into the city. Óskar and I followed Gil and Aron back to their bunks. Spread across the base of Aron's bunk was a quilt full of many different squares. One of the squares was a faded green, leeched of colour. It was almost yellow, with purple thorns that were so pale that they were nearly pink.

Gil's bunk was utilitarian. A basic but well-made blanket and a warm set of furs. I made a note to get him something to add colour to his setup. Nothing crazy, but a nice dark blue or burgundy would add just the right little something to make it a bit homier for him.

Luck swung an arm around Aron's shoulders. "What would you all say to a tour?"

"If the tour came with a tankard of ale, I would think that

you are a gods send," Aron said. "You should have seen me just now embarrassing myself before Jarl Einar."

"Worse than when you got your sea legs on our first warship?"

"I would have gone through that all over again to avoid what happened in the training ring."

Luck laughed. "Don't worry, I'll take good care of you. A tour and a drink coming right up."

FIFTEEN

BRYN

T he castle of Wolfmire was both more formal than the fortress and more informal at the same time.

There were set times for everything; meals, guard changes, and the training of different units. Groups of warriors travelled together throughout the day, going from one thing to the next as they adhered to the schedule. They only separated during their free time, which was also carefully slotted into their daily timetables.

However, a strict schedule was needed with the number of warriors at the castle. There was no other way to ensure that everyone was properly trained and fed at any moment.

The informal nature of the castle lay in how people talked to each other. How they treated each other. They shouted across the training yards, joking with each other, and laughed heartily over meal times.

I couldn't imagine the same behaviour at the fortress.

Especially with the twisted snake pit that it has become.

"Each barrack holds two hundred and fifty warriors," Luck explained. "They just hold Jarl Einar's personal force. It does not include the roughly five hundred city guards and the thousand warriors that go on the warships that live in the city. He also has several dispatches of warriors outside Wolfmire at any given time. I believe around two hundred and fifty warriors are currently in various areas of Drysden."

Gods' bones.

No wonder Ragna emphasized how important it is for us to get Jarl Einar's support.

Three thousand highly trained warriors would make a difference for us in a war. Not to mention the resources or the money that he could provide. The only problem was that I had no idea how to convince him that we deserved it—that we were worthy of his faith.

Luck led us through the fortress. Showing us the library and some smaller common rooms. A whole wing of the castle was dedicated to the military: a muster hall, war chamber, the rooms and offices of all the commanders. An armoury.

It was impressive, to say the least.

"The commanders being together makes sense logistically for multiple reasons," Luck explained. "It also allows them to gather in the war chamber quicker should the need arise."

"The commanders make up Jarl Einar's advisors, then?" Aron asked, clearly taking this opportunity for what it was—to learn more about Jarl Einar. There was so little about him in the packet of information we received before we left that anything we could discover while we were here would certainly be a boon.

Luck shrugged. "Yes and no. They all serve on his war council to help him with the military movements. But his true advisory council? That is much more diverse than them."

"How so?"

"There is a commander on the council, as well as a representative of the city guard and the raiders. There are also representatives of the merchants, the artisans and craftsmen, and the farmers."

My jaw dropped, slightly stunned. "He listens to them all?" I asked. I hadn't heard of anyone doing such a thing. Not as their main advisory council, at the very least. Usually, someone needed a title, money, or military success to even have their words heard.

"Yes. Both during council meetings and outside of it. He'll also seek them, or others, out for their insights into different topics. He is responsible for his lands and people's well-being and takes that very seriously." Luck said before studying me, the emotions dancing across my face momentarily. "You're the one that was just found, weren't you? Where are you from?"

"Ebonwell. It's a small village. You probably haven't heard of it."

Luck glanced around us, dropping his voice. "Then you've probably heard the whispers or felt the sentiment yourself. The people in the smaller villages, the more distant settlements, feel abandoned by the King Commander."

"I've heard it. I know the people in my village felt it," I said softly.

"What are you saying?" Gil asked Luck; Aron and Óskar focused on our conversation.

"We're in the north, Gil. We're one of the forgotten. I know it, the city guards know it, Jarl Einar knows it," Luck said. "That feeling, that kernel of worthlessness, can fester in a city. Jarl Einar is trying to stop the spread. If he makes them all feel heard and valued, he may cut any civil unrest off at the root."

Aron nodded towards a more deserted path. "Do you think he's been successful?"

We started down the path, each alternating, throwing a

stick for Yugar to chase down. The path winded through ever-green trees and bushes, all no doubt picked so they would still be green during the cold northern winters.

"It's hard to say. I hope so," Luck said with a shrug. "Everyone seems happy, and the city has a healthy relationship between them and Jarl Einar. But I've heard some whispers. They're quiet, but if there's whispers, there's a problem."

"And what about us being here? Do we make it better or worse?" Óskar asked, voicing the concern that had also taken root in me.

"Honestly? It can probably go either way."

Aron scoffed. "Great. Happy to hear that. No pressure on us while we're here. None at all."

"Any advice?" Gil turned to Luck. Aron seemed to trust him, which had to be enough for us. He was new, but he was now tied to us, and we needed faith in him. Not to mention that Luck had spoken to us about things bordering on treason. If he turned on us, he was just as cooked as we were.

"If you win over the military leaders, you will catch Jarl Einar's attention. You convince the city? Then you earn his respect," Luck said as we returned from the path.

Georg stood around a training ring in the distance with some of the warriors as two people sparred in the middle.

"That sounds a lot easier than it is, I bet," Óskar joked. "Guess we should have left a certain party member at home if we hoped to make a good impression."

I clipped him over the back of the head. "Watch your mouth, you idiot."

Luck and Aron snickered.

"Jarl Einar surrounds himself with people that have three core things within them. If he can see those things in you, you have a good chance," Luck said.

"And what are those?"

"Work ethic—work hard and put effort into everything you do. Show that you care, not just for the high ranks, but for everyone regardless of social standing."

We stopped, preparing to go our separate ways. "And the third?" Gil asked.

"Be absolutely fucking lethal on a battlefield."

Luck's tour helped me familiarize myself with the general layout of the castle. Still, it had brushed over one place that I was interested in.

The healing centre.

I knew where it was. Luck had pointed out its door as we walked by, but we hadn't entered it. So, the next day, I went through the castle to the healing centre when I had a brief period of free time. I was interested in seeing it, and Ma would love to hear about how they did things here.

The double doors were open when I got there. I walked in to find a bright room; long, skinny windows were evenly spaced on the largest wall to ensure plenty of light got in. Two rows of beds were placed along the walls with curtains in between that could be drawn for privacy. Shelves of healing supplies and a desk were placed along one of the shorter walls, with several doors along it and the wall opposite it.

The room was mostly empty, with only a few people in the beds.

I wandered over to the shelves on one end. Careful not to touch anything, I studied what I could see, curious if it was similar to what we used or if they had their own recipes.

"Hello," a soft voice said. I turned to find a girl close to my age standing by me. She had her black hair pulled back from her delicate face, a few strands falling free from her bun to rest against her cheeks. Her emerald green eyes were kind as she watched me with a small smile. She wore a simple navy-blue skirt with a loose white shirt tucked into it. A white apron was tied around her waist. "Can I help you?"

"I'm sorry." I stepped back from the shelves. "I didn't mean to disturb you. I was just curious about the healing centre and what supplies you use."

"The lead healers all have a healing bloodrite, but many assistants or support healers do not. They are extensively trained to be familiar with the supplies behind you."

I nodded. "I use supplies myself," I said before holding out my hand. "I'm sorry, I'm being rude, aren't I? I'm Bryn, Jarl Brynja, I suppose I should say."

"I'm Sofie, one of the lead healers." She clasped forearms with me. "And you are one of the Verndari who are staying with us. I didn't know that they taught you healing."

"They don't. Before I knew I was a Verndari, I lived in a small village with my parents. My Ma was the closest thing we had to a healer there, and she taught me to take her place one day. We made all our own supplies—creams and teas and that kind of thing. Now, whenever we are sent out into the field, I am the person that heals us or stitches us back up long enough for us to find a true healer."

Sofie's eyes sparked in excitement. "You made your own supplies? Do you still do so?"

"I do." I nodded with a smile. "I use all my own supplies, and if I have any downtime, I make some extra to have in reserve or share with the healers at the fortress."

"Would you be willing to compare our items? I also make

several of the things we use and would love to compare them with you."

"Of course. I would be happy to show you some of my own supplies in my rooms. I was also planning to make some more during my free time while I'm here. If they are up to your standards, I can provide some to the healing centre."

Sofie grinned. "I would love to."

"I have some time now. Do you want to come to my rooms to see the supplies?" I offered.

She shook her head. "Unfortunately, my shift isn't over for a few hours yet. But could I show you around here and tell you what we use?"

"I would love that," I smiled.

A WEEK PASSED, truly settling us into the coldest depths of winter. The last month of winter was always the harshest.

Snow blew through the open spaces around the castle, stinging when it hit what little skin I had left exposed to it. I trudged towards the castle with Rúna by my side. My legs had started to go numb, the cold sinking into the very marrow of my bones. Rúna's teeth chattered, her arms tucked close to her body, her hands in her armpits. She and Gil hadn't been in the final spar, so she had started cooling down faster than I had.

I pushed open the heavy, wooden side door. The warm air of the castle surrounded our bodies as we shut the door tightly behind us.

My legs began to tingle, prickling running down them as the heat worked to warm them. We winded through the hallways towards our rooms, desperate for a warm bath to burn away any lingering cold from our bones.

Sofie crossed our path, her dark black hair pulled back from her face in a horsetail. Her white, healing apron was pristine over her dress. Her green eyes danced as she took in our thawing forms. "Not used to northern winters, eh?"

"Ebonwell had cold winters, but this is absolutely miserable. How do you survive it?" I asked.

"I went into healing rather than fighting. Far less training in the weather that way." She grinned.

Rúna turned to me. "Do you think we still have time to make the switch?"

"I think that ship has sailed," I joked, causing us all to chuckle. "Were you looking for me?"

The healing centre was across the castle from the wing where we were now. I had become close to Sofie and Luck since we arrived at Wolfmire. Luck fit in easily with us because of his friendship with Aron.

But Sofie was the first friend I had made just for myself since I had left Ebonwell.

No previous ties to the Verndari, no working relationship, and no politics were involved.

We were friends simply because we wanted to. No one was forcing us to, and there was no hidden agenda for our relationship.

"I was. You mentioned that you had a new batch of supplies, and I was going to see if you wanted a hand to move them to the centre. Then I figured I would see if you were interested in seeing Wolfmire," she said, falling into step with us as we continued down the hallway towards mine and Rúna's rooms.

"I need a moment to bathe and melt the icicles off my body, and then I'd love to. You can wait in my room for me if you want?"

"There you are!" Baldur called from behind us, causing Rúna to tense. "I've been looking for you everywhere."

I brushed my hand over Rúna's.

She gave me a small smile before turning back towards Baldur.

"I was at training. I was going to take a quick bath and then come and find you," she said, her voice carefully neutral.

"Oh, were you now?" Baldur arched a brow at her before turning to the rest of us. His eyes landed on Sofie by my side. "I don't believe that we have met. I'm Commanding Son Baldur, and you are—?"

"Sofie, Commanding Son," she said with a respectful curtsy. "Pleasure to meet you."

Baldur's eyes were bright. "Sofie, the heir apparent to the healing centre? I would love to hear your thoughts about the healing system. Jarl Einar has told me that you are one of the brightest healers he has seen in many years, and your healing bloodrite is the strongest of the healing centre."

My eyes widened, stunned.

I hadn't realized that Baldur had been having separate discussions with Jarl Einar.

A sinking weight settled into my stomach at the thought of it. Who knew what he had been saying in those meetings.

"I didn't know the Commanding Son was so passionate about healing. I always thought that Hákon was the healer in the family."

Baldur's jaw clenched, his eyes blazing in fury before he banished it again. "I've always been interested in it. Since I was a little boy."

Sofie smiled softly. "I would happily show you around the healing centre while you are here. Show you how we do things around here."

"I would love that," Baldur said, his eyes lighting up. "I'm available most of the time, so please let me know when would work best for you."

Rúna and I shared a wide-eyed look over Baldur's shoulder.

I had seen Baldur agreeable, rarely, but it had happened. I had also seen him put on a front or suck up to someone.

But to show excitement like this? To be incredibly kind and willing to work around someone else's schedule?

I didn't even know that was possible for him.

"I will check my schedule and get back to you with a time that would work for us to meet."

"Thank you," Baldur dipped his head before opening the door to his and Rúna's room. He held it open for her before shutting it softly behind them.

I disappeared into my room and hopped in the bath, ready to rid my body of the chill that seemed to seep through every part of my skin.

Once I had dressed again for the day, Sofie gathered a basket of healing supplies. My healing supplies were not used while we were here, so I could dedicate my efforts to the castle.

Sofie and I made our way through the hallways to the healing wing. We walked through the main area of the centre into the back storage room. Shelves upon shelves were filled with supplies.

I had just put down the basket to help Sofie unload and put away the supplies when Óskar ran in, Yugar skidding to a stop by his side.

"Skolli were spotted last night. We leave within the hour."

CHAPTER

SIXTEEN

BRYN

I met the others in the courtyard; every sheath in my leather armour held a dagger, with more stuffed in my saddlebags alongside my healing supplies. Convincing Jarl Einar that we deserved his support was an unknown, but this was familiar. This was something we could do; this was something that we had done. Multiple times.

Our horses were waiting for us, Georg and Aron already in their saddles. Óskar and Gil were finishing their final checks and securing their saddle bags.

Rúna flew out of the fortress, Baldur close on her heels. Her blonde hair shone, her horsetail flaring out behind her in the wind. Her staff, currently in two pieces, was strapped across her back, her whip coiled at her hip. Baldur was also dressed for battle, his armour and weapons looking to be just as well cared for as our own.

Georg drew up beside him. "Are you ready for this? Have you fought them before?" His voice was quiet to ensure it didn't carry beyond our circle. It would do us no favours to show discontent between the Verndari and the Commanding Son.

"Don't coddle me," Baldur sneered. "I may not have a bloodrite, but I am gods damned lethal with my weapons."

Georg studied him for a moment. "Mount up," he ordered loud enough for everyone around us to hear before dropping his voice again. "Join us. But from the moment you mount up until the moment we return, I will be in charge. You will listen to my orders and follow my directions like anyone else on the team. I will not allow you to put them at risk by trying to control a situation that you have no fucking experience in. Am I clear?"

"As crystal." Baldur pursed his lips. "I'll follow your orders." He swung up into his saddle easily.

"You're with Bryn and Óskar," Georg said before guiding his horse to his spot beside Aron.

Baldur had a bow and quiver of arrows strapped to his saddle. Two axes hung from his belt, and a single sword was strapped down his spine. I positioned myself between the two men. If we needed them, their bows would be much more effective if they were outside our trio.

"Have you fought the Skolli before?" I asked, keeping my voice carefully neutral. Like Georg, my words were quiet, just loud enough for our trio to hear.

Baldur's lip curled into the smallest of sneers. "Once."

"Why?" Baldur's brows furrowed slightly at my question. "You've fought them once, but that doesn't exactly make you an expert. You have to know the risks of facing them. You could stay here in Wolfmire while we go, like how you stayed safely at the fortress while we faced the attack."

Óskar's gaze burned on my skin, no doubt wondering what

possessed me to talk with Baldur, let alone call him out on this. We knew what he was capable of, and I was pushing him.

"These are my people. They need help, and I can give it to them," he said. I blinked, surprised at the answer. "At the fortress, they had my darling brother and his warriors. They didn't need me. He didn't count me into his plans." Baldur's lip curled.

Was Hákon the one who dismissed him, or was it someone else? Who had made the call for him to sit in safety?

I didn't get a chance to ask as Gil and Rúna settled into place behind us.

"What are we waiting for?" Óskar said, effectively navigating the conversation away from the rocky waters it had gone to. He was leaving Yugar behind, not wanting to put him at risk in the fight. Sofie had happily agreed to watch over him when Óskar asked her when he had gotten me from the healing centre. They hadn't spent much time together, but I considered her a friend, which was enough for Óskar.

It would have been enough for me had our positions been reversed.

We held each other's lives in our hands on the battlefield. We had each other's backs. That bond leads to a level of trust that very few can achieve.

Maybe that's why it hurt so much when Pétur left.

Georg nodded towards the entrance of the castle. "For that."

Jarl Einar was dressed for battle, his furs streaming behind him as he approached a readied horse. Five other warriors, including Luck, joined him.

He guided his horse towards Georg. "Normally, I would bring more warriors, but with your team here, I felt they had more value staying behind. We are yours to guide—use us as you see best."

"Form up behind Gil and Rúna. We will lead. When we arrive, divide your team into two teams and assign one of them to each of our pairings." Georg didn't hesitate to issue the orders. "We ride out as soon as your team is in place."

Jarl Einar nodded. "Understood."

When the hoofbeats stopped sounding on the stone, Georg rose in his stirrups. "Move out!"

We kept our horses to a walk as we exited the castle grounds and made our way through Wolfmire. A scout waited at the walls of the city, dressed for travel. Georg waved her over.

"Lead us to the Skolli," he said.

She nodded, swinging her horse around and kneed it into a gallop. We all fell into place behind her.

Óskar didn't use his bloodrite; if we were careful with our pacing of the horses, we would reach the village by dusk. It was better to save his bloodrite should we really need it later.

The scout led the group, alternating between a gallop and a trot, her changing pace filtering down the line easily whenever she shifted her tempo. The cold wind whipped across my face, and the curls that had escaped my braid flew around my head, no doubt tangling. My eyes watered, leaving me to wipe them with my frosty cloak.

The terrain changed; the hills got steeper, the cold sharper as we got closer to the base of the mountains. The pathways got narrower with more cracks and crevices. There were plenty of caves filled with who knows what inside the darkness of the rock shelter. We were forced to slow our horses to ensure they didn't catch a hoof or break a leg.

The sun was setting as we crested a ridge; the village lay ahead, tucked into a small valley.

"Bryn, Óskar, Baldur. Go right," Georg ordered. "Gil, Rúna. Go left."

We immediately peeled off to head in our assigned directions. Two of Jarl Einar's warriors following us. When we reached the very rudimentary wooden wall of the village, I hopped off my horse, removing the saddle bags. "How long do we have?" I asked one of Jarl Einar's men.

"Moments at the worst, a few minutes at best," one of the warriors said. "The sun sets faster in the mountains."

"Great," I grumbled. I dropped my saddlebags against the wall as Baldur removed his weapons from his horse, propping them up next to my items. I nodded at Óskar, who sent all five of our horses into the village before the gates were shut for the night. I turned towards the two warriors. "Have you fought the Skolli before?"

They both nodded. "Multiple times," one said.

"Good," I said as I scanned their weapons. One had a bow, while the other had a war axe. "You and Óskar will be closest to the wall. Pick off any in the skies." I gestured towards the warrior with a bow before turning to the other one. "You and I are the front line."

The warrior nodded, smiling grimly. "Aye."

"Baldur, you can fight close range and distance based on your weapons. You'll have to make the call to decide which is better."

I never would have dared give Baldur an order before seeing how Georg spoke to him before we left. He may be the Commanding Son, but Óskar and I had the authority on the battlefield unless it was expressly given to Baldur instead.

The sun fully set, darkness sweeping over us like a blanket.

"Let's see what comes at us. Then I'll make the call," Baldur told me before turning towards the villagers on the walls. "Light the lanterns! The Skolli are going to come either way!"

The villagers scrambled to do as he asked.

My eyes and the skin surrounding them burned as I shifted to give myself the eyes of a Skolli. Their night vision was unparalleled, perhaps even better than mine on bright sunny days. Using it was disorienting when I fought, but I was slowly getting accustomed to it.

I scanned the area around us, drawing two daggers from my weapons belt.

There.

Crashing in the trees.

"On the ground," I said, pointing towards the trees. "They're coming."

The villagers lit the lanterns, so I allowed the burning to return to my eyes as they shifted back to normal. Now that I could see it would be better to save my bloodrite for other things during the fight.

I strode forward until I stood halfway between the tree line and the walls, Baldur and the warrior flanking me.

Skolli broke through the tree line, charging towards us. I sunk into my fighting crouch, raising my daggers before me.

I stepped forward towards a Skolli, catching its claws with my blades. I pushed the claws away, swiping at its throat.

It slashed at me again, forcing me to spin out of the way. I dropped to the ground, sliding behind it and slicing at the weak spot behind its knees.

It toppled forward, crippled. I climbed atop its back before kneeling down and cutting clean through its neck.

121

I stood, assessing the fight around me. Baldur fought nearby, an axe in one hand and a sword in the other.

Two Skolli were surrounding the warrior. He kept them at bay with large swings of his war axe but wasn't taking them down.

I sheathed my daggers, the familiar burning settling in my legs and fingertips.

I crouched, gathering all the power in my Skolli legs, jumping high in the air and landing between the warrior and one of the Skolli. I didn't hesitate as I punched my claws clean through its eye.

Leaping again, I landed behind the other Skolli and kicked it hard in the back. It stumbled forward, off balance, allowing the warrior to cut clean through its throat, its head bouncing across the ground.

I spun around, ready to attack the next monster, but none remained alive. Some lay with arrows sticking out of various weak spots, and two had deep cuts by Baldur. "Is it over?" I asked as we rejoined the archers.

"I don't know. Night just fell. It doesn't feel right," Óskar said before taking the opportunity to gather the arrows that they had used.

"They might come in waves. Try to see if they can catch us off guard." Baldur wiped the black blood off the blade of his weapons, making my stomach turn.

"Then we won't let that happen," I said. "Have a drink, care for your weapons, and be ready should another wave come."

Another wave came. A small one, easily handled between us.

Then, a few more. All small—never more than ten Skolli. It was almost like they were taunting us, teasing us.

Sizing us up.

But as the sky lightened, it became clear that the Skolli had never intended to breach the walls. At least not once there were defenders to keep them at bay.

They had been looking for easy pickings at the small village or had another goal. And that possibility scared me far more than their potential to breach the wall.

CHAPTER
SEVENTEEN
BRYN

I patted the warrior beside me on the shoulder. Dawn had broken—we had made it.

"Nice work," I said after taking a swig from my water skin.

"Just a regular day at the office," Óskar joked as he cared for his bow. "Well, night, I suppose."

One of the warriors turned to me, their face splattered with black Skolli blood. "Is he always like this?"

"Oh, this is tame." I rolled my eyes playfully. "You should see him when he's really in a mood."

"Bryn!" Aron called, charging towards us. His eyes were wide, panicked.

I dropped my water skin, immediately reaching for my saddlebags. "Who's hurt? What's happened?"

"It's Gil. He had to use his bloodrite."

"Shit. Fucking shit," I hissed, allowing the burn to once again settle in my legs. I would get there faster using Skolli legs rather than my own.

"Go," Óskar said. "I'll finish up here."

I didn't hesitate, racing towards where I knew Gil was stationed. Aron fell behind quickly, unable to keep up with me.

Rúna had Gil separated from the rest of the warriors who watched on. He wasn't attacking her, but from the way he flung his arms and the muscles in his neck bulged, I knew that he was yelling at her. Insulting her. Threatening her.

And hating himself more with every second that passed.

It took me a moment more to reach them, to allow the burning in my legs to spread until my bare feet stood on the snow. I rested my hands on his cheeks, forcing him to look at me. Pitch-black eyes met mine.

"Gil," I said. "Stay with me."

His eyes flickered to green for a second before reverting to black.

Good. The darkness hadn't sunk its claws into him too deeply.

"Go," I whispered to Rúna, nodding towards where the others stood watching us. "We're good here."

Gil felt guilty enough whenever the darkness sunk its claws into him; we didn't need to provide more people for it to target.

I was the one who could pull him out of it—I was the only one who should be there.

"Got it." Rúna backed away from us slowly, careful not to grab Gil's attention. I ignored her, my focus locked on Gil's eyes.

"Come on, Gil. Stay with me."

His eyes flickered again.

"For someone so scared of blood, you sure do like to cover yourself in it," he hissed. "Is it to give you an excuse when you inevitably get someone killed when you freeze?"

I ignored him. It wasn't Gil speaking.

And I hadn't frozen in weeks, not since I had learned my triggers and how to handle them.

I needed something to distract him. I needed something he wouldn't expect to catch the darkness that latched onto him off guard and give Gil a chance to regain control. My eyes landed on a snow bank near us.

"Do you want to hear a story?" I asked him quietly, not waiting for a response as I continued. "Whenever I see a snow bank, I am reminded of Fannar. His parents, his adoptive parents, found him in a snow bank after a massive snowstorm. He was bundled up in this green blanket covered in purple embroidery and was screaming his head off. They brought him to my mother as soon as they found him. She was pregnant with me, young, and establishing herself as a healer. She warmed him up slowly. Carefully. When she was done and he was out of the woods, she joked with his parents that he was just as much hers now as theirs. So, when I was born seven months later, my parents and his raised us together. Each other's houses, each other's families, an extension of our own."

Gil's arm wrapped around my waist, pulling me closer. His eyes fully green. Himself once again. "I had no idea," he whispered before tucking his head into the crook of my neck.

I wrapped my arms around him, my fingers brushing through his hair.

We stood there for several moments until Gil found the strength to raise his head again. "I'm sorry."

"You have nothing to be sorry for, but I accept," I said softly before leading us back toward the others. I never felt that he had anything to apologize for. Still, I would grant him forgiveness if it helped him and eased some of the guilt that seeped into his heart after the darkness seized control.

The warriors had dispersed, leaving only the Verndari, Baldur, and Jarl Einar waiting for us.

"We have secured lodgings for us to rest for the day. We will stay tonight to ensure no other attacks and then be on our way in the morning." Georg explained once we reached them. "We're split up throughout the village. I have you two," he said, gesturing to Gil and me, "in the stable loft. Unfortunately, no more beds were available, but the straw combined with your bedrolls should be fairly comfortable."

Georg often paired me with Rúna when we found lodgings in other settlements, but with Baldur here, that would be out of the question. Especially after the darkness had gotten control of Gil, he always did better when I stayed close to him afterwards.

"We'll be fine, Georg." I smiled tiredly. "Honestly, as long as I get out of the snow, I'll be happy."

Gil glanced at me, realizing for the first time the tattered state of the legs of my pants and the complete lack of boots or socks on my feet.

"You have some explaining to do, boy," Jarl Einar snapped, pointing toward Gil.

My blood heated, but not from my bloodrite. From the fury pumping through my veins.

"He has to do no such thing," I snapped, stepping close to Jarl Einar. Rúna took my spot beside Gil as Aron and Óskar flanked me. "And you have no right to demand such a thing."

"Watch how you speak to me in my lands, girl."

"Whether we are in your lands, or back at Goldhelm, or at fucking sea, you have no authority over him, me, or any of us. You are not the one in command here. That's Georg. And you are not the one with superior titles because every single one of us outranks you," I hissed. "*You* should watch how you speak to *us*."

Gil scooped me into his arms with one arm under my knees and one behind my back before he turned for the city.

Once we were inside the walls, I looked up at him. "You can put me down. I'm not going to go back to Jarl Einar."

"I am carrying you because there is snow on the ground, not because of what you did. Even if that was a very stupid thing," Gil said as we reached the stable. He put me down inside at the base of the ladder to the loft. Our things were already here, one of the warriors must have dropped it off. When we had both reached the top, he turned me towards him. "You did not have to do that."

"Of course I did," I said, swallowing thickly. "He has no right to talk to you like that. And while I hope with everything that I am that I didn't just cost us our allegiance with him, I would do it all over again."

Gil stepped closer to me. "I am not worth the cost of losing him."

"You are worth everything, Gil. *Everything*." My hands cupped his cheeks. "And I will always defend you against the people that try to paint you as a monster because that is the furthest thing from what you are."

Gil dipped his head, his lips pressing to mine. Soft at first, then desperate.

I met him, kiss for kiss, as he led me backwards until my body met one of the wooden posts.

His body pressed up flush against mine even as I tried to pull him closer to me. He broke the kiss, trailing his lips across my cheek, down my throat until he met the top of my armour. I reached for the buckles of his leather chest plate, but his hands gently wrapped around my wrists. Stopping me. He leaned back just enough to look into my eyes.

"I cannot—not now. Not so soon after," he rasped.

"I trust you."

He brushed a curl behind my ear. "I know you do. And as much as I want this—" He leaned into me, making it clear just how much he wished to continue. "—I want more than this," he said, gesturing around us. "More than a stable loft and a bedroll piled on straw."

"There is always this post," I joked softly. My heart was warming at his words, even as butterflies erupted in my stomach at their meaning.

Gil's eyes were as bright as I'd ever seen them. "There is always this post, but not for this. Not the first time, at least."

"But maybe another time?" I suggested, smiling up at him.

Gil laughed, pressing a kiss to my forehead. "I will be sure to keep it in mind, darling."

I DIDN'T cross paths with Jarl Einar until we prepared to return to Wolfmire the next morning.

Dressed in new boots Gil had packed in his belongings — having seen me rip through many pants and boots since learning to control my bloodrite— I straightened my shoulders and walked straight towards Jarl Einar.

Gil was a step behind me, close enough to support me but not close enough to take the full attention.

Jarl Einar turned towards me from his conversation with Georg.

I swallowed, tucking my hands behind my back to hide

their shaking. "Good morning, Jarl Einar. Would you mind if I borrowed a moment of your time?"

"So formal this morning, Jarl Brynja. Do go ahead," he said, giving me his full attention. Georg raised an eyebrow at me but didn't say a word.

"I wanted to apologize for how I spoke to you last night. It wasn't appropriate."

Put him in his place without jeopardizing his support.

Jarl Einar crossed his arms over his chest. "As you explained last night, you had every right, seeing as you outrank me."

I blew out a breath. So, he was going to play it that way. As though I thought I was above him now that I was a Verndari. I did outrank him, but I didn't want to be the leader who abused their rank or treated others without respect. I wanted to be a Verndari, a leader whose warriors followed me because they respected me. Not because they were afraid of me.

I didn't want to be like Baldur.

"I do outrank you, but that gives me no right to speak to you that way. You thought you were doing what was right for your people. I should have approached the situation different-ly," I told him.

Jarl Einar evaluated me for a long moment. "I accept your apology,' he finally said. "I also find the wording of your apology very interesting. You are specifically apologizing for how you spoke to me, not for what happened."

"I will never apologize for defending Gil or any of the other Verndari."

"Good." My eyes widened before he continued. "I will never fault someone for standing up for who they love. For defending their comrades. Especially when they recognize that they might not have handled it correctly in the heat of the moment. There is a difference between that and treating people poorly because you choose to. Because that's how you believe that they should be treated."

"Thank you, Jarl Einar." I nodded my head in respect before turning to ready myself to leave.

Jarl Einar rested a hand on my shoulder. "Whatever you may have lost from your outburst was regained when I understood the reasoning. You even gained some respect in my eyes by publicly apologizing to me," he said softly. Gil may have heard it, but there was no way anyone else would have. "The whole situation will not affect where my support will land. I assure you."

I swallowed, nodding again. "Thank you. I appreciate you telling me that."

He gently squeezed my shoulder before rejoining his conversation with Georg.

I breathed a little lighter as I mounted my horse and settled into my place between Óskar and Baldur. Georg signalled for us to move out, and the scout took her spot at the head of our procession to guide us back to Wolfmire. I allowed the rhythmic pace of my horse to further soothe my nerves, allowing the calming motion to settle any lingering anxieties.

I hadn't lost his support or compromised our position should the barrier fall.

We still had a chance to prove that we deserved his respect. That we deserved the support of his warriors, storehouses, and coffers should a war erupt.

By the time Wolfmire came into sight, its towers climbing high into the sky above the walls, I had recentred myself, ready to pursue our goal again.

EIGHTEEN

BRYN

A light snowfall dusted the streets as Luck led the way through Wolfmire. Aron and Óskar walked by his side, Yugar trotting alongside them. Rúna and Gil followed behind them, Rúna happily talking Gil's ear off as he nodded along to what she was saying. Sofie and I brought up the rear, our heads bent close in conversation as my eyes danced across the city around us, trying to take it all in.

"It's a shame that the Commanding Son and Georg couldn't join us," Sofie said. Both Georg and Baldur had been pulled into a meeting with Jarl Einar. Georg hadn't been able to deny it or didn't want to risk leaving Baldur alone with Jarl Einar, so he had had to back out of our trip into the city.

I gaped at her. "I wish Georg was here too, but you also wish Baldur was here?"

"He's quite nice. He's really helpful whenever he visits the healing centre." Sofie tilted her head. "Do you not agree?"

"No, I don't agree," I said, not wanting to say more in public. I had gotten the feeling from our discussion with Luck when we first arrived that the King Commander would not find his most fervent supporters in Wolfmire. But there was always a price for information, and sometimes it was tempting enough to sway someone even if it didn't align with their personal beliefs.

Sofie was quiet for a moment. "He does act differently in the healing centre. Maybe I see a different side to him than you do."

"Or maybe I have seen something he has yet to reveal to you."

"I'll be careful," Sofie promised as we entered a square larger than the entirety of Ebonwell had been. Some large evergreen trees grew in the square with flowerbeds, currently covered in snow, and benches around them.

A faded piece of parchment lay on the ground, mostly distorted by water. I could only see the title—Criers of Justice. It looked hastily made, handwritten, with no design.

Luck turned to face us with a smile. "So, what does everyone want to do? We can visit two large marketplaces if you want to do shopping. They are also filled with various food and drink stalls if that's what you are in the mood for."

Gil stepped towards Luck, saying something under his breath. Luck's eyes flickered over to me before he nodded to Gil and pointed down one of the roads.

Gil stepped back to stand beside me, his cloak pressed against mine.

"I, for one, would like to do some shopping," Rúna said, her eyes alight at the chance to explore new shops. She enjoyed the merchants in Goldhelm and regularly patronized many of them. Still, the opportunity to explore something new had a smile on her face since we left the castle.

"I'm game as long as we hit those food and drink stalls Luck talked about," Óskar agreed.

Aron nodded by his side. "I second that. A drink sounds wonderful right now."

"Follow me," Luck said, leading us down one of the roads that branched off the square.

Gil wrapped his hand around my wrist when I went to follow the group. "Come with me," he said quietly.

Sofie had paused by my side when I did, but I waved her on. She skipped to catch up to Rúna. "Where are we going?" I asked him as he led me down a different road.

"It is a surprise."

"Does this have anything to do with what you just talked to Luck about?"

Gil looked at me out of the corner of his eye. "Patience, darling."

He led me to an eating house, holding the door open for me to enter. It was warm, a fire going in the fireplace in the corner. A small stage was built next to the fire, and a man sat on a stool, strumming his instrument. A long bar went along one wall while tables filled the rest. Gil gently took my hand and led me through the space until we found an empty table.

He unclipped my cloak from around my neck, hanging it on a hook with his own. Gil pulled out my chair, tucking it in once I was seated, and trailed his fingers along my shoulders as he made his way to his spot.

"What's all this?" I asked with a smile.

"I promised we would make time for this," he told me. "We never know when we might get called away, so when I saw the chance today, I took it."

One of the serving ladies came to the table with two bowls of stew and a plate with crusty bread. A winter staple up in the north. My own family ate our share of it when we lived in Ebonwell. She returned shortly with two tankards.

"Do you realize this is the first time we have gone out together like this?" I asked him.

"We've gone to the shops together in Goldhelm."

"That's not the same as this, and you know it," I teased him before shrugging. "But with how busy everything is and the attacks, it makes sense that we haven't had the time."

Gil took a drink from his tankard. "That is no excuse. It is easy to say that there isn't enough time. To stay where we are comfortable." In our wing, away from the judgemental stares and expectations constantly laid upon our shoulders. "But if we do not make the time or choose to push our comfort zone, then our world will slowly narrow. It will limit itself to the confines we have set upon it, which is not a life I want to live. That is not a life I would want for you."

I reached out to take his hand. "You could have just said that you want to do this more with me," I joked before sobering. "But I agree. I want to be more than a Verndari, see more than just the fortress, and explore it all with you."

A MESSENGER ARRIVED during the midday meal a few days later.

They strode straight for Jarl Einar, handing him a sealed letter. He opened it at his table, his face going red after a moment. He stood from his chair, saying something we couldn't hear to the messenger. Jarl Einar made his way out of the hall, the messenger close behind him. When he reached the door, he turned back towards us and waved for us to follow.

"That can't be good," Óskar muttered as we immediately pushed away our plates to join them.

"No, it can't be," Georg agreed grimly.

"Good luck," Sofie said quietly as Luck grimaced from where he had been sitting beside Aron.

Jarl Einar strode through the castle confidently, straight to his office. Once we were all inside, he nodded to the door. I shut it before rejoining the others.

He held up the missive in his hand. "A request from the fortress. The King Commander is hosting a ball in a week. We are all requested to be there."

"We must leave within the next two days," Georg said.

Jarl Einar placed the missive on his desk and crossed his arms over his chest. "You are going then?"

"That missive is not a request for us. That is an order."

"You are here to earn my support. To show me—to show everyone—that you are here to get us through these attacks. That the King Commander is here to get us through these attacks."

Rúna stepped forward. "Have we not shown that to you?"

"Not if you leave to return for a ball." Not if we chose to attend a party rather than stay and defend the people who needed it. Over winning his support for the inevitable war looming on the horizon.

"We have orders," she said. "We don't have a choice."

"Bad orders shouldn't be followed. You will lose support if you do this."

Georg stepped forward. "Just as many allies are made over swords and desks as they are a tankard of ale and a dance. We have our orders. We need to fulfill them."

"With every day that passes, the King Commander loses support." Jarl Einar let out a humourless chuckle. "He doesn't care about us up here and doesn't do shit to support us in these attacks. When word gets around that he's pulling his warriors back to the fortress to dance and be merry rather than protecting his people—" He shrugged. "I wouldn't blame them if they decided they've had enough with him."

"You border on treason."

"I'm issuing a warning. If you do this—if the King Commander does this—he doesn't just stand to lose any opportunity for my support. His own country may turn on him."

I swallowed, stepping forward to stand beside Georg. "We have a duty to fulfil. I have faith that they wouldn't call us back unnecessarily. Every order they issue, every task I fulfill, and every battlefield I enter counts for something. I am securing alliances, gaining resources, and saving lives. There are only six of us. We can't cover the entire country. We can't do everything. I have to believe that what I do counts. That going back for this ball *will matter*."

"You know what I think? I think that ensuring my support is very important to the King Commander. Whether it is my warriors or my resources, he needs them. Otherwise, he wouldn't have stationed you in Wolfmire, far from the fortress, with no return date set." Jarl Einar continued, not giving us a chance to retort. "You are right. Returning to the ball will matter. You will be returning without me declaring my support."

Gil rested his hand on the small of my back.

I had opened up to him and admitted how I truly felt.

And all he did was fling those words back in my face.

"I had great respect for you, Jarl Einar, just based on the stories I had heard of you," Rúna said softly. "And it only grew when I arrived here. But after how you just spoke to Bryn?" Her eyes went cold. "You just lost all of it."

"When we arrived, it was clear that you were most intrigued by Bryn and I. For our choices, role in the Verndari, and completely different circumstances to the other Verndari." Aron gestured to me. "You know what I heard Bryn say? There are hundreds of places we should be right now, a hundred things we should be doing. We can only be in one place and do one thing at a time. And everywhere we should be but can't be, people are losing their homes. Children are being orphaned. People are dying. That weighs on every single one of us, and you just threw that back in her fucking face."

Jarl Einar's face fell momentarily, his eyes darting to me. I straightened my shoulders, forcing every scrap of emotion to fall from my face. Jarl Einar composed himself seconds later.

"Rúna, Aron, that is enough. You just pointed out that we should be doing plenty of things but can't. We should return to the ball and be here helping. We fight not just over the orders that we have been issued, but what they mean. What we won't be able to do because of them. There is nothing else to say here. There is no way for us to be in both Wolfmire and Goldhelm simultaneously, and we have our summons." Georg strode for the door. "Thank you for your hospitality. We will only impose upon it until we leave tomorrow morning to fulfil our orders. I will inform the King Commander that you have chosen not to attend."

Georg held open the door, and Aron left without another word, Rúna close behind him.

"I know that you are facing attacks up here and have to defend your people. But you know that you can't face it alone, which is exactly what will happen if you don't align with the King Commander. You'll see no support. Don't do that to your people," Óskar pleaded. He was quiet for several moments, giving Jarl Einar the chance to answer. He didn't utter a word. "You're a fucking fool," Óskar snapped before spinning on his heel and gesturing for Yugar to join him.

Gil guided me with the hand still on my back towards the door.

"Bryn," Jarl Einar said behind me, causing all three of us to pause.

I turned to face him, my face cold. "That is Jarl Brynja to you. Only my friends and comrades get to call me Bryn, and you have made it quite clear that you are neither of those things." I stepped forward. "I see no need to have any further conversation with you unless you declare your support. You need us just as much as we need you."

Jarl Einar pressed his lips together, his fingers drumming on the top of his desk.

But he didn't say a word.

"That's what I thought."

I strode straight for the door, Gil, Óskar and Yugar flanking me. Georg was the last to leave, closing the door behind him.

Gil rested his hand on my shoulder as Óskar said quietly. "That's our girl."

CHAPTER
NINETEEN
BRYN

I t was a somber journey back to the fortress. None of us liked accepting defeat; none of us liked failure. Especially when it was something so vital. When our failure meant that more people would suffer, more would die.

And we were returning with nothing but bad news.

We had failed, and it left behind a bitter feeling that had taken root in the pit of my stomach.

And as much as Jarl Einar had said that he allowed us to prove ourselves and that my outburst didn't affect things, I didn't think we ever had a chance. From the moment we arrived, Jarl Einar had acted the same way. By making us prove ourselves to him, he was delaying the inevitable. Delaying the time when he had to declare that he wouldn't side with us.

We arrived with very little fanfare as everyone went about their daily activities. It suited me and the other Verndari just fine, but Baldur was frustrated. He commanded more simply by being the Commanding Son. Still, everyone was distracted by Hákon and a line of Royal Regiment across the courtyard.

"Typical," Baldur spat under his breath before flagging

down a stable hand to take his horse. He stormed into the fortress a moment later, Rúna finally relaxing by my side.

I dismounted and grabbed my saddlebags before handing my horse to the stable hand.

Hákon noticed us then, raising a gloved hand in greeting.

Georg nodded in return before heading towards the Striking Shadows buildings, no doubt to inform Ragna of how things had gone. Rúna also disappeared into the fortress, leaving Gil, Óskar, Aron and I to approach the Royal Regiment.

"I wasn't expecting both of your teams to return so closely together," Hákon said. "Saves me a trip down here."

Óskar winked at Hákon. "You know we're worth the trip."

Hákon laughed, clapping Óskar on the shoulder. "Good trip?"

"It was fine," was all Gil said, aware of everyone around us.

"I see." Hákon's face was carefully neutral, used to life at the fortress filled with eyes and ears. How bad had the fortress gotten while we were gone? How divided was it? Now was not the time to ask.

Lúdvík approached Hákon's side, and I realized exactly which line this was. I stretched onto the balls of my feet, searching through the various warriors.

"Miss me?" Fannar asked from behind me.

I spun with a laugh, throwing my arms around his shoulders. His arms wrapped tightly around me, lifting me slightly from the ground before placing me back down.

I stepped back, scanning him for any injuries. There were a few bruises here and there, and a cut was mostly healed, but there was nothing concerning.

"Of course I did," I said, lightly punching his shoulder. "Didn't you miss me?"

"Sure I did, of course." Fannar nodded with a smirk. I

punched him again, making him tip his head back with a laugh.

"I thought she was with Gil?" Aron said behind us.

I turned to face the others, Fannar by my side.

"She is," Gil said.

"Then who's he?"

Óskar leaned down to scratch Yugar's ears. "Her brother. You see, Bryn is a very affectionate person. Give her enough time, and she'll greet you like that, too."

"She can speak for herself," I said before turning to Aron. "I forgot that you and Fannar hadn't met yet. Aron, this is my brother Fannar. Fannar, this is Aron. He replaced Pétur."

They shook hands, Aron scanning Fannar's face with furrowed brows. "You remind me of someone."

Fannar tilted his head. "I don't think we've met. Maybe you've seen me in the fortress."

"I'm going to go visit Ma, I just need to wash up," I told Fannar.

"I was planning to do the same. I'll meet you there," Fannar agreed.

Hákon stepped forward. "She has been doing well. Either Ragna or I visit her daily."

"Thank you. We really appreciate it." I smiled.

It didn't take me long to wash up, excited to see Ma. I wore a comfortable outfit, messily braiding my hair to deal with later.

I paid close attention to the people I passed on the way to the fortress. Emilía was sitting close to a young warlord, practically draped over him. Her lips were by his ear, as Aron had hinted before we left.

The message from her father no doubt hidden as a pair of sweethearts flirting in the hallways.

Just how many messages were being communicated that way? Through whispered conversations in hallways, across pillows in beds, in letters carefully delivered by the most trusted servants?

On the outside, the fortress didn't look too different from when we left, but if you looked closer, it was clear that lines were being drawn. Small groups still chatted in the hallways, but their voices were lowered, and their eyes constantly darted around their surroundings, keeping a close eye on the people around them.

People were choosing their sides, and I could practically feel the tension as I made my way to Ma's rooms.

Fannar was already there, pouring three cups of tea.

Ma was seated in her favourite chair by the window. Her eyes lit up when I entered, and she stood from her chair. I went straight to her, reaching for her hand and squeezing it.

"I'm back, Ma," I said quietly, causing her to smile.

We took our seats as Fannar brought over the tea.

She still didn't speak, but she sipped at her tea as we talked, her eyes alert and following the conversation. We took turns filling her in on what we had gotten up to outside the fortress, her more aware of us than ever.

My chest filled with renewed hope as the conversation continued. She hadn't regressed while we were gone. Hákon had said she had been doing well, but hearing and seeing it were different.

Maybe we would get her back.

"Where is your partner?" my crotchety old dance teacher asked. Her snow-white hair was harshly pinned back, not a single strand escaping. She was short and leaned heavily on her cane, snapping it harshly on the ground whenever she had a correction. And she had plenty of those, the clack of wood on stone almost as steady as the beat of the music.

"I'm sure Óskar will be here any minute," I said, glancing at the door.

Óskar had endured every minute of her teaching with me the day before as she led us through each step of the opening dance. The dance instructor had no patience for his antics, which put her in a worse and worse mood as it went on.

The Verndari were required to perform the first dance to open the ball, and unlike the others, I had not been trained in the dance throughout my training. There hadn't been time. Now I had to cram all my dance instruction into a couple of days and hope I didn't make a fool of myself.

My hopes weren't too high.

The door opened to reveal Gil. He shut the door behind himself before joining me.

"You are not her partner," the dance teacher said.

"Óskar will have the opening dance as her partner, but I intend to have the rest. Or as many as she will let me. It makes more sense for me to be here for this," Gil explained, his eyes locked on mine the whole time.

"As long as she is okay with it, you can stay. You are much better to teach than that other rascal anyways."

I stepped closer to Gil, my body a hair away from his. "Show me what to do," I whispered. The dance teacher stepped away to talk to the musicians as Gil took one hand in his and rested the other on my waist. "I never thought that you would like dancing."

"Dancing is safe. There is a prescribed set of rules—how close to hold someone, where to put your hands, how to move.

And no chance I may be asked to use my bloodrite. Dancing was the one time that I felt safe enough to allow myself near people," Gil explained. His words cracked my heart.

The sound of the dance teacher's cane alerted us that she was returning to us. Gil stepped back a half step, releasing my waist just long enough to guide my hand to his shoulder.

He was patient with me, never rushing me as the dance instructor walked me through the steps. Gently correcting me when I got the steps wrong as she led us through multiple dances. Some were fast, filled with spins and lifts, while others were slow, the movements smooth.

"You just need to know the basics of each dance," he softly reassured me. "I will guide you through the rest. I've got you."

Finally, the dance teacher cued the musicians, and a beautiful song filled the air. It was a slow, melodic song. Gil moved me smoothly around the floor, his steps never faltering. He spun me under his arm and dipped me, holding me close to him.

As the song came to a finish, the dance teacher stepped forward. "Good, you can take it from here. Run through it a few more times with her."

I turned back to Gil as she slowly made her way out of the room. "I can tell you love dancing. There is something so beautiful about how you move."

"The rules made me feel safe to enjoy it," he explained as the door shut behind the dance instructor. Gil nodded to the musicians, curing them once again. "But with you, I want to break all the rules." He started to dance effortlessly, guiding us across the floor. "I do not need to worry about where my hands are." His hand on my waist dropped lower before pulling my body closer to him, only a breath of space between us. "Or how close you are to me."

He gently twirled me before pulling me close once again.

I looked up at him. "And what about the third?"

"Follow my lead," Gil said as he changed the steps.

I didn't know these steps and didn't know what came next. But I trusted him—I knew that he had me. The smallest touches from his fingers told me which way he would move. A gentle squeeze of my hand before a spin.

His hands settled on my waist as he lifted me in the air, spinning us once before letting me down. My body slid down every inch of his until my feet rested on the ground.

Gil began to guide me across the floor again, but the movements took on a new quality with my body this close to his. More sensual than graceful.

As the musicians began their final notes, Gil stopped moving, shifting his hands down my body to slowly dip me. The song's last notes floated around us as he leaned down, pressing his lips to my throat. He effortlessly helped me back to my feet.

I wrapped my arms around his neck, standing on my tip toes. "I like it when there are no rules," I whispered.

Gil chuckled, pulling me closer with a hand on my hip. "Do you now?"

I pressed my lips to his, not bothering to answer his question.

"I thought you were supposed to be teaching Bryn how to dance, not letting her climb you like a tree," Óskar said, startling me.

I dropped my arms, spinning to face him, my back pressed against Gil's chest.

"Gods, Óskar, you scared me. I didn't hear you come in," I said, glancing around the otherwise empty room. I hadn't heard the musicians leave either.

"And you scarred me, I don't think I can un-see what I just saw." He dramatically rubbed his eyes.

"If you had come in a little later, I am sure it would have been much worse." Gil's voice vibrated against my back.

Óskar gaped at him for a moment before viciously shaking his head. "No, that's enough of that. Bryn has to go to her rooms—her dress is ready for her fitting. And your sisters were looking for you, Gil. They said they would be in your rooms."

CHAPTER
TWENTY

GIL

My sisters were waiting in my rooms. Klara was pacing back and forth in front of my fireplace as Violet sat on the couch watching her. I shut the door behind me, drawing the attention of both of my sisters, but that wasn't enough to stop Klara's pacing.

"She's been like this since we got here," Violet told me quietly as I sat beside her on the couch. I watched Klara warily, leaning back on the sofa and stretching my arm behind Violet.

"What's wrong, Klara?" I asked. While Violet was definitely the calm one out of us, Klara didn't often show her nerves like this. She was more likely to bottle it up and unleash it on the poor warrior willing to spar with her on the training grounds.

Klara continued to pace. "I can't believe him."

"Him?" I turned to Violet for clarification, but she just shrugged at me.

"She was riled up when I found her. I don't know who she is talking about," Violet admitted.

I sighed, refocusing on Klara. "You need to give me more than that, Klara. Who is he?"

"The King Commander," she spat, her eyes blazing in fury.

My body went rigid, my back straightening. Klara wasn't meant to have anything to do with the King Commander. Yes, he ultimately ruled over all his citizens, but I had carefully shielded her and Violet from him. As head of our family, they only needed to answer to me, and I would never issue them orders. I would always grant them the freedom to make their own choices. I had promised myself that when I was old enough to know how the King Commander treated Mother, how he ordered and used her until the darkness consumed her.

Until she had turned into a monster fit for nothing but to be locked away.

I may be caught in his twisted web, but I would allow the darkness to overwhelm me before my sisters were caught up in the King Commander's manipulations.

I would bear that burden for them.

"What did the King Commander do?" I asked, carefully keeping my voice calm.

"He summoned me to his office today," she said, her hair flaring out around her as she spun on her heel, continuing to pace. "With how things have been here, I didn't think I could refuse."

I leaned forward in my seat, bracing my arms on my thighs. "You have every right to declare that your head of house be with you when you meet with the King Commander." I took a moment to process the other things she said. "What do you mean 'how things have been here'?"

"Things have been different since Pétur left, but when you all left for Wolfmire, things got worse," Violet said quietly, her green eyes, mirrors of my own, focused on Klara. "The King Commander is...temperamental. Lines are being drawn between people depending on who they support and who they suspect others are supporting. Who they trust, who they don't trust."

"And you did not want to risk being the subject of his anger," I said softly, turning my attention back to Klara.

"I know how he treats you and our family." Klara finally stopped moving. "I couldn't risk it."

I took a deep breath. "What did he say to you?"

"He knows how strong our family's bloodrite is and doesn't necessarily believe that Violet and I don't have it."

"There was no guarantee that someone would inherit their parent's bloodrite. If you or Violet had it, we would have known by now."

Klara bit her lip. "The King Commander has seen your increased control over the darkness and believes that Violet and I may be using that newfound control to hide the bloodrite. He says that if he discovers that we are hiding it, he will use whatever means necessary to make us reveal it." Her voice broke.

I stood and made my way to her, pulling her close. "I will not let him touch you," I promised her. Klara's fingers gripped the back of my shirt, her arms tight around me.

This was exactly what I have always tried to protect her and Violet from. I had always been relieved that they hadn't inherited the bloodrite, that they would never be at risk of becoming a monster like our mother had. Like generations of our ancestors had.

The only thing that scared me was the darkness that lingered in the shadows of my own life, waiting for the opportunity to sweep in and take control. Bryn had soothed those fears and had shown me that there was a future where I would not end up in the prison designed for my family below the fortress.

But my control, hope, and dreams for the future now put my sisters at risk.

"I am sorry that I have done this to you. This is my fault," I told her quietly, but in the room's silence, the words felt quite loud.

Klara pulled back, her hands resting on my cheeks. "Don't you dare apologize, Gil. This is not your fault."

"If I had not shown him that there was the possibility of our family maintaining control, he would not have the grounds to threaten you and Violet." My voice wavered.

A hand on my back told me that Violet had joined us.

"This is not on you, Gil," Violet told me. "You have nothing to apologize for. Nothing."

"This control that you have? That means we will not lose our brother or be separated," Klara said, her green eyes meeting my own. "I think I speak for the both of us that that makes all of this shit worth it."

"Absolutely," Violet agreed.

I swallowed thickly, letting their words settle over me like a warm blanket. "Thank you." I reached out an arm to each of my sisters, pulling them close. "But we face this together. If he tries to get one of you alone, you do whatever you need to do to get me. And if you cannot get me, you get one of the Verndari. Please. Promise me."

"We promise," Violet said for the both of them.

I FOUND Georg in his office, parchments stacked over his desk, only a small portion of the surface clear for him to work. I knocked on the door frame, not wanting to startle him.

Georg glanced up, setting aside the parchment he was

reading with a smile. "Gil, come in." I walked in and shut the door behind me. "What brings you to my office?"

"Is this a result of our trip to Wolfmire?" I asked, nodding towards the parchments.

Georg grimaced. "Yes, a rather unfortunate side effect of being away from the fortress for so long." He watched me take a seat in front of his desk. "What's wrong, Gil?"

"The King Commander has set his sights on my sisters. He is not convinced that they do not have the bloodrite and is threatening to force it out of them," I said, focusing on the edge of the desk in front of me. "He cornered Klara, and I am worried he will do it again. I have told them to only speak to him if I am with them or one of the Verndari."

"Good. That will help protect them," Georg said, leaning back in his chair and crossing his arms over his chest. He was quiet for a moment. "The King Commander has always enjoyed power. Whenever something threatens, his true colours reveal themselves."

"You sound as though you are speaking from experience."

Georg ran a hand over his bald head. "When I went through the trainer's tournament, he showed who he was, but I noticed it too late."

When the next generation of Verndari was born, each family chose a representative to enter the trainer's tournament to determine who the trainer would be for their children. Although tournament was too weak of a name for what they went through. The demands of them, the trials, the tests were dangerous. Life threatening. And sometimes, the winner of the trainer's tournament was simply the last person standing.

"Would you have chosen differently if you could? Would you not have not become our trainer?"

Georg considered my question for several moments. "I still

would have become your trainer. Not having you all in my life doesn't sit right with me. But would I have made some different decisions? Yes. Absolutely."

"Are my sisters at risk?" I knew that Klara and Violet were being threatened by someone who had the power to fully capitalize on that threat. But I needed to know just how big the risk was.

"I think that we all are," Georg said quietly. His eyes met mine. "If he is threatening your sisters, it will not be long until that focus shifts to the rest of us. We are all going to need to be on guard. For both ourselves and each other."

CHAPTER
TWENTY-ONE
BRYN

The maid had intricately braided my hair before carefully pinning it up to leave my neck bare. A few curls hung free to frame my face. She had darkened my eyes and painted my lips blood red.

"All done, Jarl Brynja," she said with a pat on my shoulder. "You can slip on your shoes now."

I stood, lifting the hem of my dress to slide on my heeled slippers. I had spent an hour the night before making sure I could walk in them without falling on my face.

"Don't you look marvellous," the maid gushed. "Come, look in the mirrored glass."

The grey material clung to my upper body, highlighting every curve I had before gracefully draping once it hit my waist, and the light material practically floated as I moved. But the back of the dress captured all of the attention.

My back was bare, bracketed by many silver metal pieces, like feathers on a wing. The two sides were held together with three jewelled strips.

My scar from the attack on the village was there, but it had paled in the months since it happened. The only physical reminder that I carried of the night that I had lost my Da.

The maid handed me a pair of beautifully decorated staffs only about a foot long as a knock sounded on my door. Óskar stood there, elegantly dressed with his own staffs in his hand.

"It's good that I came to get you rather than Gil. If he had seen you looking like that, you both would have been late for the ball," he joked, tucking my hand into the crook of his arm. "Especially after what I saw yesterday."

My cheeks warmed, but I lifted my chin, feigning ignorance. "I have no idea what you're talking about."

"Of course you don't. Just do me a favour and don't start undressing each other at the ball. Save it for later." He led us out of my rooms. "I don't think I'll be able to dance all that well with my eyes bleeding."

I rolled my eyes. "You're ridiculous."

"You're right. I'll still be able to dance marvellously and look fabulous if blood's your thing."

I laughed as we reached the entry to our wing, where we were meeting the others. We were the last ones to arrive, and Gil's eyes immediately landed on me when we joined them. They slowly scanned down my body, then back up again, before locking with mine.

Georg and Aron led us out, and Óskar and I settled into our places behind them.

"Gods," Gil muttered behind me as he caught a glimpse of the back of the dress. My cheeks warmed, my stomach fluttering at his reaction.

"Be careful not to drool there," Rúna laughed.

Óskar raised his brows at me, a small smirk on his face. He knew he was right about what he said earlier, but I wasn't going to give him the satisfaction of admitting it to him.

"Don't you start," I warned.

He snickered but said nothing as we arrived at the entrance of the gathering hall. The rows of tables and benches had been removed, and the room had been transformed. Decorations filled the space and hung from the rafters above. A group of musicians were set up in the corner with a spread of food and drinks against one of the walls.

The space was filled with people as we were supposed to be among the last to arrive. Only the King Commander and his family were to come after us.

We took our places to the side of the dais as the King Commander and his family entered. I sunk into a graceful curtsy, the metal pieces on my dress gently tinkling against each other.

"Welcome, everyone. Tonight is a time for us to come together, to bond together, before we move forward. Together." Everyone applauded, some more enthusiastically than others. "I would like to invite the Verndari to open the celebrations, with my daughters joining them."

Georg and Aron walked up to the dais and bowed before holding their hands to the princesses. Ragna went to Georg, while Sigrún went to Aron. She had always paired up with Pétur before. They had been very close, and with him gone, it was yet another hole he had left behind.

Another bond broken.

Óskar led me up to the dais, where I sank into yet another curtsy before we took our places on the floor. I held one of the staffs in each hand as the musicians started a quick song full of heavy beats.

Óskar and I paired off against each other, the dance like a choreographed fight. Our staffs clacked against each other in time with the other pairs. We spun around each other fluidly, flowing from step to choreographed step, and the music swelled to a crescendo.

We came into the final few steps, and I allowed Óskar to knock the staff out of my hands. He dipped me, and the staff pressed gently to my throat as the last note hung in the air.

Everyone applauded before we made our way off the floor and handed our staffs to a servant. The musicians started another song just as an arm snaked around my waist.

"May I have this dance?" Gil asked, his breath tickling my ear.

"Of course you can." I took his hand and let him lead me onto the floor.

Gil pulled my body close to his, his hand on my back warm against my bare skin. It was a fast-paced dance that Gil easily guided me through. He spun me around him and lifted me from the ground as though I weighed nothing. The song ended with an elaborate series of spins culminating in a dip that left me trying to catch my breath with a grin as Gil kissed my forehead.

He helped me get back to my feet as the next song started, the music taking on an upbeat tune that was not unlike those played back in Ebonwell. I lifted a hand to Gil's as we circled each other, my other hand holding my dress so that the hem was above my feet. The steps took on a skipping quality as we circled each other. Gil spun me away from him as we switched partners. I found myself face to face with a man from the Royal Regiment. He was fun to dance with, but I counted down every step until I was back in Gil's arms. And when I finally spun back to him, his hands catching my waist, I laughed, the sound ringing around us and harmonizing with the music.

We stayed on the floor for every song, rejecting everyone who came forward to try and interrupt our dance. Until the music stopped, the King Commander standing to draw every-one's attention to himself.

I hooked my hand around Gil's arm, and he guided us to our places by the dais. My fingers shook against his arm, so he raised his hand to cover mine. To comfort me and to hide the shaking from the others.

The King Commander cleared his throat. "We are all aware of the return of the Skolli and the dangers that they pose to Drysden. As enjoyable as it is, this ball was not just for us to gather together, share food, and dance." The crowd was silent as they watched him. "With the attacks increasing, it is time for us to prepare for more drastic measures, and we need to know who we can count on for those measures. It is time for you to declare your loyalties."

Óskar leaned closer to me. "This will be interesting," he muttered.

Ragna stepped up to her father and passed him a rolled scroll. She immediately stepped back to join her family, pulling out a matching roll for herself.

The King Commander unrolled the scroll. "Verndari."

Our allegiance was to the Commanding Family; everyone knew that. But it was a formality that we must be called upon as we are all Jarls in our own right. We were technically encompassed in the same laws as the others, even if we took different vows upon being named a Verndari.

Georg stepped forward into the open space before us and bowed. "We are yours to command." He stepped back into place.

Hákon stepped forward to pledge the Royal Regiment and Ragna the Striking Shadows.

"Jarl Ottó," the King Commander read out.

I found Ottó in the crowd. He stood near the front of the

crowd with Emilía by his side, a new Warlord on her arm. Sigrún stood apart from them as she was by Gier's side with some of the other Striking Shadows. A non-verbal declaration of where her support truly lay.

Ottó didn't say a word.

"Jarl Ottó," the King Commander repeated.

Ottó stayed quiet, simply crossing his arms over his chest. Very clearly saying that he wasn't going to declare his support.

Ragna made a note on the scroll she was holding as the King Commander continued reading his list of names. One by one, people began to step forward and declare their loyalty.

But not everyone did.

People hung back, deliberately not making a move or saying a word that would give away where their loyalties lay.

Not against the King Commander, but certainly not for him either.

The ball started to wrap up quickly after that. A few people lingered on the dance floor, while others left chatting or couples disappeared off together.

Gil swept me into one last dance before leaning down to whisper in my ear. "Do you want to leave?"

"Lead the way."

CHAPTER
TWENTY-TWO
BRYN

Gil walked me back to my rooms, keeping me close to his side. My arm wrapped around his waist, holding him as close to me as I could. We reached my door too quickly—I didn't want him to leave yet. His words from the stable loft ran through my head as I pushed open my door.

I stepped in, our hands lingering on each other until they could no longer reach. I turned back to face him. "Do you want to come in?" I asked.

His eyes heated, no doubt remembering the same conversation I had.

"I would love to." He stepped in after me, shutting the door behind us. He shrugged off his jacket, draping it over the back of a chair before he stepped closer to me. "Have I told you how breathtaking you look tonight?"

"Not in those exact words, but some version of them." I smiled coyly. I spun in a slow circle, his eyes burning into me the whole time. "What's your favourite part?"

"Do I have to choose just one?"

I laughed, stepping into my bedroom. "As much as I love how my hair looks, all the pins are murdering my head." I sat at my dressing table, my fingers already searching for the first pin.

Gil appeared in the mirrored glass a moment later, standing so close behind me that the warmth of his body sunk into my skin. He methodically searched for every pin, gently freeing them from my hair. When my curls and various braids finally hung freely down my back, he shifted his attention to unravelling them so each strand hung freely. Gil ran his fingers through my hair before massaging my scalp.

I tipped my head back, my eyes closing.

Gil chuckled. "Does that feel better?"

I moaned before saying, "You have no idea how good that feels." His fingers froze in my hair. I opened my eyes, locking gazes with Gil in the mirrored glass. "What is it?"

"I'm just thinking about all the things I could do to make you make that sound again," he said, his voice gravelly.

"I'm pretty sure it would happen if you keep doing what you were doing."

"I was thinking of some other things."

I rose, turning to face him. I stepped closer to him, my body practically touching his. "Like what?"

Gil wrapped an arm around my waist and pulled me flush against him. He pressed a kiss to the crook of my neck, tracing his lips up the column of my throat. His teeth found my ear, gently tugging at it. I gasped, my fingers tunnelling through his hair.

"I like that sound, too," he admitted before finally pressing his lips to mine.

I stood on my tiptoes, matching his every movement, desperate for more. He deepened the kiss, wrapping my curls around his hand while the other slipped through the open back of my dress to rest on my bare skin.

I slid my hands to the top of his shirt, lingering at the first button there. Giving him plenty of time to stop me if he wasn't ready.

But he made no move to do so.

I undid the first button before starting on the next. And the next. And the next. Until his shirt hung completely open, allowing me to push it off of his shoulders.

Gil pulled just far enough back from me to let it slip off his arms and onto my floor. I stood there for a moment my eyes slowly drifting down his revealed skin and back up. His body toned and defined from the hours we spend training. My eyes finally locked with his again, the corner of his mouth quirking. "Like what you see?"

I trailed a finger from the hollow of his throat to the top of his pants, following every dip and ridge of his body. "I do."

He caught my hand, interlacing our fingers and kissed the back of it. His other hand fiddled with the sleeve of my dress. "May I?"

"You'll need to unhook the chains too," I said as I turned around so that he could reach the buttons on the dress' skirt. I gathered my hair, holding it over one shoulder.

Gil pressed a kiss to my throat before he unhooked the first chain. He placed each one carefully on my dressing table before turning to the buttons. I held the dress to my chest with my other arm as it continued to loosen on my body.

When he finished, taking a step back, I took a single, deep breath to calm my nerves before I turned to face him. I released my hair so that it fell freely down my back, and Gil gave me a soft smile.

I let go of the dress, allowing it to flow down my body and pool on the ground by his shirt.

Gil sucked in a breath, his green eyes blazing as they drifted down my body before locking with my own once again.

"You are beautiful," he said before kissing me again. His arms wrapped around me, pulling me close, our bare skin pressed close for the first time. Our hands trailed over each other's bodies as he drew a moan from me. "There it is," he said against my lips.

He guided me back towards my bed. My legs bumped against it, so I finally broke away from him and climbed atop it.

Gil hesitated momentarily, his hands on the waist of his pants. "Are you sure?"

"Yes," I breathed.

His eyes blazed as he quickly took off his pants and joined me.

He kissed me once, twice, three times before slowly making his way down my body. Gil took his time, his lips and hands finding every place that made me gasp. Every place that made me moan.

He kept going, his actions more and more deliberate as he started to learn my body. The pleasure continued to build, my fingers tingling, my toes curling until it finally burst, my back arching slightly off the bed.

Gil let me pull him back up my body as he settled between my legs. He pressed a gentle kiss to my forehead. "Are you sure? We don't have to—"

I cupped his face in my hands, my thumbs drifting across his cheekbones. "I want to," I said quietly, the words floating around us. "Kiss me."

He bracketed his arms on either side of my head and dipped to kiss my lips. It was slower than the earlier ones, every movement of his lips against mine drawn out. Soaking in every moment.

Gil pushed forward, joining us, pausing his movements to allow me to adjust to him. He brushed a curl from my face, tucking it behind my ear. He peppered my face with kisses until I lifted my hips, urging him to move. Gil began to move, his hand tracing down my body until it reached my thigh. He hooked my leg over his hips, quickening his movements.

The pleasure built once again, my fingernails digging into his shoulders and back.

And when it burst once again, I cried out, clutching him closer. A few moments later, he stilled, groaning my name into my ear.

We lay there momentarily before Gil rolled us to the side, slipping off the bed and disappearing into the bathing room. He returned with a cloth, gently wiping off my body before joining me again.

I rested my head on his chest, looping my leg over his.

He pressed a kiss to my forehead, his arm wrapping around me.

It didn't take long for me to fall asleep to his fingers mindlessly tracing across my back, drawing designs that only he could see.

Rúna sought me out the next afternoon, finding me in the middle of making new healing supplies to replenish my stores. She burst through the doors, her hair tied back in a messy horsetail and her clothes loose and comfortable.

She studied me momentarily, noticing I was wearing Gil's

shirt from the night before over a pair of the close-fitting leggings I wore to train.

"Something you want to tell me?" she teased as she flopped down on one of the couches by the fire.

My cheeks warmed. "It's new."

"I wouldn't call you and Gil that, so you must be referring to other things." She waggled her eyebrows.

"Yes—the other things are quite recent."

"How recent?"

I finished mixing the herbs into the cream and turned to face Rúna. "Last night."

Rúna squealed, her face lighting up. "You need to tell me everything. Wait—Gil is like my brother. Don't give me details. Tell me, was it good?"

"It was incredible," I giggled with a big smile. "It was absolutely incredible."

"I'm happy for you," Rúna grinned before pretending to gag. "But let's leave it at that, shall we?"

I laughed, flopping on the couch across from Rúna. We lay in comfortable silence for a moment. I had a feeling that there was a specific reason she had sought me out, and sometimes, it was best to wait for her to open up. If I pushed her, it could cause her to withdraw into herself.

"I haven't been able to find anything," she finally said. "I haven't found any fucking proof that Baldur is the traitor."

My spirits dimmed. Rúna was in an impossible position, and I would be the first to pull her out of it. Well, the first person after Gil. But she was also our best bet to keep an eye on Baldur, and I would do everything I could to support her as long as she thought it was necessary.

"How has he been?" I asked.

"Better, surprisingly." Rúna rolled onto her side to face me.

"Ever since we left the fortress, he's been better. He'll never be my favourite person, but I certainly wouldn't call him a bad person since we left for Wolfmire."

I propped my head up an elbow. "Sofie mentioned that she thought that he was nice." I made a face. "What do you think is different?"

"I don't know if it was getting out of the fortress or if something else happened. Maybe he could put something in motion while we were in Wolfmire that I'm unaware of. He's never wanting to be around Hákon. Still, he's always offering to help Ragna and is the first person to track down Sigrún whenever she disappears."

"What do you mean Sigrún disappears?"

Rúna brushed away my words with a hand. "She's still upset about the arranged marriage and shows it by disappearing on them. I think she's trying to see who cares enough to come and find her, but I don't know."

I was quiet for a moment, shocked. "Do you still think Baldur's the traitor?"

"I think he is the most likely person to be the traitor," Rúna said. "I don't know who it would be if it's not him. I don't know what to do if it's not him."

Georg and Aron faced off against Rúna and Gil in the training ring the next day.

Óskar and I watched on, Yugar by our feet with his head on his paws.

Georg and Aron attacked as one, dividing Gil and Rúna. Georg pushed Rúna back with a swing of his axe while Gil stood his ground against Aron.

"Fuck him up, Aron!" Óskar cheered from the outside as Gil and Aron's blades clashed together. I chuckled quietly beside him. I refused to cheer against Gil, but I wanted Aron and Georg to finally get a win. To finally click in a way that they hadn't been able to yet.

It wasn't just important for them.

It was important for all of us. The longer it took them to click, the more dangerous it would be for us on the battlefield.

We needed this to work.

Gil and Aron were evenly matched, their weapons a blur, easily attacking and blocking. Georg and Rúna's bout was more of a dance as Georg pushed closer before retreating from her longer reach.

"Wanna bet on who will win?" Óskar asked me. "My money is on Georg and Aron."

I studied the spar for a moment. "Fine. I'll bet on Gil and Rúna, but I honestly think this can go either way. It all depends on what happens if Gil and Rúna manage to push them back together."

There was no doubt that Aron was an incredible fighter and that he and Georg were best suited for each other. However, they still hadn't had the moment where everything clicked into place. The moment when they finally start anticipating the other's moves before they make them.

And that hurt them the most when they fought side by side.

We all knew it, so there was no doubt in my mind that Gil and Rúna would try to push them together and force them to fight side by side.

And as Gil pivoted to the side, snapping out a kick at Aron as Rúna swung her staff at Georg's middle, I knew they were making their move.

Georg and Aron spun to avoid being hit, but they didn't crash into each other. Each spun past the other to attack the other person—Aron engaging Rúna while Georg took on Gil.

"There it is!" Óskar yelled as I clapped and cheered by his side.

That was it.

That was the moment when everything finally clicked.

Aron placed his blade against Rúna's neck, effectively winning the bout.

Rúna dropped her weapons, jumping to wrap her arms around Aron's neck. "You guys did it!"

Georg laughed, clapping Gil on the shoulder, before making his way over to Rúna and Aron. Rúna gave him the same enthusiastic hug she had given Aron.

When she was done, Georg wrapped an arm around Aron's shoulders. "Nicely done."

"Think we can work with that?" Aron grinned.

"I'd say," Óskar added from the sidelines.

Georg nodded. "We can absolutely work with that."

TWENTY-THREE

BRYN

We all gathered in Ragna's office, spread out on all the seating we could find, and even then, it wasn't enough. Gil sat on the arm of my chair to save space. But, when Hákon joined us a moment later, he was forced to stand, leaning against the wall with one leg propped up behind him.

"How do things look?" Georg asked Ragna, his face grim. We had all been at the ball and seen how many people had stepped forward and how many people had not.

The question was how that matched what Ragna thought would happen and how we could work with the people we had.

And how the people who had not declared could hurt us.

"Five Jarls have declared their full support, and two declared they would support us with supplies. Ten Warlords have also indicated they will give us their full support."

We were silent for a moment. "And how many have not declared?" Georg finally asked.

"Double that," Ragna said with a sigh. "And some of the

hold-offs are some of the most powerful people in Drysden, such as Jarl Ottó and Jarl Einar."

"How bad is it?" Gil's voice was grim. "Did it match up to what you think would happen?"

Were we prepared for this outcome, or were we in dangerous waters with how things had played out at the ball?

Ragna let out a humourless chuckle. "Not the worst. But I wouldn't feel comfortable in a war anytime soon."

"What can we do?" Rúna asked softly.

"I need Jarl Einar. How close were you to convincing him?"

I shook my head with a sigh. "I wouldn't count on him anytime soon. It felt like we were progressing with him, but he didn't agree with our decision to return for the ball. He made his opinion of our actions very clear."

"With Jarl Einar an unlikely ally and Ottó a dangerous one at best," Ragna pursed her lips, "we need as many of the remainder that we can get."

"What are our odds if we don't get the support?" Georg asked bluntly. He wasn't one to dance around a question, especially if it affected his tactics or put us at risk.

And this would do both.

Ragna's face was grave. "The odds are bad. We would be severely outnumbered and underfunded."

"And out monstered," Óskar added, no doubt trying to lighten the mood. There were very few things more depressing than discussing your odds of survival. Especially when those odds did not look like they were in your favour.

Aron scoffed. "He's not wrong. Those monsters alone put them at an advantage. Only one person can tangle with them on a somewhat even footing." He gestured towards me. "We need everyone we can to give us a fighting chance."

"He's right," Ragna sighed as she rubbed her eyes.

"Send us out," Óskar said, his voice now uncharacteristically serious. "Use us."

Hákon pushed off the wall, joining his sister. "We will—we don't have another choice. But we have to approach this systematically. Because we would be fooling ourselves if we thought that the exiled royal family weren't campaigning for the same thing as us."

"They can't leave where they were exiled," Rúna said.

"They have allies. They made that very clear by the nature of their survival. And they will use as many of them as possible to gather their armies until they can do it themselves. I'm pretty sure they even have one in the fortress."

"Ottó." My voice was soft.

Ragna nodded at me. "That's what we believe, but we haven't been able to catch him doing anything."

"He's doing it, but he's doing it from behind the scenes." I exchanged a look with Aron and Ragna. We suspected how he was doing it.

Hákon crossed his arms over his chest. "What do you mean?"

"We think he is using Emilía," I said, tucking a curl behind my ear. "No one expects her to be plotting when it looks like she is flirting her way through the Warlords and sons of Jarls. Especially when we all know how obsessed with power Ottó is."

Hákon swore.

"I will put someone on my team on them both. We need evidence before we can do anything, especially now." Ragna sighed. Especially now when we are doing everything to gain the support of the people. They won't likely side with us if we violate their rights. "If we are desperate, I have someone I can send inside to get information. Unofficially. But that would be an absolute last resort."

Svanna—Ottó's daughter, member of the Striking Shadows, and Ragna's lover. She wouldn't ask that of her unless we had no other choices. Or we were out of time.

"What are our next steps?" Georg asked. "What can we do?"

"I am almost done compiling the list of who we need to target for support. You will be riding out within a week to visit everyone on the list. You can stay no longer than three days at each location before moving on to the next."

"Jarl Einar will be on the list. He is too important not to be," Hákon said, joining his sister by her desk. "But if you do not think he will likely provide support, you should prioritize the others. Focus on them and then follow up with Jarl Einar. He's important, but we can't ignore all the other potential supporters hoping he will join us."

I drummed my fingers on my leg until Gil rested his hand on mine. Stilling me. Soothing me. "And if we aren't successful in convincing them in that time?"

"Then you move on," Hákon crossed his arms over his chest. "You make our need quite clear, but you move on. Because every day we spend trying to convince someone is a day that the exiled royal family can be doing the same with the others."

"We are racing against an unknown clock. If we have time, we can circle back, but we need to guarantee as much support as possible," Ragna explained.

Óskar leaned forward, petting Yugar's back. "And if we fail?"

"Then we battle with what we have and get struck down one by one."

TWENTY-FOUR

BRYN

I led Aron through the hallways towards my mother's rooms. With all the others busy with their own things, Aron had asked if I would be interested in going down to Goldhelm for some light shopping. Rúna had grumbled on her way to meet Baldur, upset that she was missing out, but I was happy to join him.

I needed to visit Ma on the way. It had been a few days since I had seen her, and with the chance of us being called away at a moment's notice, I made sure to visit her whenever possible.

She seemed to be doing the tiniest bit better each time I visited her. She had her bad days, but on the whole, she seemed to be getting better slowly.

I knocked on the door to her rooms. Aron had already been warned what to expect, so I wasn't too worried about his reaction.

Ma opened the door, her eyes brightening at the sight of me. She stepped aside to let us in before shutting the door behind us.

"Hi, Ma," I smiled as she hugged me.

Ma rested her hand on my cheek, her eyes darting across my face before scanning my body closely. With a nod and a soft pat on my cheek, she turned towards Aron.

"Pleasure to meet you, ma'am," he bowed his head in respect. "I'm Aron."

Ma looked towards me with an eyebrow lifted. Her question as clear as though she had spoken aloud.

"Aron is the newest member of the Verndari," I explained. "He took Pétur's spot."

Ma turned back towards Aron with a new look in her eye. She finally nodded, apparently deeming him worthy of the position. I stifled a laugh as Aron stood patiently throughout the inspection as though he were a prized horse.

"Don't laugh," Aron said, following me toward the sitting area. "If she raised you, I'm sure that she is more than able to hurt me if she wanted. I wasn't going to give her a reason to."

Ma grinned as she poured us some tea.

"Ma isn't much of a fighter. She's more likely to poison you."

Aron studied the tea before him, a new suspicion in his eyes. "That's wonderful to hear."

I couldn't hold it then, my laughter ringing through the room. Ma leaned forward and sipped Aron's tea before settling into her chair.

"That does make me feel better, thank you," he said as he picked up his tea.

I sipped my drink as Ma reached into her mending basket and pulled out Fannar's baby blanket. I knew he no longer slept with it, but Ma always ensured it was in pristine condition since it was the only thing Fannar had left of wherever he came from.

The last part of who he was before he was found in that snow bank.

Aron went rigid beside me. "Where did you get that?" Ma tilted her head, her brows furrowed. "Where did you get that blanket?"

"It's mine," Fannar said.

I whirled around towards the door. Fannar stood there, his hair damp as though it were freshly washed. "Fannar! I didn't hear you come in!"

"I just got here," he said before quickly giving Ma a kiss on her cheek. He turned back towards Aron. "Why were you asking about my baby blanket?"

"Your baby blanket," Aron repeated. His words were rough, his eyes misty.

Fannar turned to me, a question in his eyes. I shook my head—I had no idea what was going on.

"I'm sure you've heard I'm Bryn's adoptive brother." Fannar took a seat, Aron's eyes locked on his every move. "I was found by my adoptive parents when I was just a baby. They were merchants travelling back to Ebonwell after a big snowstorm." Aron's breathing hitched. "They found me in a snow bank wrapped in that blanket."

"Why are you so interested in his blanket?" I asked softly.

Aron didn't answer me; his focus was entirely on Fannar. "Your hair—it's almost the exact same as hers. And I can see him in your eyes." I don't think he even realized he was talking. He wasn't entirely aware of anyone in the room besides Fannar.

"Aron," I said, waiting until he finally looked at me. "Why are you so interested in his blanket?"

"Because it's the symbols and colours of my family. I have one exactly like it." Fannar's eyes widened. "We fled from

Graythorn to Goldhelm. But early in our journey, we were caught in a snowstorm," Aron started, summarizing the story he had told me before.

"And you lost your baby brother during that snowstorm," I said softly, my eyes darting towards Fannar. "Going from Graythorn to Goldhelm would have taken you right by Ebonwell."

Ma's eyes darted between us, her fingers drifting idly across the blanket.

"How can we be sure?" Fannar asked, swallowing thickly as his eyes darted between us. For support and clarification.

Aron took a deep breath before turning back to Fannar. "My—our—mother always joked that my brother was my mini-me because we had the same birthmark on our shoulders." He stood, pulling his shirt off. "Can you take your shirt off too?" Aron asked Fannar hesitantly.

Fannar stood wordlessly, watching Aron with wide eyes. He pulled his shirt off before they both turned their back to me.

I gasped, jumping from my seat.

There, on each of their shoulders, was the exact same birthmark.

"It's there," I told them.

"Brother," Aron whispered brokenly before pulling Fannar into a tight hug. Fannar held him just as tightly. After a moment, Fannar reached out to me, pulling me into their arms as well. Aron laughed, wiping his tears from his eyes. "I guess that makes you my sister, then."

I laughed, my own eyes going misty. "I guess so. Welcome to the family."

We finally separated, and Fannar was quick to ask for details about his birth family. His face was pure shock at learning his father was a Warlord, making him a member of a titled household. When Aron explained his father's almost bloodrite-style connection to weapons, Fannar's eyes whipped to mine.

"Do you remember what Hákon said when he started training me?" he asked breathlessly.

"He was amazed at how fast you took to the training; how easy it was for you to pick up the weapons and how natural you seemed with them."

Aron smiled. "I'm the same."

"Does your mother, or I guess our mother, live in Goldhelm?" Fannar asked, stumbling over his words.

"She does. Would you like to meet her?"

With Aron and Fannar otherwise occupied, I finished my tea with my mother before heading back towards the Verndari Wing.

Knowing the others would be busy, I poked my head into the library to see if I could find anyone. I drew the stares of the people in the room, a consequence of being a Verndari these days. There was no one there that I recognized, so I continued on. Baldur and Rúna were in one of the common spaces throughout the halls, but I had no desire to join them. I waved to Rúna but kept moving before I got drawn into whatever the group was doing.

I decided to give it one more try and looked into the Gathering Hall to see if anyone was there. I was about to return to my rooms to work on healing supplies or read a book when I spotted them.

Gier and Svanna were seated together, a game board in

front of them. I hadn't seen much of either of them—the Striking Shadows were being kept as busy as we were.

And it had been a long time since I had sat in front of a game board.

I approached them, noticing Sigrún sitting a table over, her head bent over a book. She didn't acknowledge me, so I carried on towards the pair of Striking Shadows.

I studied the game board and winced. "Black wins in two," I said.

Svanna groaned. "No. I thought I had a chance this time."

"This is a game of logic," Gier said matter-of-factly. He didn't need to say anything else. Gier had to be one of the smartest people in the fortress and one of the strongest tacticians.

Two moves later, he officially captured the win and turned toward me. "You saw that I was going to win."

"I did. I played this game a lot growing up. I may not have won every time, but each time I lost, I tried that much harder to figure out the strategies." I took a seat beside Svanna.

"Interested in playing?"

My fingers immediately reached for the white pieces that Svanna had been using. "Absolutely."

Svanna rested her head on an elbow on the table as we set up the board. "This will be interesting. I've heard that you are decent at tactics, Bryn."

"I'm still getting used to battlefield tactics, but I'm alright," I agreed as I placed my last piece on the board. "Did your whisper networks tell you that, or are you trying to hide that it's your own observation?"

Svanna grinned. "A lady never tells."

"It should be that a spy never tells. Ladies gossip more than anyone else," Gier scoffed as he made the first move.

"Men gossip too. You just don't notice it since you don't participate." Svanna rolled her eyes.

I made my move, earning a twitch of Gier's eyebrow. It wasn't one of the moves that most people use.

I had caught him off guard.

"Interesting," he said before making his next move. "This will be fun."

We exchanged moves back and forth in silence, my respect for his skill growing with each one.

"This is tense," Svanna said. "It's been a while since anyone has lasted this long against Gier."

"She's still not going to win," Gier argued as he took one of my pieces.

I moved one of my last pieces back away from his own.

"At least she's putting up a fight," Svanna studied the board for a moment. "She's got options,"

"Or she does not know when to give up." Gier took his turn.

"I prefer to think of it as skill," I said as I took one of his pieces. "And perhaps a little stubbornness."

The door to the hall creaked open, drawing my attention. Hákon entered and waved to us before heading towards Sigrún. I turned my focus back to the board as Gier took another of my pieces. "Shit," I muttered. I had two pieces against Gier's five, and my paths to victory were quickly dwindling.

I had two, maybe three, moves before Gier won. But I was going to make him work for it. Perhaps he was right—maybe I don't know when to give up.

"I've looked everywhere for you, Sigrún," Hákon said quietly behind me as I made my move.

"Well, you found me," she bit out.

"You never spend time here. It was one of the last places I had to check."

Gier took another of my pieces, a smirk already on his face. He knew that he was going to win.

"You've got the Royal Regiment and your healing. Ragna's got the Striking Shadows. Baldur's got his training as Commanding Son. I've got nothing. I've got no one of my own."

"And you thought you would find it here?" Hákon asked. "Not to mention the Treaty. That's yours. You play the biggest role in it."

Sigrún scoffed. "Yes, because it is something to be proud of, something exciting, to be dealt and traded like cattle."

I moved my piece backwards, forcing Gier to chase me. Drawing out the inevitable.

"You aren't being traded like cattle, Sigrún. You're marrying to secure a treaty to avoid a war."

"And that's exactly what I dreamed about growing up, wasn't it?" Sigrún laughed, but there was nothing happy about it.

Gier took my last piece, and I helped him pack up the game.

"I know it's not what you wanted. Gods, it's not what I would have wanted for you. But it's not a death sentence, sister."

"Baldur's got Rúna, Ragna has Svanna. And don't think I haven't noticed how you look at a certain someone when you think people aren't watching. I've got—" Her book slammed closed behind me. "I've got no one. No one to make me smile, no one to make me laugh, no one to make me feel loved. Father condemns me to marry our enemy, and none of you have taken my side."

Sigrún stormed out of the room, but her words kept ringing in my head when I eventually made my way to the Verndari wing.

Sigrún had had that person. The one that would make her laugh.

I had seen him spinning a small cyclone on his hand to make her smile.

But Pétur had abandoned her just as much as us when he went behind the barrier.

CHAPTER
TWENTY-FIVE
BRYN

I woke suddenly, my body alert.

I studied the darkness of my room, the lingering embers of the fireplace casting the barest of light, searching for what woke me. But nothing was out of place, no sign of what caused me to wake. I turned over, curling closer to Gil. His arm wrapped around me, pulling me tighter to him, the warmth of his body seeping into me.

I shut my eyes, hoping Gil's steady breathing would lull me back to sleep. We had shared a bed since the ball and I was quickly becoming used to his presence. His steady breathing, warmth in the blankets, and scent on the pillows.

Something banged on the door.

I shot up in bed, the furs pooling around my waist. Gil was equally alert next to me.

"Jarl Brynja!" someone called before banging on the door.

"Dammit," I muttered as I flung myself out of bed. I pulled Gil's shirt on before stumbling towards the door. It only fell to the middle of my thighs, but I didn't care that my bare legs were able to be seen under the hem of his shirt. They wouldn't be waking me in the middle of the night if it wasn't an emergency. "This can't be good."

"No, it cannot be," Gil agreed as he quickly pulled on his pants and joined me, his chest still bare.

I pulled open the door to reveal a frazzled maid. She looked from me to Gil and back again with wide eyes before catching herself. "The War Council is being summoned."

My heart pounded in my chest. "We will be right there."

She nodded before hurrying on to the next door.

I swallowed thickly and shut the door. Gil stepped forward, wrapping me in the briefest of hugs before leading me back into the bedroom to get changed. We dressed in silence, the thoughts in my head racing.

There was only one reason they would call the War Council in the middle of the night.

There had been another attack.

Where was it?

How bad was it?

"Bryn." Gil placed his hands on my cheeks. "We both know that whatever awaits us in the War Chamber will not be good. But we will face it as a team—we will face it together. Breathe, darling."

I wrapped my fingers around his with a nod. "Together."

"Exactly." He pressed a kiss to my forehead. Gil led the way to the door, taking my hand as we entered the hallway.

We walked to the War Chamber silently as I braced myself for whatever awaited us. I prepared myself for whatever we were asked of once we crossed the threshold. The only bright side was that since Ottó had not declared his support of the King Commander, he was barred from the War Chamber until his alliance was clear.

Once everyone was in the space, Ragna wasted no time.

She rolled out a map, and Gier helped her secure the corners. His clothing was creased, his face drawn.

As though he had ridden for hours without a break to get here.

To tell Ragna about whatever we were about to learn.

"Large amounts of Skolli are on the move, and it appears that they are preparing to launch large-scale attacks," Ragna said, her face grim.

"Attacks plural?" Óskar asked as he rubbed the sleep from his eyes.

"How many Skolli do you consider large amounts?" Georg added.

"Two attacks that appear to be at least the size of the one on the fortress," Ragna said.

The blood froze in my veins. I took both Óskar's and Gil's hands in mine. We had survived the attack on the fortress, but we had been able to put all of our focus into one fight. Not two.

"That is impossible," Gil said, leaning forward in his seat. "The barrier is still up. It still limits how many monsters they can send."

"I know." Ragna took a deep breath. "But we have no way of knowing which is the attack's true target and which is the diversion."

"I suspect that one group of Skolli is being ordered to double back to make their group size seem larger, but there is no indication which one it is." Gier sighed. "I lingered as long as I dared, but there was no sign which one we needed to prioritize, and I had to return with the information."

Aron braced his arms on the table. "Then it appears that we don't have a choice—we need to treat both as though they are the true target."

"We will need to use the Royal Regiment," Hákon said,

pursing his lips. "We will have to divide them up between the two responses. And we will have to divide the Verndari amongst the two as well."

My fingers started to shake. Gil pulled my chair closer to his, pressing his leg against mine as Óskar squeezed my hand.

"We need to keep our pairings together. Two pairs will go to one, and the remaining will need some support for the other."

"I can go," Hákon said immediately.

"I will ride as well," Gier added.

Gier and Hákon were formidable warriors in their own right, and should the barrier fall, they would be playing a leadership role on the battlefield alongside us.

And while they had both faced the Skolli, the very thought of dividing up the Verndari twisted knots in my stomach.

However, with things looking as dire as Ragna had made it sound, we would have no choice.

Georg nodded; his hand rubbed his chin. "Knowing that, I suggest that Gil, Rúna, Aron, and I go to one attack while Bryn, Óskar, Hákon and Gier go to the other."

My heart sank at his words.

I wouldn't be able to face this with Gil.

And whoever got the true attack wouldn't have numbers in their favour. They would need to fight for their lives and hope for a stroke of good luck. The odds of us all surviving were slim, and that was being optimistic. I studied Gil's face, trying to memorize every part of it. I was most likely never going to see it again.

"We do not have confirmed targets for the attack, but based on the path of the Skolli, we predict that one group is targeting Wolfmire and the other is targeting the mines near

Fairguard," Gier explained, pointing out the two points on the map.

"Bryn needs to go to Wolfmire. She had the best relationship with Einar," Rúna pointed out.

"Good. We may be able to use that," Gier agreed.

Ragna crossed her arms over her chest. "All of you know the challenge that awaits the team that has the true attack. As soon as you are *absolutely certain* you are the diversion, leave enough warriors behind to handle it and ride like hell for the others. They will need you."

"I need to alert the Royal Regiment. They will be ready to ride at first light." Hákon stood with a nod to his sister. "I will ensure that there are enough healers assigned to your team since I will be with the others."

"I appreciate it," Georg said. "Gil may be able to assist with minor injuries to help spare their workload."

"I will make sure they know to turn to him for support. I will see you all in a few hours." Hákon left the room.

Gier and Ragna followed shortly behind.

"Get a few more hours of sleep. We will reconvene shortly before we leave to plan," Georg said as he led us back to the Verndari wing.

I intertwined my fingers with Gil, pulling him into my room.

I wanted to spend every moment of our limited time with him.

CHAPTER
TWENTY-SIX

BRYN

Neither one of us had gotten much more sleep that night.

We had tried, of course, but for every minute of sleep I got, there was another where I was awake, wrapping myself as tightly around Gil as I could. For every moment he slept, there was another where his fingers traced idle designs on my back, and he pulled me closer to him.

I knew that I needed to sleep, that there was a chance I was about to ride to a battlefield. But how was I supposed to make myself lose those last moments with Gil? How was I supposed to close my eyes when I just wanted to look at him, to study the green of his eyes, the curve of his lips? My bed had suddenly become a sanctuary, the furs a shield between us and the world we would face when the sun rose.

And I didn't know how I was supposed to leave it.

Eventually, we both gave up trying to sleep and lay facing each other.

"Gil," I whispered, my voice breaking. My eyes welled with tears, but I refused to let them fall.

He pressed his forehead to mine. "Bryn. Darling."

"We both know what's waiting for us out there." My lip quivered. One of us would go to the diversion, but the other—the other would go where they were no doubt vastly outnumbered. Unprepared. The odds stacked against them.

Death more likely than survival.

And we didn't know which one we were riding to. Which one the other was riding to.

Gil pressed a brief kiss to my lips. "Look at me," he said softly. I immediately found his vivid green eyes. "I hope that I am riding to the true attack." I lost the battle against my tears, one slipping down my cheek. He wiped away a tear from my skin. "But gods, Bryn, if it is you, then you must give it everything. You can bend, but you cannot break. You have to fight like hell until we can get to you—until I can get to you. Because you must know that as soon as I discover it is a diversion, I will be riding for you as though Hell itself was chasing me."

"I will," I promised, kissing him. "You have to do the same. I'll be with Óskar, so we will need less time to reach you."

Gil gently rolled us so that he was on top of me, his weight resting on his arms as he smiled sadly down at me. "I promise."

I reached up, looping my arms around his neck and pulling him closer. "You better," I mumbled against his lips. "I need you to come back to me."

He kissed me as I threaded my fingers through his hair. Our lips moved together, matching each movement the other made. His hand drifted down the side of my body until it found my hip, as though he was trying to pull me even closer to him.

I wrapped my leg around him, desperate to have him as close as possible.

His lips found my jaw, then travelled down my throat as

my fingers trailed down his bare chest. Gil caught my hands as they reached the waistband of his pants.

"We have to pack and meet the others. We do not have time." His voice was rough as his lips quirked into a smile. "Besides, it will give us something to look forward to after this." I ignored the forced lightness in his words and allowed the playfulness to wrap around me.

"Someone thinks highly of himself," I teased with a soft laugh, my thumb brushing across his jaw. If he was trying to lighten the mood, if he was trying to picture a future where one of us doesn't end up bleeding out on a battlefield, I would embrace that wholeheartedly.

"I am learning to." His eyes were soft, open, as they met my own. "Because of you."

Because I refused to see him as a monster.

Because I was teaching him to heal, not to destroy. Helping him learn to control the darkness rather than succumb to it.

He was Gil—*my Gil*—not some monster to be used and locked away.

I kissed him softly. "I'm glad."

Gil lifted himself from the bed before reaching down a hand to pull me out after him. I dressed in silence before braiding my riotous curls back from my face. He helped me pack, then double-check, my saddlebags before we went to his room for him to do the same. When we were both packed and dressed there was nothing left for us to do in our rooms. We had to face the world outside the walls.

Gil wrapped gentle fingers around my wrist and pulled me tight to him. I pressed myself as closely to him as possible, wrapping my arms around his neck. Maybe if I hugged him tightly enough, I could borrow some of his strength and share some of mine. His hand cradled the back of my head, his lips pressed to my temple. Gil's mouth moved across my skin, forming words I couldn't hear.

Bells rang through the fortress—a summoning.

We were out of time.

We made our way to the armoury, hand-in-hand and helped each other with our armour, securing every buckle and checking for any weak points. Gil slid the daggers into the sheaths on my weapons belt and legs while I filled every sheath on my torso and arms. I tucked as many daggers as possible into my bags as Gil attached a pair of swords across his back and another to his belt. He grabbed two extra pairs of blades to strap to his horse before he left.

When we were both ready, we entered the meeting room. Within moments, we were all there, in addition to Hákon and Gier, with solemn looks on our faces. Gier had harsh dark circles under his eyes. He had been the one to share the information, having had to ride from Wolfmire to the fortress. He most likely hadn't slept more than a few hours each night while travelling and hadn't had enough time to catch up last night. Hákon looked lethal in his Royal Regiment uniform beside Georg.

"I have assigned more Royal Regiment members to the group going to the mines by Fairguard. It's a smaller settlement there. They won't have the same warriors that Wolfmire will," Hákon said, crossing his arms over his chest. "Both teams have also been assigned support staff and supplies for the war camp. I'm sure you will be able to use them to the best of their abilities."

Georg turned to me; his face grim. "You will be the best bet at getting Jarl Einar to support you. His city needs protection, but with the Royal Regiment there, he may not be willing to risk his warriors. You'll have to convince him otherwise."

Jarl Einar and I hadn't left things on the best terms, but he had to see the risk to his city. That we wouldn't have the numbers to hold the monsters off ourselves. As frustrating as Jarl Einar was, he was logical and cared for his people and Wolfmire.

"I will do my best," I said with a nod. I had no other choice. If I failed and we were the sight of the true attack, then we were destined to be a feast for the crows.

We wouldn't stand a chance.

"You have all fought the Skolli before. You know what to expect." Georg's gaze landed on each of us. "I don't like being split up like this, but we don't have a choice. I expect whoever is at the true attack to fight until we can reunite. I don't care what you must do, how tired you are, or how grim things are. You will still be fighting when the others can finally join you."

We all nodded. Gil squeezed our intertwined hands. I had promised him, we had pledged to each other and would fight like hell until we reunited. And I would do everything I could to keep that promise.

"I expect to return to the fortress with every one of you," Georg continued, clearing his throat. "So don't you dare give up regardless of whatever odds you will face. We will be reunited and returning to this fortress. Every one of us." He looked at us all one last time. "Let's go."

Georg and Hákon led the way to the courtyard. The Royal Regiment was forming outside the open gates since there wouldn't have been enough space for us inside them. Only the sergeants lingered in the courtyard, no doubt waiting to tell whoever was leading their force that they were ready to move out.

I gently stroked my horse's nose before strapping my saddlebags to my horse and seeking out the others.

Rúna wrapped me in a tight hug that I gladly returned before mounting her horse.

I turned to find Aron already waiting for me. "Sister," he said with a small smile. A similar one appeared on my own face. "If you have Fannar with you, please take care of him. I just got him back."

"Only if you promise to do the same if you have him."

"Of course." He wrapped me in a gentle hug. "You and Óskar will take care of each other. Yeah?"

I smiled. "We will always have each other's backs. Be careful."

Gil lingered by my horse as I made my way over to him. He kissed me, not caring who in the courtyard saw us. Ignoring any looks we received, any whispers that the action would no doubt spawn. "I will see you soon."

I swallowed thickly. "I'll see you soon."

I went to Óskar and helped him secure Yugar to the carrier on the back of his horse. We didn't mount up; instead, we waited for Georg to finish meeting with Hákon and the Royal Regiment sergeants. The sergeants had divided into two groups, one speaking with Georg and the other with Hákon. I immediately saw Lúdvík with Hákon, meaning that Fannar was with me.

It was a comfort to have my brother with me and to face this together.

The meetings didn't take long to wrap up, and the sergeants left to rejoin their forces outside the walls. Georg made his way directly to Óskar and I. He wrapped us each in a brief hug. "I know I will see you two again. Don't prove me wrong now." He gave Yugar a scratch behind his ears and joined his team.

I mounted my horse, my eyes finding Gil one last time in the crowd. Sharing one last look with him.

Óskar settled by my side as Hákon and Gier took their positions behind us. The King Commander exited the fortress, the old horn in his hands. He didn't pause until he reached the platform on the walls designed for our departures. He lifted the horn to his lips, the sound ringing through the courtyard.

"Strike hard, strike fast," the King Commander's words easily carried over the crowd. Óskar and I were the first to move, Hákon and Gier following behind us. We bowed our heads to the King Commander as we reached him, echoing his words. Strike hard, strike fast.

"Ready?" Óskar asked quietly as we left the gates and assembled at the head of the Royal Regiment warriors assigned to us. I recognized Fannar's face among them immediately. He was in the line closest to us, right beside Lúdvík. A position of honour reserved for some of the most skilled warriors.

"Ready as I can be," I answered softly, carefully hiding my nerves from the warriors we were leading. The horn rang out inside the walls again as the King Commander officially dispatched the others into the field.

"Then we ride."

CHAPTER
TWENTY-SEVEN
BRYN

We rode hard for Wolfmire, leading our contingent of warriors. I had expected Hákon to take the lead, but he had deferred to us. Even with the Royal Regiment present, this was very much in the Verndari's specialty.

It was ours to lead.

We couldn't risk using Óskar's bloodrite to get us there faster. If we were on the scene of a large-scale attack, we would need every fighter, every drop of our bloodrites, to give us a fighting chance.

My horse surged below me in the middle of one of the carefully monitored gallops Óskar allowed. We were quite strict with the horses, alternating between gallops and slower paces at regular intervals to protect them. We rested, never for more than a few hours at a time, to ensure that our horses were still in decent shape when we finally arrived.

Wolfmire began to take shape in the distance, the tall towers jutting above the walls. The midday sun hung high in the sky when we finally reached the gates. Hákon, Gier, Óskar and I gathered as a few of the Royal Regiment came forward to collect our horses before rejoining their comrades.

"Bryn has to be the one to speak to him," Óskar said to the others, his voice just low enough to be sure it did not carry to the Royal Regiment. "She was the closest to building a relationship with him."

I glanced at the closed gates with a wince. "The last few days before we left were rough. And he was pissed when we left for the ball."

"You had orders," Gier defended.

There was a clear line for Gier, who said exactly what he thought and dealt with it in logic, not emotions. We had orders, we followed the orders, and there was nothing else to it. He struggled to understand the feelings behind our actions, both on our end and on Jarl Einar's side. Just because we had orders didn't mean it made sense to Jarl Einar, nor that our feelings could affect how this next conversation would play out.

"Jarl Einar was quite clear about those orders and what he thought of us following them. He claimed that bad orders were not meant to be followed. Leaving Wolfmire and our attempts at convincing him to support us to return to the fortress for what he saw as a party? To him, that is a bad order, and we followed it," I said, explaining exactly what I thought Jarl Einar's mindset would have been.

As much as I disagreed with him not declaring his support, I could understand why he was frustrated that we had returned for the ball. People were dying in the attacks, and instead, we were dancing.

But how were we meant to balance our responsibilities on the battlefield with our political responsibilities without letting one of them down?

And which one was the right one to choose?

Hákon ran a gloved hand through his hair. "Do you think you can get through to him?"

"He respected me. From the moment we arrived, he respected me and Aron the most," I said before sighing. "What he thinks of me after we left, after I, well—" I cleared my throat. "I know how he thinks and what he values. I can push that even if his view of me has shifted."

"It has to be you," Gier agreed. "We cannot bring all the regiment with us. It will come across as a threat, and he will have his defences up. He would not be open to what we have to say."

I turned to survey the regiment. They had all dismounted and were in various stages of caring for their horses. Lúdvík's line—Fannar's line—lingered the closest to us. "We need to bring some with us. Jarl Einar may connect with them. It needs to be one of your strongest lines. They must have seen battle and will be central to our plans when night comes. His eyes will be on them."

"Then that's the line we take." Hákon nodded to Lúdvík. "There's a reason that they stayed the closest. Lúdvík is my second in command. If his line is not fighting by my side, they are fighting where the combat is the thickest."

I swallowed thickly. I knew that Fannar being named to Lúdvík's line was an honour, but I had no idea the required skill level.

I hadn't realized just how dangerous and important that line was.

"Then it's settled. We need to do it now," Óskar said.

"I agree. Every minute we spend here is a minute of preparation we lose before dusk," Gier turned to survey the walls.

"They will have been watching us since we arrived. Every moment we linger, the more uncertain we seem."

"I will get them to join us, and we will go." Hákon started towards Lúdvík. "We won't need to brief them since Bryn will do most of the talking."

It only took a moment for the line to join us. I straightened my shoulders, heading straight for the gate. Óskar and Hákon naturally flanked me, Gier and Lúdvík behind them, with Fannar and the others taking the rear.

The gates were closed, the city clearly preparing for an inevitable attack. I banged on them with my fist and it only took a moment to open to reveal Jarl Einar. Proving Gier was right.

They had been watching us. They would have had to send someone to get him if they hadn't been. Instead, he was there waiting for us to make the first move.

"Jarl Einar." I nodded my head respectfully.

"Jarl Brynja. Jarl Óskar." He studied the others. "Hersir Hákon."

He didn't acknowledge the others, but I don't think it was because he was being rude or overlooking them. I think he didn't know who they were.

"We have reports that a Skolli attack is coming," I said, getting straight to the point. "We have come to aid you."

"And when do we expect this attack?"

"Shortly. Tonight. Tomorrow, if we're lucky."

He was silent for a moment. "And you have been dispatched to deal with it."

"Yes, sir. But we were hoping that your forces would join us. We won't know until tonight exactly how big the attack will be."

Jarl Einar was silent for a moment, no doubt considering

every possible option we had. His gaze drifted from Óskar and me to the warriors at our back, to the host we had just outside the gates to Wolfmire.

He finally shook his head. "No."

I blinked, shocked. "What do you mean no?" Out of all the responses I had expected from him, a flat-out no had been one of the least likely. I had thought he was logical—tactical. He had to know that by refusing to help us, the defence's strength would be significantly weakened.

"With you all here, I have no reason to put my own warriors at risk. Especially when I will need them at full strength when you inevitably leave," Jarl Einar said, his arms crossed over his chest. "You seem to have a track record of leaving."

I took a minute to consider my words. "You will not allow your warriors to participate in our defence, but would you provide your support in other ways?"

"No. My warriors are not yours, but neither are my healers or my supplies. You cannot use my city in your defence, and you cannot use it for your lodgings."

He was going to force us to launch our defence from outside the city and without the benefit of the high ground of the walls. We wouldn't be granted the brief respite of safety, of comfort, of providing us with lodging in Wolfmire. The Royal Regiment had packed all the supplies we would need for a war camp just in case, Hákon had told me during one of our brief breaks.

Turned out that we were going to be using those supplies. Just like we would have to hold the line and heal any warriors with just the people we had brought. Anger flared in my chest.

"How dare—" I cut myself off.

"You didn't hold your tongue when you yelled at me before, Jarl Brynja. Don't start now."

I stepped closer to Jarl Einar. "How dare you turn this attack into one of your fucking tests. As though this is an opportunity for us to prove ourselves to you. If you withhold your warriors and this is a large-scale attack, people will die. Our warriors will die protecting your people," I hissed. "I hope that you sleep well with blood on your hands."

I spun on my heel, walking right back out of the gates that shut again behind us.

Fannar stopped by my side. "Did you really yell at him before?"

"He deserved it," I muttered.

He chuckled quietly as we gathered together. Without the warriors of Wolfmire available for us, we would need to pivot.

"We need to prepare," Gier said. "We are going to need every minute we have until nightfall."

"We can set up the tents closest to the city. We'll leave the pathway to the gate clear and put the healing tent closest to the wall. It's the most sheltered we'll get with the city barred to us," Hákon added.

Óskar turned towards the Royal Regiment that had taken care of their horses and were lingering in groups, chatting and laughing with each other. "Fear runs through them faster than you can blink if we ever give the impression that we are worried."

"Then we don't let on." I took a deep breath. "We have more than enough warriors if we are the diversion. We should have enough to last the night, hopefully more, if we are the scene of the full attack."

"Give them a good plan, Lassie. Give them their positions, roles and who they report to in the fight, and they will be fine."

Lúdvík ran a hand over his head. "They are warriors, not children. If they feel unprepared, fear will travel through them, so prove that we aren't."

"Then let's plan."

We sent Fannar and the rest of Lúdvík's line to supervise the setup of the war camp and the positioning of our supplies. Hákon, Gier, Óskar, Lúdvík, and I huddled around a map. Due to the positioning of Wolfmire, the attack was most likely to come from one direction. We debated back and forth about different scenarios before finally settling on one as it settled into the early evening.

I sat between Fannar and Óskar as I ate a quick dinner. When I was done, I changed into my armour and made my way to my half of the field.

Óskar and I would lead the defence on one side of the road to the gates while Gier and Hákon led the other. The sun threatened to sink below the horizon as the last warriors took their place. Óskar shifted by my side as I double-checked all of my daggers.

"You ready?" he asked quietly.

"As I can be." I turned towards him. "Are you?"

"I was born ready, Talon." Óskar grinned.

I gave him a small smile. "We've got this, right?" Only allowing the worry I was harbouring to show itself to Óskar. To the person I knew would be by my side, protecting my back against anything we would face.

"You bet we do."

The sun began to set below the horizon, casting long shadows across the ground. We lit several bonfires to light our surroundings. The Skolli were going to come for us either way.

"Now we wait," I said, pulling two daggers to ease some anxious energy thrumming through my veins.

"Now we wait," Óskar repeated.

A distant thunder-like sound started. But it didn't roll through and stop like thunder typically did. The noise grew louder and louder.

Closer and closer.

"Ready your weapons!" I yelled to the warriors I led. Óskar, Hákon and Gier echoed me down our line.

Óskar nocked an arrow. "Now's the moment of truth."

Were we the diversion, or were we the main focus? The next few moments would define how our next several days went.

Wave after wave of Skolli charged towards us. There were so many I couldn't count them as they tore across the ground towards us.

I swallowed thickly.

It certainly was the moment of truth—we were the site of the true attack.

TWENTY-EIGHT

GIL

T he attacks came in waves—the next launching when the previous one was all dead.

I took a sip from my waterskin in the brief respite we seemed to be getting between each attack. The breaks were never long enough to put me at ease. Instead, it only increased my anxiety. My nerves became more shot with each break as I wondered if this was the attack where they finally used their full strength.

And trying to ignore what it meant if they didn't. Where they would be focusing their attention instead.

Who would be facing the brunt of that.

"Have you heard from the others?" I asked Rúna. She typically took the lead when we were in the field so that if I had to use my bloodrite, I could use my full focus on trying to keep the darkness under control. I still issued orders when needed but often left them for her.

"No. I've heard sounds of battle from the other side, but if I had to guess, they would be facing something similar to us."

She ran her hand along the length of her whip, cleaning the black blood off it as best as possible.

We couldn't just mount one defence with how the mines were situated about the town. We had to split our forces, leaving Rúna and I to lead one and Georg and Aron to lead the other.

The next wave of Skolli appeared on the horizon. I unsheathed my swords again, spinning them before settling into my stance.

I slashed a Skolli across the neck, the black blood spraying across my face. I spun on a heel, my sights immediately set on my next target. I crossed my swords over the Skolli, cutting its head clean of its body. The smell of burnt flesh grew around me as Rúna's whip cracked in a steady rhythm nearby. Her light cast long shadows on the warriors closest to us.

A Skolli knocked me roughly to the side, its wing landing a heavy blow to my ribs.

I staggered to the side with a curse.

Allowing my momentum to carry me, I sunk to a crouch and slashed at the back of the Skolli's knee. I popped up, my ribs complaining, and stabbed my sword through its neck.

The world around me quieted, the latest attack done.

Rúna was immediately in front of me. "Are you okay?"

"It is nothing serious. A bruise at the worst. I have some of the bruise paste in my things. I will be fine in the morning," I said, stretching my side carefully.

"Good. I can't lose you." Rúna watched as the horizon began to brighten. "Not to mention Bryn would kill me."

I smiled softly. "I would not be surprised."

The sun finally rose with no further attacks, so Rúna and I left to find Georg and Aron after assigning one of the Royal Regiment sergeants to command in our absence.

Some blood ran down Rúna's arm. I gently took her wrist and took a quick glance at the cut. "It does not look too bad. I should be able to patch it up fine if the healers are too busy to."

"I see Bryn has been rubbing off on you." She smirked. "In more ways than one."

I rolled my eyes, ignoring her innuendo. Whether she was pushing for information or trying to make me blush I wasn't going to play into it. "You have seen me helping her with the healing before. It should not surprise you."

"I've seen you helping her with the healing or taking on smaller tasks, but this is the first time I've seen you take the lead. It's a good look on you, Gil," she said softly, her eyes bright.

Rúna knew me better than anyone else except for possibly Bryn. She knew how much it would mean to me for her to say that. That I was able to show a gentler side to me that most people believed didn't exist.

We finally found Georg and Aron. They looked quite similar to us—tired, dirty, and a little bruised. But nothing significant. Nothing that signified that they experienced a large-scale attack.

Which meant that we were the diversion and Bryn was at the sight of the true attack.

Fuck.

"It is not us," I said, my throat tight.

Georg's face was grim. "We don't know that for sure yet. They could have spent the past night trying to soften us with the attacks."

"You don't actually believe that, Georg. Be straight with us." Rúna brushed some hair out of her face with a blood and dirt-stained hand.

"You're right. I don't believe it," he sighed. "But we must be

204

certain before leaving with most of the forces here. If we are wrong, we don't just lose the mines. People will die."

I swallowed. "The longer we linger here, the more likely the others will die."

"They know how to handle themselves. They're smart, and they're strong. Bryn, Óskar, Hákon, and Gier will make a solid plan and shift it as often as needed."

Rúna nodded. "They have some really good warriors with them. And there's no way Jarl Einar wouldn't have his own forces defending his city."

"And they have my brother," Aron added. "He is just as skilled and drawn to weapons as I am."

"I thought your brother was dead," Rúna's voice was soft. I wrapped my fingers around her wrist. Grounding her.

Rúna knew exactly how it felt to lose a brother. She had lost her own brother, Heimir, when he was just a kid, along with her mother.

"I did, too, but we recently discovered that he didn't die. He had been lost in the snowstorm only to be found by a couple in a snow bank once it had passed. They took him in and raised him in Ebonwell."

My eyes shot to Aron. "Fannar."

"Fannar's my brother. And he is there with them." Aron cleared his throat. "I just got him back. Don't make me lose him again."

"We won't lose him. We won't lose any of them," Georg said, looking us each in the eye. "We stay for another night to be sure and then ride hard for Wolfmire. They are fighters— they can do this."

"They will fight like hell," I agreed.

～

THE MINERS HAD CLEARED out one of the storage rooms for our use. With a table added and some chairs it made as good of a command centre as we needed. We had a map of the area spread across the table, along with various lists. How many people were at Fairguard, along with their different skills, weapons, and even the incredibly short list of wounded from the night before.

"We all believe that we are the site of the diversion and are only staying tonight to be certain of the fact," Georg said once some people from the village had dropped off some food for us. It was lunchtime for the villagers, but breakfast for all of us as we had slept once dawn had broken and were likely to go for another nap before dusk. "But that doesn't mean that we don't have to treat tonight as an opportunity for the Skolli to attack. We must treat it as though the threat is still just as high."

"I believe that our strategy last night was sound. It worked having a pair of us on each side to lead the defence in the area," Aron contributed. He was right. It had worked with a clear command structure and a good balance of warriors on each side.

Rúna nodded. "The warriors we had on our side worked well together. The different lines integrated seamlessly and complimented each other's strengths well."

"Does anyone have a reason we should not continue with the same strategy as last night?" Georg asked. No one spoke, all of us in agreement it was the best way forward. "Very well." He leaned back in his chair and crossed his arms over his chest. "Now, if we believe that we are the diversion. What must we do tonight to ensure a smooth transition when we leave?"

"We need a clear command structure for when we leave," I said. It was easy with us here. We outranked the Royal Regiment and had more experience in command, so the sergeants naturally turned to us to lead. But when we left, there would be the Royal Regiment left behind, and the sergeants were largely all considered on the same level as each other. We needed to make it very clear who was in command.

"We could nominate a second on each side," Aron suggested. He tapped his fingers on the table as he spoke, as though it was helping him work through the thoughts in his mind. "That way, we can ensure that they know everything they need to, and by serving as second by our sides tonight, it will provide plenty of credibility when they step up to command when we leave."

Georg considered his words for a minute. "That would work. How severe were your attacks last night? How many warriors would be needed to hold that side?"

"A line would be enough. We were able to spell off our warriors throughout the night last night so that they didn't get too worn down. Gil and I were the only ones that fought the whole time." Rúna shifted in her seat. "They won't need more than a line of the Royal Regiment, especially if the archers of Fairguard can hold the walls."

"We are the diversion, which means the Skolli have limited forces for their attacks. They need to draw this out and conserve their numbers. Otherwise, our full force would be able to go to Wolfmire. The monsters are not going to launch a full attack. It would eliminate them too quickly," I pointed out. I didn't know who controlled Skolli's tactics, whether it was one of the exiled royal family members or if Pétur was providing the plans. But whoever it was wasn't stupid. They were clever enough to divide our force into two and wouldn't waste it by showing their hand too early.

Georg nodded. "You're right. Both of you. We must be

careful which sergeant we choose to lead each side as their line will be one to stay."

"It should be the strongest line on each side." Aron grimaced. "As much as I want to take all of the best warriors when we leave for Wolfmire, that would be a disservice to Fairguard. The strongest lines in the Royal Regiment are used to the tougher assignments. They will be able to face whatever the Skolli throw at them. Not to mention it is their sergeants that Hákon usually assigns command roles to."

I wanted to argue against Aron's logic, to find a way to take the strongest warriors with us when we rode for Bryn and the others. Every warrior would count when we reached the site of the true attack. But that would leave Fairguard at risk, and I couldn't justify that.

Not to mention, Bryn would never forgive me if Fairguard was forsaken for them.

"That is the best plan," I agreed, the words feeling like ash in my mouth. "I already know the best line on our side."

"I do as well," Georg said. "Find the sergeant and explain their new role before you get a few more hours of sleep. Be ready and in your places an hour before dusk."

TWENTY-NINE

BRYN

I walked through the hastily built war camp.

It hadn't taken long for the camp to take shape the day before; the warriors and the people we travelled with were well-versed in what they had to do. The Royal Regiment tents were in the front, grouped by their line. Behind them, between the regiment and Wolfmire's walls, was command, the commander tents, and the food stations. And at the back, closest to the walls and most protected, were the healers' tents.

The healers were quiet in the late afternoon, finally done their work from the night before. Only a few of them milled about preparing the space for the night ahead. In contrast, the others rested before their services were again called upon.

"Bryn!" Luck called. I turned, but the gates to the city were shut. "Up here!" He stood on top of the walls, waving down at me. "I'm coming down!" He disappeared from sight, and a few minutes later, the gates to the city opened just enough to let him out.

"What are you doing? Are you allowed out here?" I asked him.

He shrugged. "Probably not, but he can't punish me too severely since I'm not picking up a weapon just yet."

"Don't do anything that would get you into trouble." Things were bad enough on our side of the wall, and I didn't want to risk conflict behind them either.

Not to mention that Aron would be upset if I got Luck into trouble.

"I can't fight but will do everything possible to help. Sofie is going to do the same."

My stomach warmed as my knees threatened to wobble in relief. "Thank you."

"Are you okay? How are the others doing?"

"Nothing that we weren't able to heal. We had some casualties, but not as bad as we thought." The words tasted like ash in my mouth. It felt wrong to talk about someone's life like that, but as the commander, I didn't always have the luxury of my emotions. I had to deal with facts and strategy so that I could ensure that my warriors were able to get through the fight.

"Sofie and I are pushing him, Bryn. And some of the other leaders in the city are joining us, but I don't know how much ground we are making."

I rested a hand on his arm. "Just the fact that you are trying means a lot to me."

"Did you get any sleep?" he asked, his eyes lingering on dark circles under my own.

There wasn't much time to sleep. As soon as the sun rose, Óskar and I were hauling wounded warriors to the healers. Once everyone had been brought to the tents, we lingered, helping tend to the lesser injured so that the healers' bloodrites could be saved for those who needed them. Óskar wasn't as versed at being my assistant as Gil was, but he worked diligently by my side.

We had only left when Gier pulled us out and into the command tent, where Hákon was changing his bloody gloves for a clean pair. Our strategy meeting started with deciding what to do with the dead before it shifted into a review of the night. I fell into my bedroll when the sun hung high in the sky and woke only a few hours later to join the others in the command tent to review the lists from the healers and develop our strategy for the night ahead of us.

"I slept enough. As much as I could." Luck grimaced at my words, no doubt knowing what I didn't say. Sleep was now a necessity that I could no longer afford. I glanced at the sky towards where the sun was starting to sink. "I need to get ready for the night."

Luck's face darkened. "Your strategy from last night was sound. Do it again."

"That's the plan."

"I may not be able to fight, but I will do my best to help. Tell me what you need tomorrow—food, weapons, anything."

I glanced around us before lowering my voice. "Jarl Einar made it very clear that he would not provide us with supplies."

"What is it that he said to you before? Bad orders are not meant to be followed?" Luck smiled sadly. "I would much rather be out on the line with you both, but until I can, I will do everything I can to help. And if that means smuggling you illicit food and weapons, that's what I am going to do."

I nodded and gave him a hug. "Thank you. You better get behind those gates before you get caught with us."

"I would rather be out here with you all than watching it

from the walls," Luck said before reluctantly returning to Wolfmire, the gates shutting behind him.

After briefly stopping in my tent to pull on my armour and grab my weapons, I made my way out to the front line. Óskar was already there as the warriors also began to take their positions in the ranks. He looked as tired as I felt. How would we make it through more if we felt like this after one night?

Yugar had been stuck to Óskar's side throughout the day, but he was nowhere to be seen now. He was undoubtedly hidden away in his tent's relative safety.

I took a sip from my waterskin as the sky began to darken. It would be the last time I would have for a drink until the morning if tonight was anything like the night before. One of the many young boys and girls that travelled with the Royal Regiment collected mine and Óskar's waterskins.

We didn't travel with the full host of people we normally would have. But we did have some healers, some cooks, and boys and girls in their late teenage years who were currently training for the Royal Regiment. They were there as another set of hands, a trusted set of message runners, aides to the healers —anything we may need.

But they weren't there to fight. They would be around the fighting but always behind the front line. If they were called to fight, then we were out of options.

If they were called to fight, we would be out of time. Out of warriors. Out of luck.

Once they were done collecting our waterskins, they would disappear behind the front lines unless there was an urgent message they had to send to us.

I walked through the lines of warriors, ensuring that everyone was in their proper positions. After last night, we had to shift things around to account for the holes in our lines. Both from injuries and deaths. I ensured that I knew every sergeant by name and made sure that I introduced myself to them. Not just as their commander but as a warrior that they would be fighting beside.

I figured they would respect me more if they knew my name and I had found time to meet them. I was younger than most of the sergeants and wanted to ensure they didn't see me as naive or inexperienced. When they looked at me, I wanted them to see a warrior. A leader.

I cracked jokes with some of the warriors I passed, forcing laughs out of them so their nerves didn't suffocate them. Some made dirty jokes that I responded to with my own innuendos, and some wanted to clasp hands while we exchanged well wishes for the night ahead.

Óskar passed by me a few times as he did his own walk. These were not just the warriors we were commanding; these were our comrades. These were the people we would fight beside and bleed beside. I knew that more people were going to die, and I didn't want their final moments before the battle to be filled with fear. I wanted them to spend the final moments laughing with their comrades over a dirty joke or making plans for the following day.

When I finished my walk, I returned to the front of the lines, my place front and centre beside Óskar. If the relationship I was trying to nurture with these warriors didn't make them want to follow me, I would convince them with my fighting.

Óskar joined me a minute later, the sun hovering above the horizon. Night would fall in only a matter of moments.

"You ready?" Óskar asked, turning to me, a pink line across his cheekbone. He had gotten cut by a Skolli claw the night before, but Hákon healed him in moments, with only the pink line hinting at the injury.

Another day, I wouldn't even know it had happened.

Luckily, none of our healers had had to limit themselves and could fully heal anyone who needed it. But it would only be a matter of time before that wasn't the case anymore. Before they had to start making some very tough choices.

But luckily, they weren't there. Not yet, at least.

I took a deep breath, holding it in my lungs for a moment before releasing it. Centring myself. Preparing myself. "As ready as I can be. You?"

Óskar grinned at me. "I was born ready, Talon."

I smiled softly at his joke, so quintessentially Óskar to lighten the mood before a battle where we would be outnumbered and outpowered.

The sun sunk behind the horizon, and the fires were again lit. I pulled two daggers from my weapons belt. "Let's do this."

"Let's do this," Óskar repeated, nocking an arrow on his bow as the first Skolli appeared. "Archers!" he yelled; his call echoed down the line by Hákon.

"Fire!" he ordered, the air around us filled by the twanging of bowstrings. "Nock! Fire! Nock! Fire!"

Regardless of how fast they shot, the archers could not kill all the Skolli. But the more they could take down before they reached us made every difference in the world.

For every Skolli that went down, another replaced it, never stopping their push towards us.

"Prepare yourselves," I screamed over the growing noise around us. Gier was also yelling his own instructions from his place by Hákon.

Óskar and I had fallen into an easy rhythm. He

commanded the archers while I was responsible for the rest of the fighters, only echoing each other's orders when needed.

I adjusted my grip on my daggers and settled into my fighting crouch. I took another deep breath, holding it again before slowly releasing it. Taking the last moment of stillness until day broke to sink into the predatory focus I would need to maintain throughout the night.

Then I struck.

A slash across the neck of the first Skolli. Its body hadn't hit the ground before I was on to the next one.

I kept moving, always aware of where Óskar was.

I struck to kill, but it wasn't long until we were overrun. Outnumbered.

Then, plans changed. I didn't strike to kill—I aimed to maim. To injure. A strike at the back of the knee to hobble them, shredding their wings to throw them off balance. Strike and move on.

Leave them to be finished by the lines of warriors behind us.

Let them bear some of the brunt of the attack even though every instinct screamed at me not to. I wanted to give everything I had, to take every blow and injury so the warriors behind me wouldn't.

But that wasn't going to happen.

We would all have to take our blows and land our strikes to survive long enough for support to reach us.

CHAPTER
THIRTY
GIL

I knew part way through the second night that our instincts were right. It was the same as the day before. Small attacks, easily handled and spread out just enough to keep our nerves on edge. A distraction and nothing more.

We were the site of the diversion, and the others were at the true attack. I wanted to go now—I had wanted to leave right after the first night.

But I couldn't leave in the middle of the attacks. I couldn't disrupt the command system and the entire defence plan while we were in the middle of these skirmishes.

It would be setting the warriors up for failure. It would set them up for unnecessary injuries or worse.

Instead, I had to wait. Every minute of these distractions was another minute when the others faced an onslaught.

Rúna and I pulled aside Greta, the sergeant that we had named our second, during one of the breaks between attacks.

"We are the diversion," I told her bluntly. "That means that Wolfmire is the location of the true attack, and the majority of us will have to ride for them tomorrow." I didn't bother concealing anything; it would be common knowledge in a matter of hours when we left.

"We made you our second so that you would assume command of the defence on this side of the wall when we left," Rúna explained.

Greta nodded, her hands resting on her weapons belt. "I understand, but why are you telling me this now?"

"I want you to take a more active role in the command during the remaining attacks," I said before taking a drink from the waterskin one of the young hands brought over. "Get a feel for the area and the attacks before we leave."

"Yes sir," she said, glancing over her head to the still-empty tree line. "I'm going to get in position before they attack."

I nodded, and Greta quickly returned to her position near the centre of the line. Rúna and I also retook our spots, ready for the night to be over. For us to be freed from the binds of our duty here to race towards where we were truly needed.

The attacks dwindled closer to sunrise, disappearing at the first hint of the sun lightning. I assigned one of the other sergeants to take charge and ensure that the Skolli bodies were burned and that anyone injured was healed. I also set up a watch so that people could get some sleep.

I sought out Greta, Rúna close by my side. She was still in her position, speaking to the warriors around her. "Tend to your line, then report to Georg on the other side," I told her, not waiting for her response before I spun on my heel. I didn't care if I was being rude. Every minute that we spent here was another minute delaying our arrival at Wolfmire. Another minute that the others, that Bryn, would have to hold the line without us.

"We need to go," I said to Rúna, already heading towards the side that Georg and Aron were stationed on.

217

"I've been packed since this afternoon." She took her place by my side as we made our way through the warriors, congratulating them on a good night of fighting as we passed by. "I knew, just like you did, that we were the diversion. We just had to be sure, Gil. Now we can go to them."

"I know. It does not make it any easier, though."

Rúna scoffed. "Knowing that something is the right thing to do doesn't automatically make it any easier. Trust me, I know."

Rúna was one of the best people I knew, especially when she was putting herself at risk with Baldur. She thought she hid her fear well and could disguise how scared Baldur sometimes made her. But I saw through it. I knew that she struggled. She was facing things that she was uncomfortable sharing with me, which was hard enough.

What made it worse was that she had chosen this before Baldur was the traitor. That he had something on her that she was so desperate to protect that she let him beat her to a bloody pulp and still stayed with him. And she still hadn't confided in me about what that was, and there was only one reason I could think of for why she did it.

She was protecting me.

If anyone knew that the right thing was not always easy, it was Rúna.

"How are things going with Baldur?" I asked, glancing at her out of the corner of my eye.

"People really don't give you enough credit for how observant you are," she mused before flipping her blood-stained blonde hair over her shoulder, several strands falling out of her horsetail. "I've got nothing. No proof at all that he's the traitor. It didn't help that he's had to track down Sigrún more than ever before. I don't know what else I can do to find proof."

"Does that mean you can leave him now?"

Rúna gave me a sad smile. "Not yet. I can't risk it."

I was quiet for a moment. "What does he have on you, Ru?"

"I can't tell you, Gil. It's the only secret I have kept from everyone, from you, in my life. If I were to tell you, it could put you in danger, too."

"You know that I would be the first person to stand beside you at the first hint of danger," I told her, meaning every word. I would face anything for her—battle, prison, death. I would stand with her beside them all, a sister to me in everything but blood.

She just had to give me the chance to.

"I know you would," Rúna said as we finally caught sight of Georg and Aron ahead. "And I am sure I will ask you to help me eventually. But I want to keep you out of it for as long as possible. I want to protect you just as much as you want to protect me."

We had almost reached Georg and Aron, effectively ending our conversation. While we were all open with each other, or as open as we were comfortable in my case, some things were too personal and raw to expose to everyone all at once.

Rúna was opening up to me, trusting me, and I wasn't about to expose her feelings about her situation with the others until she was ready.

Georg was standing with Aron, both engrossed in their conversation with most of the Sergeants we brought. I should quietly join the discussion or wait for them to be done. But I didn't have the patience to wait. Every moment we waited delayed our arrival to Wolfmire. We all knew the odds for the others decreased every minute that we weren't there.

"We have to leave," I interrupted. Rúna sighed by my side but didn't make any move to stop me. She agreed. And from the look on Aron's face, he was clearly glad that someone had said it.

"We will leave within the hour," Georg said. I wanted to push it sooner, but I knew it was irresponsible. We weren't just our group of six Verndari travelling. Warrior hosts like the one we were leading took time to pack, and they took time to travel. "We will stop for a few hours break around midday and then set up camp before the sun sets."

Aron shook his head. "We don't have time. We should ride straight through to nightfall."

"We can't. All of us have been up all night. If we ride straight through to dusk, we will be exhausted and useless to anyone in a fight."

"He has a point," Rúna said softly, sending me an apologetic look.

Georg gave her a look that said *of course I do.* "Not to mention that we don't have Óskar with us. We will be limited to our horses' natural speed and abilities. If we don't care for them carefully, we won't reach Wolfmire until too late."

He was right.

Georg gestured to the sergeants. "We will take these sergeants and their lines and leave the others to handle the skirmishes if any others pop up in the coming nights." He looked at us all. "I know this is more than just another attack, more than our job, for all of us. Every warrior riding for Wolfmire has someone there for whom they care. We will do everything we can to reach them in time."

I knew he chose his words carefully, hiding what he meant behind them.

We were going to do everything we could to reach them before they were all dead, was what he actually meant.

GRETA MET us in the command room. I was dressed for travel, my saddle bags at my feet; this meeting was the only reason we were lingering. Which meant that I was more than ready to be over.

Another sergeant joined her, the grizzled warrior the second Aron and Georg had selected for their side. Georg stood from his chair and clasped hands with both of them. "Well met," he told them.

"Well met, sir," Greta echoed, nodding in respect.

"As you have probably gathered just as we have, we are the site of the diversion rather than the true attack. We had been forced to divide our forces between here and Wolfmire, neither group having enough warriors to withstand the true attack without support," Georg crossed his arms over his chest, his face serious. "Now that we know this is the diversion, the vast majority of the warriors assigned to Fairguard will be riding for Wolfmire."

The grizzled warrior stepped forward. "What does that mean for Fairguard, sir?"

"We will leave two lines behind, one for each side. Your lines."

"We chose you as our second for a reason," I said, hurrying the conversation. As necessary as it was, I was desperate to get on the road. "Your lines will be the ones left behind to protect Fairguard. The village will post their archers on the walls, but it will be your responsibility to hold the lines on the ground."

Greta nodded, already prepared for the information that I had shared. "The attacks are already lessening in strength. Last night was less than the night before."

"That's why we feel comfortable leaving just one line for

each side," Georg explained. He ran a hand over his bald head. "I'm sure you both want to join us at Wolfmire, but we cannot knowingly leave Fairguard at risk. Your lines were chosen for a reason. You both lead the strongest line we had on each side, and by leaving you here, we can take the maximum number of warriors with us."

"I understand, sir," the grizzled sergeant said. "The war camp is already being dismantled. Is the village willing to house us?"

"They are, and they have already begun preparations for your lodgings. You will sleep inside the walls today. I will also leave behind one of the apprentice healers should anything happen." Everyone was quiet for a moment. "Do you have any questions before we continue our preparations to leave?"

The grizzled sergeant shifted his weight between his feet. "When do you leave?"

"Within the hour," I said, grabbing my saddlebags and slinging them over my shoulder. "We will leave as soon as we are ready to ride."

"With your permission, I would like to go and see to my line so we can take full advantage of the day for some rest before tonight."

"You're dismissed," Georg agreed.

The grizzled sergeant nodded his head in respect and left command. I turned my focus back to Greta. "Anything else you would like to ask?" I asked her.

"No." She shook her head. "I just wanted to wish you luck."

We would need it.

THIRTY-ONE

BRYN

The second night had been harder than the first. Our numbers were already concerning, and our healers were starting to feel overwhelmed. It wasn't dire yet, but we could feel it approaching.

I had managed to squeeze in about four hours of sleep after our post-battle responsibilities and before our pre-battle strategy meeting. My body ached from overuse and injury, my eyes were heavy with exhaustion, and my mind was overwhelmed with the responsibilities resting on my shoulders. My heart was heavy with all the lives that I was in charge of leading. And all the lives that had been lost or irrevocably changed as a result of the fighting already.

I wasn't hungry but knew I needed to eat to get through the night ahead. I had ducked into the mess tent, grabbing my serving before seeking out a quieter section of the war camp to eat. My tent was too easy to check, and the other options were too public when I needed a few minutes just to be me, Bryn, before I once again had to don the mantle of commander.

The back corner of the war camp was primarily supply

tents, and very few people travelled through it. I found a spot just beyond it against the city walls to sit down. I balanced my food on my crossed legs as I leaned back against the walls, my head tipping back against the stones and tilting to the sky.

"Is that spot taken?" Fannar asked, drawing my attention over to him. He was pointing to the ground by my side.

"Feel free to have a seat." I smiled at him.

"Fair warning, I think Óskar is on his way, no doubt with his dog in tow. If you were hoping for some alone time, you should probably run now," Fannar warned as he took his seat, setting his food aside instead of resting it on his lap like I was.

I laughed quietly. "I didn't need to be alone. I just needed a moment to be myself and not worry about putting on a strong face or being the strong commander."

"Talon!" Óskar cheered as he joined us, flopping down in front of Fannar and I, Yugar mimicking his actions. "Nice hiding spot you found here. We should put a sign somewhere claiming it's ours."

I kicked him lightly. "Oh hush, at least it's quiet."

"Or it was," Fannar mumbled under his breath.

Óskar scowled as I giggled. This was exactly what I needed when I sought out this quiet corner of the war camp. And even though I had initially sought it out by myself, I was much happier with Fannar and Óskar with me.

Running footsteps approached us, and Sofie appeared around the corner, a cloak wrapped around her shoulders. Luck wasn't far behind her, his steps much more relaxed with his hands tucked into his pockets. Sofie dropped to her knees, wrapping me in a hug before doing the same to Óskar. She covered Yugar's muzzle in kisses, causing him to give her a canine grin.

She froze as she turned towards Fannar as though she had

just noticed him. Sofie's cheeks reddened. Fannar had a similar dumbstruck look on his face. I giggled. "Sofie, may I introduce Fannar, my adopted brother. Fannar, this is Sofie, the heir apparent to the healing centre."

"It's a pleasure to meet you, Sofie," Fannar said, his voice rough. His hand took hold of hers and brought it to his mouth, pressing a kiss to the back.

Óskar rolled his eyes, making a face, forcing me to smother my giggles behind my hand.

"It's nice to meet you too," Sofie stammered as Luck joined us.

"How are you guys holding up?" Luck asked as he sat between Óskar and I. Sofie looked around for a moment, blushing again when the only open spot in our little circle was between Fannar and Yugar. I would have to ask her about it later.

Or, based on the look on Fannar's face, maybe I would have to push both of them on it.

"We're alive. Can't ask for too much more than that," Óskar said before stuffing a bite of food in his mouth.

Sofie studied each of us carefully. "None of you seem too badly injured."

"So far, we have only had minor injuries that Hákon has healed or Bryn's supplies have taken care of," Fannar reassured her.

"And how does your defence look?" Luck leaned back on an elbow.

I tilted my head back against the wall with a sigh. "It's not great, but we should be okay." I didn't say for how long because I honestly didn't know. It all depended on how tonight went. And the night after. And the one after that.

It depended on how long it would take for the others to get to us.

"Is there anything that we can do for you?" Sofie's voice was quiet, her fingers twitching as though she wished to reach out and heal us. She subtly passed some rolls of bandages hidden under her skirts to Fannar.

"There's nothing you can do unless you want to risk getting in trouble with Jarl Einar," Fannar pointed out as he took the bandages, tucking them under his cloak and acting as if he wasn't helping her break Jarl Einar's verdict.

"If you want to give us something, maybe something to brighten the warriors' spirits," I said, remembering Luck's offer from the day before. "It would be nice to fill the war camp with some joy, even for a little while."

No doubt, whatever joy would be gone after another night of fighting, but everyone would welcome the reprieve.

"I'll see what I can do and bring something tomorrow," Luck promised. "Is there anything that you guys want? Something just for you."

"Do you have any funny stories?" Óskar asked, rolling onto his stomach.

"I could tell you about Aron having to get his sea legs on our first raiding ship."

Óskar perked up, his eyes lighting up like a child getting a present. "Yes—perfect. Do tell."

Luck hesitated with a wince. "On second thought, based on your reaction, Aron may kill me if I told you."

I DIDN'T KNOW up from down. I didn't know left from right.

All I knew were the daggers in my hands, the rasp of my

breath in my throat, and the never-ending tide of Skolli in front of me.

The moon hung high in the sky, painting the battlefield in harsh shadow as I swung at the next monster, my muscles screaming.

Our healers welcomed the bandages Sofie had given us. Their supplies had already severely diminished after only two nights of fighting. And based on the number of warriors already fallen tonight, those supplies would be gone before sunrise.

I sliced across the throat of a Skolli before spinning on my heel. I pushed off a Skolli falling with an arrow in its eye and launched myself at the next one.

The twang of Óskar's bow beside me was almost completely drowned out by the din of battle. Screams of pain, cries of rage, and screeches of the Skolli combined to create an all-consuming cacophony of sound.

My arms were already tiring, soreness pooling in my joints as it had the previous two nights. But this was earlier than before, a sure sign that the fighting was taking a toll on my body.

"Jarl Brynja," one of the young messengers screamed from where they were somewhat safely tucked behind the first line of warriors.

"What?" I didn't mean to snap or to be rude, but with hundreds of Skolli in front of me, dwindling daggers in my sheaths, and a collection of bruises and cuts forming on my body, I didn't have the luxury of providing them with my undivided attention. Especially when I was also trying to lead our defence.

"Gier says that we need to divide some of the stronger teams amongst both sides instead of keeping them together."

I threw a dagger at an approaching Skolli, and it sank to the hilt in its throat. "Tell him that he can do as he sees fit. I'll handle the placements of the warriors on my side."

The messenger didn't respond, no doubt already carefully weaving her way back across the battlefield toward Gier.

A scream sounded to my left. A sound that was becoming more and more familiar as the third night of attacks wore on.

But this one was close. Too close.

Risking a glance, I found one of our front-line fighters down, one of the young hands already trying to push through the crowd to pull the wounded warrior to the healers. The warrior that had been by his side fell to the ground, cut in half by the Skolli, as another one lost her head.

With them down, it left a hole in the heart of our front line.

The Skolli were already pushing, trying to take advantage of our weaknesses. They charged forward, threatening to widen the gap through the sheer mass of their bodies.

If they got through the front line, past the defence and to the war camp behind us, the wounded and the healers wouldn't stand a chance.

And then it would be a clear shot to Wolfmire's walls and every man, woman, and child behind them.

"Fill the gap!" I roared, my voice beginning to crack from overuse. "Fill the gap!"

The warriors were trying, but it was taking time.

Time that we don't have.

Óskar and I moved in unison, fighting down the line. We had to reach them. If I could get there, I could shift and hold off the Skolli long enough for the warriors behind to reform their defence.

Or, at least, I thought I could.

I had to. It was our best chance.

"I'll hold the line," I yelled when Óskar and I finally reached the buckling section of the line. "You need to reform the defence behind us."

I risked a look behind me to see the state of the warriors in the area and if I would need to call for reinforcements. Some warriors were pushing from behind us, no doubt coming to support the efforts.

A heavy thud landed on my back, knocking me to the ground.

My whole body smarted as the breath left my lungs in a rush. The Skolli slashed down at me, its claws raking across my arm. Hissing, I rolled to my back, allowing the familiar burning to spread through my legs. Allowed it to pool in my fingers and my mouth.

I lifted both of my feet, putting every ounce of the shifted Skolli strength into them, and landed a kick to the monster's chest.

It stumbled back several paces, giving me a second to scramble to my feet. I winced at the movement but ignored the pain throbbing in my body. Ignored the blood running down my arm. I was still off-balance, my weight on my back foot instead of balanced evenly between them, when it charged at me again.

Not ready to defend.

I twisted my body, preparing for the blow. I could take it. I just had to last long enough to recover my balance or for Óskar to get a good shot.

But the blow never came—instead, I got covered in a spray of blood.

I turned back to see Fannar pulling his axe from the corpse.

"What are you doing here?" I asked above the din of the battle as I shifted so that Óskar was once again near me.

229

"Too much of the core line on this side has been wounded," Fannar grunted as he beheaded another Skolli. "Hákon sent some of my line over here. I volunteered."

We had made it through the first two nights relatively unscathed, but it appeared as though our luck had run out.

"I told you we would be fighting together," Fannar panted.

I grinned; my mouth full of fangs. "Watch how it's done."

CHAPTER

THIRTY-TWO

GIL

We had pushed the horses hard throughout the day, desperate to reach Wolfmire before it got too dark to travel safely. Every hour that passed tightened the knots in my stomach further. They were all very capable warriors, but a wall could only stand against a tsunami for so long before it crumbled.

And I knew that if things were dire, Bryn and the others would be the very last to run away. If they even considered the possibility.

We had to reach them before they had to consider whether to die fighting or abandon the city and live.

But we hadn't made it and were forced to camp for the night.

My fingers shook as I cared for my horse, fully aware of what another night might mean for the others. What our absence might have already meant for them.

This made three nights away from them. Three nights of not knowing what they were facing but expecting the worst.

Every fibre in my being screamed for me to climb back on my horse and ride until I reached them. Until I reached Bryn. But I would be useless to them if I showed up alone. I wouldn't make any difference by myself.

And as much as I knew the other Verndari were feeling the same way, and the four of us would not be enough to turn the tide without the warriors that rode at our backs.

They just had to hold on.

They had to hold on until we got there.

Bryn had promised me she would fight like hell until I got to her, and I had to believe that was what she was doing. I had to believe that she was still able to fight.

Georg finished talking to our guide and made his way over to Aron and me with a grim look.

"How close are we?" I asked Georg.

"We're not," Georg said grimly. Aron cursed. "We might make it towards the end of tomorrow night, but we likely won't make it until the night after that."

Aron paled. "Two more nights after this one? Georg, three nights was asking a lot of them with the warriors they have, but *five?*" He let out a breath. "I just got my brother back, and now—" he cut himself off with a shake of his head. "*Fuck.*"

"I know. It's bad, and they will be in a rough spot. But they are smart. They can get through this."

"They are also stubborn. And Bryn will throw herself in front of a blade if it meant that someone else would not be hurt," I said, equally proud of who she was and frustrated that she thought so little of her own life on a battlefield. Like when she threw herself from the fortress walls to keep a Skolli from breaching them. "Óskar is the same."

Georg sighed, running a hand over his bald head. "I know. *I know.* But they knew we would come for them as soon as we learned we were the diversion. They just need to last until we get there."

"But that's two days, Georg. Can you honestly tell me that they can last two days?" Aron demanded, frustrated as I was with the situation.

He was silent for a moment. "I hope they can."

Even Georg was down to hope, not logic, not strategy, regarding the odds of their survival.

"They will fight. They have to," I said, swallowing thickly.

I grabbed some of my rations before slipping into the tent I shared with Rúna. Without Bryn and Óskar, it made the most sense for us to share. Rúna was already in there, sitting cross-legged on her bedroll, her rations untouched by her side.

I shut the tent flap behind me before settling on my bed roll facing her. I forced myself to eat even though the meat felt like a weight in the base of my stomach. I mechanically made my way through the rations, ignoring how they tasted like ash in my mouth. There was no worse feeling for a warrior than knowing your comrades, your loved ones, were fighting for their lives, and you weren't there to help them.

"You need to eat," I said quietly.

"I'm not hungry."

Rúna was always hungry, always up for a snack or a meal, eating way more than she should be able to for a person the size she was. But when she was anxious or stressed? It was a struggle to get her to have a single bite.

"They will keep fighting until they have absolutely nothing left to give," I told her softly, the words just as much for me as they were for her. "We will make it in time."

Rúna broke a piece of cheese off, holding it in her fingers. "Is this my fault?"

Her question caught me off guard.

"How could this be your fault, Ru?" I asked softly.

"I've spent all that time with Baldur, but there hasn't been a single instance of proof that he's the traitor. He acts differently away from the fortress—nicer, interested in healing, a strong warrior. He's the first to volunteer to look for Sigrún when she throws a temper tantrum and disappears. In the fortress, he's a mean and vicious person who does anything he can to insult the Royal Regiment and avoids the healing centre like a plague." She paused, gathering her thoughts. "It makes no sense, but it doesn't prove he's the traitor. If I had proof, could we have stopped him? Could we have prevented this from happening?"

She had voiced her frustrations about him in Fairguard, but the self-imposed guilt had taken root in her. Whether it was guilt talking or frustrations, it was clear that she was trying to sort out the riot of thoughts coursing through her head.

I knew exactly how she felt. I experienced it every time the darkness gained control over me, regardless of how often Bryn and Rúna told me it was not my fault.

Once that guilt sinks its teeth into you, it is hard to free yourself from it.

"Not a single person blames you for this because you have done nothing wrong. You have been doing everything you can in an impossible situation. Even if we knew who the traitor was, this attack still could have happened."

Rúna shut her eyes. "I'm so tired, Gil," she admitted, her lip trembling.

My chest tightened to the point of pain as I set my rations aside and pulled her into my arms, her tears wetting my shirt. "I know," I swallowed. "I told you yesterday that when we return, you no longer need put up the charade. We will find a different way."

Rúna pulled back, a sad smile on her face. "I don't have a choice," she admitted. "We might as well try to use it to our advantage."

THIRTY-THREE

BRYN

My body was one large ache; bruises littered my skin, pockets of blue, green, and purple to show every hit I had taken the night before. Hákon had to stop healing our bumps and bruises last night to ensure he had enough in reserve for tonight.

The fourth night.

And likely our last.

The Skolli had almost overrun us last night, the front line buckling multiple times. We have been able to reform every time it happens, but each one took more and more effort.

The healers we brought were nearly spent, their bloodrite reserved for only the most serious injuries. Stitches and our rapidly evaporating medical supplies were the most we could do for everyone else. Which left some warriors still recovering today and unable to fight.

I stood in the command tent with Óskar by my side. Hákon stood across the table from us with Gier by his side. Lúdvík and Fannar were there; Fannar had stepped up into a leadership role on our side of the road.

236

Óskar finished reading the healer's report with a curse and passed it to me. I scanned it quickly. It was even worse than I had thought.

We wouldn't have enough warriors to get us through the night.

I swallowed, placing the report on the table and looking at the others.

"Still no word from Georg?" I asked, my voice soft.

"None," Gier said. "But the odds of a messenger getting to us through the Skolli is slim."

I nodded, having already known what his response would be, but I needed to ask it regardless.

"We don't have enough warriors," Gier continued bluntly. "Based on what we have faced the last few nights, we do not have enough healthy warriors to make it through tonight."

"You're right," Hákon braced his hands on the table, a beard gracing his face as though the effort of shaving was too much. "We have the trainees. They will bolster our numbers."

"To die," Óskar said bitterly. "You put them on that line with us, and they will die."

Fannar cleared his throat. "They wanted to fight the first night and every day since. They know what they are facing and have been begging to join the defence."

"It will be their choice," Hákon said. "But I will emphasize our desperation. Every minute we hold the line is another minute for forces to reach us."

I momentarily shut my eyes, accepting what awaited us in a few hours. "Send a healer to the gates. Have them ask for Sofie or Luck. They may be able to help us to at least get the wounded behind the gates."

To help save at least some of the lives we had brought with us.

"I will," Hákon agreed. "I will send someone as soon as we are done."

"Thank you." I straightened my shoulders. "We can't let on that this is the end. That we don't have any hope. We need the warriors to believe we will make it like we have any other night."

"I will go out and start preparations. I have a better time hiding my emotions than you all do," Gier said as he made his way to the exit. He paused. "It has been a pleasure."

Then he disappeared into the camp beyond to ready the troops one last time.

"I'll follow his lead, Hersir. It's been an honour to fight alongside you," Lúdvík said, holding a bandaged hand out to Hákon. Hákon's throat bobbed as he clasped his hand.

"The honour has been mine," Hákon disagreed. "I will meet you on the line one last time, my friend."

Lúdvík hugged me tightly, causing tears to escape my eyes before he did the same to Fannar. He whispered something to him, causing Fannar's eyes to well with tears. Lúdvík clapped Óskar on the shoulders, scratched Yugar's ears and left the tent without hesitation.

It was silent for a moment, but I knew what I had to do. Gier may have been the primary leader on his side of the road, but I was the commander of mine.

And I had to go out and rally my troops one last time.

I walked around the table and wrapped Hákon in a tight hug. "Thank you for everything you have done for me and my family," I whispered.

"I would do it all over again," he said as his gloved hands gently squeezed me.

"So would I."

I turned to Yugar next, dropping to my knees before him.

He tucked his head into my chest in a canine hug. I gave him one last scratch and kiss on his snout before I stood. I jumped into Óskar's arms, and he spun me gently in a circle. I gave a wet laugh.

"I'm sorry it's ending like this," Óskar said. "But I'm still happy that you were found, Talon, and if I am going to die, then I am happy that it will be by your side."

Tears slipped down my face. "As much tragedy as my family faced in the last few months, you and the other Verndari were a light spot in the darkness. And I am so happy that I got to be your partner, even if it was for a short time." I took a shuddering breath. "But you cannot die with me today. You need to save your bloodrite and use it when it has all gone to shit to get out, Óskar. Take Yugar and find the others. They need to know what has happened to mount their own attack."

"You can't ask that of me, Bryn." Óskar's voice broke.

"I have to. They have to know."

"She's right," Hákon agreed. "And you are the only one who stands a chance of getting to them."

Óskar shut his eyes as though what was being asked of him was too much to bear. I knew it would have broken me. He finally sighed and pressed a kiss to my temple. "Fine. But I will fight with you until the very last moment."

I nodded before turning to Fannar, my face crumpling as my tears fell steadily.

"I didn't want this for us," I admitted.

Fannar brushed the tears from my face with his thumbs. "The moment those Skolli attacked our village, this would always be ahead of us. Because there was no way I would have my sister fighting on the front lines without me."

"But you just found your family, Fannar, and you won't have any time with them."

"You are my family, Bryn. My sister from the day you were born. And I cannot think of a person I would rather spend my last moments with."

I wrapped my arms tightly around him, tucking my head into his shoulder and balling my hands in his shirt. "I love you," I whispered. My brother. My family.

I stepped back after a moment. "Together?" I asked weakly.

A tear dropped from his eyes. "Together," he agreed. "As it should be."

I didn't want to die. I wanted to live, spend time with my family and friends, and fall deeper in love with Gil. I hadn't even realized I loved him, truly loved him, until I knew that I wouldn't see him again. That I wouldn't hold him again or kiss him again.

That I wouldn't get to say goodbye.

And that I wouldn't get to tell him that I loved him.

But if I had to, then I wanted to die doing something that would have made my Da proud. He had died to save his family, and now I would die to try to save a whole city full of families. And while every fibre of my being wanted to send Fannar to safety, to protect him from what lay ahead of us tonight, there was some sick, twisted comfort in knowing that I would have my brother by my side.

We had faced life side by side; we would embrace death together, too.

I took a deep breath and went to the washstand in the corner, washing away every trace of my heartbreak and sorrow from my face. Wiping my skin dry with Gil's handkerchief, I hid my emotions until no one could see my heart-shattering in my chest.

I took a deep breath and turned to Hákon. "I will go to the

gates with the healer to ensure that the wounded are granted shelter."

"Thank you," Hákon said with a nod.

I ducked out of the tent and went to our crude healing centre. The ground around the tent was stained red, as though the blood of the wounded could no longer be contained within the tent walls. I ducked my head inside to find Tyl, the chief healer behind Hákon, preparing his supplies.

We had a few hours before night fell, but it didn't feel like enough time to prepare.

"Tyl, I need you to come with me," I told him.

"Healing?"

"No." My tongue darted out to wet my lips. "We have another job that we have to do."

It didn't take us long to reach the gates. Once again, they opened as we approached. Proof that we were still being watched. Still being judged.

Too bad that we would receive the verdict too late.

Luck was the first one to reach us. "Gods, Bryn." His eyes darted across my face. "Are you okay?"

"It's all superficial," I reassured him, although the words felt hollow in my chest. "I'm just sore."

Sofie reached us next, throwing her arms around my shoulders. "We watched last night, Luck and I. And so many people from the city that the walls couldn't hold anymore. I was so scared that you weren't going to make it."

"We made it through last night," I said, my voice emotionless. Luck and Sofie immediately narrowed their eyes but had nothing else to say as Jarl Einar approached us.

I bowed my head to him in respect. "Jarl Einar."

"Jarl Brynja. What brings you into my city?"

"I have come to ask you to allow the wounded refuge in the

city. Most of our healers will go with them so that it does not burden your resources."

Jarl Einar was quiet for a moment. "Just the wounded."

"Yes. The rest of us have a job to do outside the gates." I gestured to Tyl. "Tyl will help coordinate the move if you accept."

Jarl Einar studied me closely for a moment. "I accept."

A young kid ran from the crowd, a basket in his hands. He grinned at me, showing his missing baby teeth and the adult teeth growing in their place. "My Ma made this for you, Jarl Brynja!"

I knelt down to be at eye level with the little boy. "Thank you. What did she make?"

"She made stew! Da always loves to have stew before he goes out on the ships. And there's enough that you can share it with your friends!"

I took the basket from him, ruffled his hair and gently nudged him back to the crowd. Once he was gone, I stared at the basket in my hands.

"Did you know that stew was the last meal that I ate with my Da before the Skolli killed him?" I asked no one in particular. "I think I will enjoy sharing it one last time with my friends."

Sofie gasped as Luck cursed.

"You do not expect to make it through the night," Jarl Einar said, careful to keep his voice quiet so it didn't carry.

"No, we do not. I'm sure that you've been watching each night, Jarl Einar. You know how many of our warriors have been injured or killed. Tonight, we will hold the line one last time."

"You could have fled during the day. Put as much distance between the Skolli and your forces as you could."

I adjusted the basket in my hands. They were a bit raw from the hilts of my daggers. "We have orders to hold the line. But it's not just that. Look behind you, Jarl Einar. We are standing between the Skolli and that little boy. All the children, the families, and the people of your city. We would not have abandoned them."

Einar said nothing, his eyes fixed on my face and then to the gates behind me.

I turned to Luck and Sofie. "Thank you. For everything. Tell them I love them whenever you see the others, okay?"

Sofie sniffled. "Of course we will."

"Fight, Bryn," Luck urged. "You don't know for sure that it's the end."

"I will fight until the very end," I promised. "Now, if you all will excuse me, I have a stew to eat with my friends before dusk falls."

The gates shut behind me as I returned to the war camp. I did a lap to ensure that all of the warriors were in the midst of preparations before doing my own. I buckled on my armour, still stained with Skolli blood from the night before, as I had lost the energy to clean my armour the previous day. I sharpened my daggers before sliding them into their sheathes. I filled my waterskin and threw my saddlebags over my shoulder with the last healing supplies.

I dropped the supplies off at the healing centre before heading towards my place at the front of the lines. The lines would slowly fill over the next hour as everyone finished their preparations.

Óskar and Fannar were already there when I joined them. We settled on the battle-torn ground and passed the cask of stew between us until it was gone and the sun had started to set. We threw the basket and cask as far as we could in front of us, leaving it to be trampled by the monsters.

The Skolli came at us as soon as the sun had fully set, a rolling black tide of talons and claws. Some had taken to the skies but were easy prey for our archers.

I pulled two daggers and sunk into my crouch with a wince. Taking one last moment to look at Óskar and Fannar before refocusing my attention on the Skolli.

We fought through the night but began to falter when the moon hung high in the sky.

Warriors fell with a scream, and there were fewer to take their place.

"Fall back!" I bellowed above the noise of battle. "Fall back to the walls!"

We gradually made our way backwards, putting the walls at our backs.

Our final stand.

The Skolli continued to charge, ripping tent poles from the ground, shredding the covers with their claws, and crushing them beneath their feet. I could practically smell the fear of the warriors behind me. I had to give them something to rally behind.

I sheathed my daggers and stepped forward.

Fannar and Óskar were just a step behind me. Hákon and Gier doing the same thing on the other side.

I allowed the burning to consume my body more than ever before. My feet. My legs. My arms. My hands. My teeth.

I stood tall with my Skolli legs, my reach longer with my Skolli arms. My feet, hands, and teeth my weapons.

People shouted behind the walls, Jarl Einar's warriors preparing for the moment we began to fall. When the Skolli would be at the doors to the city and they would be called upon to defend it. Wood scrapped against the gate, no doubt reinforcing the main entry to Wolfmire.

A horn blew behind the walls, and the gates slammed open. Jarl Einar led his forces out, and they effortlessly filled and bolstered our ranks. Luck and Jarl Einar joined us as I unleashed myself on the Skolli, a new hope blooming in my chest.

Maybe we would survive this after all.

We fought hard, even managing to push the Skolli back a few metres with the renewed energy from the Wolfmire forces.

As the sun rose, the Skolli retreated, and we still stood there.

Alive.

I had reverted to my normal state part way through the night and had been forced to finish the night fighting in bare feet that were now cut to shreds and bloody. But I barely felt the pain as I laughed in amazement and surprise.

We were alive.

I turned towards Luck and wrapped him in a hug. "Thank you."

"I fight with you," Luck said, squeezing me.

"I would have it no other way," I said with a grin. "I know you briefly met Fannar, but did you know he is Aron's brother?" I gestured to Fannar. Luck stared at me with wide eyes before hurrying towards Fannar, no doubt knowing what finding his brother meant to Aron.

Óskar carried me inside the gates, where Hákon met us a few moments later to heal my feet. He may be able to let bruises slide, but if he left my feet, I wouldn't be able to fight the next night, and even with the forces from Wolfmire, we couldn't afford to lose me on the battlefield.

Luck and Fannar joined us, cut and bruised, but nothing serious.

Hákon had just left when Jarl Einar walked up to me.

"Thank you for joining us," I said.

"We would have been food for the crows if you hadn't," Óskar added.

"You chose to fight for my city and my people even though you didn't stand a chance," Jarl Einar said. "You had orders, but you fought like it was more than just that."

Fannar stepped forward. "I've had my village destroyed and the people slaughtered by Skolli. We would do everything we could to stop that from happening here."

Jarl Einar cocked his head as he studied Fannar. "You look familiar."

"That is Fannar," I said as I stood with a wince. "My adoptive brother and Aron's blood brother. He is the lost son of the Spirit Sword of Greythorn."

Jarl Einar nodded and refocused his attention on me. "You've not only won the respect of my warriors and healers but also that of my city. You were right. I watched all of you every night, and you fought with everything you had." He paused before holding out his hand. "You have my respect and my blade. I hereby pledge my forces and whatever else I can provide you."

I clasped his hand. "Thank you. Drysden stands a better chance with you."

"That it does," he agreed. "But I want to be very clear. My forces and supplies are yours. Not the King Commander's, not the Royal Regiment's, but *yours*. You're the one that has earned it."

"I understand."

Gier, Hákon, and Lúdvík joined us. They were all more battered than they had been earlier, but they were all still alive.

"Well, with all your forces here, I think we can change some of our strategies, don't you think?" I asked Jarl Einar.

He nodded, observing us. Hákon and Gier. Lúdvík and Fannar. Óskar and I.

The warriors that had held the line for days without support. The warriors that had protected his city and his people from the Skolli.

"Seems like we have some strategizing to do before night falls," Jarl Einar agreed with a small smile.

Gier grinned. "This will be fun."

THIRTY-FOUR

GIL

I t was the first night that we rode through the darkness. We would make it tonight—I would be back with Bryn before sunrise. She just had to last that long.

Two days had never felt longer.

We had just finished the final stream crossing between Fairguard and Wolfmire and were charging towards the city. My horse was surging below me, carefully paced throughout the day to ensure it had enough energy for this final desperate push towards the town. Or whatever was left of it.

They had to still be fighting. *They had to.*

Rúna rode beside me with Georg and Aron ahead. The warriors behind us were in an endless line, the hoofbeats a thunder around us.

My breath was ragged in my chest, my heartbeat pounding. We were finally close. We could finally make a difference.

A distant scream reached us. Followed by another.

The battlefield.

"Push!" Georg yelled as he tried to urge any remaining speed out of his horse.

I did the same. The sounds of battle grew around us. The clash of blades, the thundering of Skolli legs and wings. The screams of warriors.

We finally reached a hill to the side of Wolfmire and could see the battlefield.

"Oh, holy gods," Rúna gasped by my side as we stopped to survey the ground ahead of us.

Multiple large fires lit the sides of the battlefield, along with several fires on the walls. The ground before the walls was churned and scored, stained with blood. Piles upon piles of Skolli were spread throughout, with countless bodies throughout the grounds. The remains of a war camp were destroyed, and tents crushed. And in front of the walls a desperate fight between the warriors holding the line and the never-ending tide of monsters.

Georg held me back from joining the fight. "Not yet."

"What do you mean *not yet*? They have been holding off that force for five days, and you want to sit here?" I growled.

"We need to evaluate what's going on down there. Assess the situation, find out where the key players are, and launch our attack."

"Can you see them?" Aron asked.

Rúna leaned forward in her seat, pointing. "Hákon and Lúdvík are leading the far side!"

"Jarl Einar and Gier are leading the near side," Aron said.

"Where are Bryn and Óskar?" I demanded. They should have been the easiest to spot since they were supposed to lead the defence. Had something happened? Were they hurt? Were they—

"Óskar's on the walls leading the archers," Georg said, cutting off the spiral my thoughts had taken. "He and Bryn must have split up."

My eyes searched the fighters on the front line again. Why would they have split up? She would be at risk if she was alone. My focus snagged at the centre of the line where the fighting was thickest as they defended the gates—the one weak spot on the wall.

There she was. Slightly ahead of the rest of the front line, Fannar and Luck flanking her, she led the heart of the defence.

"Bryn is in the centre with Fannar and Luck. She is leading the core of the defence," I said, my words filled with pride even as worry had taken root in my throat.

That's my girl.

I couldn't tell if she was injured. We were too far away to see anything in any detail, but the fact that she was still holding the line was enough to bring me to my knees.

Bryn was still alive and still fighting like hell.

"We'll need to leave the horses here. They don't have the agility we need against the Skolli," Georg said before turning towards the warriors around us. "Dismount!" he yelled. "Phalanx formation!" Everyone scrambled into position behind us so that we resembled an arrowhead. "Don't stop moving until you reach our own forces!"

I drew my swords, my eyes still fixed on Bryn.

I was here—I just had to reach her.

"Attack!" Georg bellowed, his voice easily carrying around us.

I charged towards the Skolli, spinning my swords once before we slammed into the side of their offensive. We caught them by surprise, easily cutting down the first couple of monsters before they realized they were now being attacked on two sides.

I didn't pay attention to the warriors around me, only

ensuring I kept track of Rúna beside me. Georg and Aron would look after each other.

Rúna's whip cracked over my head, the flickering light of her bloodrite lighting the battlefield even further. The sizzling smell of fried flesh filled my nose as she struck the Skolli down.

We kept moving, slashing and stabbing as we fought towards the centre of the line where the fighting was the thickest. Not only was that where we would be most useful, but it was also where Bryn was. And Rúna knew just how desperately I wanted to reach her side.

"Push!" Bryn yelled, her voice soothing me to my very bones. It boomed and cracked from use, but the sound of it still nearly brought me to my knees. "They're buckling! Push!"

"Let her know we are here, Rúna," I panted as I took down another Skolli and gained another few feet towards Bryn. "They will not be able to see us."

"On it," Rúna said as the light on her whip grew. "Watch my back." She snapped her whip into the air three times, the light easily coiling fifteen or twenty feet high like a beacon.

Óskar whooped on the walls. "We've got friendlies! Pick your shots carefully!"

"Push!" Bryn yelled again. "We've got support! This is our chance!"

I kept pushing, Rúna right by my side. Finally, I broke through the front line of monsters.

And there she was. Taller than she normally was, her legs those of a Skolli.

She was bruised, her eye black, and her lip split. She had a cut somewhere on her head, spilling blood over half her face. But she was alive.

She was okay.

Bryn's eyes widened; a second later, her dagger was whizzing by my ear and sinking into a Skolli behind me.

"Boy, are we happy to see you," she told us, her voice cracking from days of battle. She pointed to the left, towards Luck. "Join the line."

We quickly took our spots, seamlessly folding into the defensive setup that Bryn, Fannar, and Luck had organized.

With our forces united, we could get through the night easily, even pushing the Skolli back further and further as we could mount attack after attack.

The last Skolli fled as the sun began to rise.

THIRTY-FIVE

BRYN

They had made it.

Gil and the others had reached us before it was too late. I had lost them in the chaos of the fight, but they were here.

I stepped forward with a wince, my legs long since returned to my own. My ankle screamed as I had rolled it in the last minutes of the battle. It must have done more damage than I thought it had.

Fannar stepped forward, draping my arm around his shoulders and his hand bracketing my waist. Luck joined him on my other side, mirroring his movements.

"You don't have to do this," I told them as we slowly entered the city. They could easily take my weight as I kept my left leg from touching the ground.

"I saw your wince, Bryn, and that ankle is probably about double the size it should be," Fannar said.

"Not to mention that you burst through your shoes again, and your other foot is probably all cut up," Luck added.

I smiled. "Thank you. It does help." I looked at them both a little closer. "The two of you could use a trip to a healer."

Fannar snorted. "You need one too."

"Unless the blood on your face was intentional? Then I think you would need to speak to someone else," Luck joked.

I snorted. The blood was definitely unintentional.

Georg and Aron stood just inside the gates, talking to Óskar. I studied them all for injuries and was relieved to see nothing to be concerned about. Aron's eyes brightened at the sight of us.

He quickly made his way over. "Brother," he said, relieved. "Are you alright?"

"Nothing that can't be healed," Fannar reassured him.

Aron nodded before turning to us. "I just need to be healed and get a few hours of sleep, and then I'll be right as rain," I said.

Fannar snorted. "I don't think either of us will be right as rain for a little while, but we'll survive."

"I'm in much better shape than these two. I'm fine," Luck said, brushing away Aron's concern. "I'm happy to see that you made it."

We had just reached Georg and Óskar, Georg ruffling my knotted hair in greeting, when Gil appeared in front of the gates.

"Gil," I whispered, viciously blinking away the tears in my eyes at the sight of him. I tried to run to him, ignoring the pain in my ankle. I only made it a few steps before nearly falling, biting my lip to keep my pained cry inside. Fannar and Luck were back by my side instantly as Gil rushed towards me.

As soon as he was close enough, I flung myself into his arms, my own wrapping around his shoulders. I tucked my face into the crook of his neck. He reeked of sweat and blood, but beneath that all he smelled like Gil.

He smelled like home.

His arms wrapped around me gently as though he wasn't sure where was safe to touch. His hand tangled in the curls on the back of my head as he pressed a kiss to my temple. "Bryn," he whispered, his lips moving against my skin. "Darling."

"You made it." My voice broke.

"I made it. I am here now." His breath danced across my face.

Suddenly, Sofie was there, pulling me away from Gil to study my injuries. "They told me that you were the worst out of them. Anything outside of the usual besides the head and ankle?"

"Outside of the usual?" Gil asked me, but I ignored him to answer Sofie's question.

"No, I think those are the only things you need to focus on besides what you did last night."

I leaned against Gil's chest as she rested her hands on my arms, her healing bloodrite flowing into me, pink lightning flickering under my skin. Gil's hands rested on my waist, his thumbs rubbing small circles against me. I let my eyes fall closed while she worked and struggled to blink them open again when she was done.

"The ankle is healed, but it would be best to keep weight off it for the next hour," Sofie told me before starting towards the others. "Go get some sleep. Your body needs it."

"Thank you," I told her as Gil scooped me into his arms. I pointed him toward the room I had been given near the gates. It was a basic tavern room with a bed big enough for two people, a washstand, and a standard clothes chest, but very little else.

Gil sat me on the bed and began peeling my armour off me. "The usual?" he asked, echoing his words from earlier.

"Sofie has started doing a scan of all of us, healing any deep bruises and cuts." I didn't mention that she had only been allowed to heal us after Einar had joined our forces the night before. "The bruises that are more surface level have to stay. She also healed my hands and feet."

He set aside my armour and pulled my shirt over my head. "Gods, Bryn." My body was a patchwork of different coloured bruises in various stages of healing. Some red lines marred my skin from where the slashes I had taken from Skolli claws were still healing.

"I'm okay," I told him, cupping his cheek in my hand, my thumb brushing over his cheekbone.

"This is not okay," he said, gesturing to my body.

"I'm alive," I corrected myself. "And I will heal and be okay."

Gil swallowed, quickly helping me undress the rest of the way and wiped the dried blood, dirt, and sweat from me with a damp cloth. He pulled one of his shirts over my head for me to sleep in before quickly removing his armour. I shuffled back in the bed, pulling the furs over myself as he wiped his skin clean before joining me.

We lay on our sides facing each other, our fingers intertwined. I leaned forward to press a kiss to his lips. He eagerly responded, his fingers tangling in my hair.

But he didn't once try to turn it into more.

No doubt thinking of every single bruise he just saw on my body, every cut, and the pain and soreness that would be associated with them.

Gil finally broke the kiss and pressed his forehead to mine. "How close was it?" he finally asked.

How close was it to the Skolli breaking our lines?

How close was it to them being too late?

How close was it to us dying?

"Too close," I whispered, recalling those moments in the command tent when we knew it was the end. How it felt on the battlefield when Fannar and I stepped forward, prepared to fight until we were struck down. A tear slipped from my eye. Gil immediately brushed it away, his hand lingering, its warmth sinking into my skin. "It was too close."

He swallowed. "Will you tell me about it? About what you faced and how you got through it?"

"I will," I promised. "But later, once I've had some sleep."

Gil nodded. "Is there anything I can do?"

"Can you lay here with me?" My voice broke. "Can you just lay here with me and hold me?"

"Of course, darling." He gently shifted us so that he laid on his back, with my head pillowed on his chest and his arms wrapped around me. I lifted a leg to drape over his, wanting to be as close as possible to him.

His fingers began tracing mindless shapes over my back as usual.

"I never thought I would get to do this again," I confided in a whisper.

His fingers froze, and his body tensed at my words. At what I had admitted in them.

A hint at just how bad it had been.

"I am here, Bryn," Gil finally said, his words rumbling in his chest under my ear. "And we can do this every night if you wish."

∼

I awoke around midday, stretching with a wince. I tentatively rolled my ankle, but no pain lingered.

Gil was still asleep, so I carefully eased out of bed to ensure I didn't wake him.

I did a lap of the walls. The warriors all knew me by name now. They called out greetings, shared jokes or bites of their food. Some looked at me as though I were untouchable, as though I was above them, but I tried to ignore that. Wanted to show them that I was a warrior just like them.

I grabbed a warm bun from one of the mess stations and entered our command room. Hákon and Gier were already there, bleary-eyed but in good spirits regardless.

"Morning," I said, taking my usual spot at the head of the table. "Have you two been waiting long?"

"No." Hákon shook his head. "Jarl Einar and Luck are up too. They just went to find something to eat. I'm sure the others won't be long."

As if he summoned them, Óskar, Fannar, and Lúdvík entered with steaming tankards in their hands. Yugar slumped onto his bed as soon as he could, no doubt desperate for more sleep, much like Óskar, who slumped in his chair as though he was still half asleep.

"Did you let the others know about our meeting?" I asked him quietly as he passed me one of his tankards.

He didn't have to answer as the other Verndari filled the room, followed by Jarl Einar and Luck, each carrying two platters of steaming buns.

It was only then that I realized there weren't enough seats. I sat at the head of the table with Óskar at the foot. Hákon, Lúdvík, and Fannar sat on one side, with Gier, Luck, and Jarl Einar on the other.

I stood from my chair and made my way towards Georg. He stood between Gil and Aron with a steaming bun in his hand. "Would you like my spot?"

He looked past me to the table for a moment before returning his attention to me. "No, Bryn, you earned that seat. The eight of you around the table have led the defence for five days and done a fine job. We are here to help you, not take over."

I swallowed with a nod. Gil stepped forward to kiss my forehead before I returned to my seat.

Georg, Gil, Aron, and Rúna stood around the table. They didn't have seats but could see everything and participate in the conversations just fine.

"Alright, let's get started," I said, my voice filled with confidence. "The other Verndari arrived and brought fresh warriors and healers. How do we best use them?"

"We intermix them into the lines and push some of the more tired warriors towards the back to give them some respite," Gier suggested.

"Divide the pairings of Verndari between the two sides, but don't change the command structure." Luck leaned forward in his seat. "The warriors don't just fight for you because they have to. They respect you."

Georg cleared his throat. "I agree. I just have one question. How are you determining the warriors that will move to the back?"

"The warriors that have fought for longer will be moved back," I said, my eyes scanning the lists of warriors to determine who to shuffle.

"How is that decided?" Aron asked. "Wouldn't that be the same for everyone if you don't consider any injuries?"

I grimaced as Luck shifted uncomfortably in his seat before he answered. "Their forces have held the lines for five nights. Ours have not. Sofie and I, as well as some of the others, did whatever we could, but we were bound by orders."

"How many nights did they hold it alone?" Rúna's voice was shocked. Gil's wide eyes landed on me, his eyes once again scanning the injuries that I had, that he knew were hidden beneath my clothes. Realizing the true brunt that I had borne, that we had carried.

"Three and a half."

Gil's fists clenched. "They would not have survived."

"No, we wouldn't have," Hákon agreed, running a gloved hand down his cheek. "By the fourth night, we knew we weren't walking away."

"And when did your forces join, Jarl Einar?" Gil's words were threaded with anger.

"When Bryn and Fannar stepped out in front of the line part way through the fourth night to make their final stand," Jarl Einar said, causing Gil to practically vibrate with anger. But his eyes weren't angry when they locked on mine. They were heartbroken.

I sighed. This wasn't the time to get into this.

"We know how we are going to approach tonight. But how are they able to keep a sustained attack like this?" I asked, diverting the conversation down another path. From the look in Gil's eyes, he knew exactly what I was doing.

"My men have a theory on that," Jarl Einar said. "The caves."

Luck nodded. "That makes sense. There are caves all around us and in the mountains. It would provide them with shelter from the sun during the day. The question is, which ones?"

"We don't know."

"Then we find out. Tonight. When the fighting is done, we send our best trackers after the Skolli as we flee," I lean back in my seat, crossing my arms over my chest. "When we know where they go, we strike them when they're at their weakest."

THIRTY-SIX

BRYN

W e were finally able to gain some ground that night.

We were no longer back on our heels, waiting for the Skolli to rush us. We finally had the numbers to take the fight to them. To launch a counterattack alongside our defence. No longer victims of circumstance but active players in the battle unfolding before us. We had planned like we had every other night—defence first and offence second. But when the moon finally rose, and the Skolli attacked, I quickly realized we could do much more than hold our ground.

We could push.

We could regain the ground that the Skolli had taken from us. The ground that the warriors, that *we*, had bled for. That some had died for.

I signalled the warriors around me and sent the call down the line. *Advance.*

"Warriors with me!" I yelled, Luck and Fannar echoing my orders. A similar cry rose from the sides. From Hákon and

Lúdvík. From Jarl Einar and Gier. Supported by the other Verndari.

Time to push.

I took the first step, Luck and Fannar flanking me with every pace. With every Skolli that went down, with every slash of our blades, we advanced a step.

Over crushed tents from the nights before, over the deeply scarred earth of the battleground, we continued to advance.

Never halting, never stopping, we continued to push.

No longer retreating, no longer folding.

Our forward progress paused at various times throughout the night but never regressed. We kept moving forward until the sun began to brighten the horizon.

Jarl Einar's best scouts, specifically chosen for this job, followed the fleeing Skolli, hopefully able to track the monsters to whatever cave they hid in during the day.

Cheers rippled down the lines, weapons thrust in the air, heads thrown back in laughter. I grinned, my own shoulders shaking with silent, relieved chuckles. The stinging of my cuts, the aches of my bruises, fading in the rush of elation coursing through me.

Fannar slung an arm over my shoulder, grinning. "You know that night was just as long, but it felt so much shorter when we were in control than when we fell back with our tail between our legs."

"I don't think I would have described any of you as having your tail between your legs," Luck chimed in, his voice husky from the battle. "Out of options? Yes. Desperate? More than likely. But cowed? Never."

The spirits were higher amongst the warriors as they chatted and joked with each other and made their way back into Wolfmire for the day. Two days ago, you could practically feel the fear rolling off of them in waves, and now they laughed with a lightness in their eyes.

A renewed hope that we would get through this.

I walked through the lines, clasping hands with the warriors. I shared laughs, exchanged compliments, and clapped people on the back. Fannar and Luck stayed by my side as we made our way through, helping people we passed to the healers and congratulating everyone we passed on an incredible night.

But for every person I stopped to talk to, three more stopped us. The grins on their faces were a welcome change to the grief and fear they had shown every other night. Their jokes replaced their screams of pain, their cries of anguish.

We should have been the first people to reach Wolfmire as we were stationed in the centre of the line, but Georg and Rúna had beaten us and stood just inside the gates. They were dirty and sweaty from the fight, but neither seemed noticeably injured. I eased out from under Fannar's arm and approached the pair with a wave.

"The scouts got away without any problems," I told Georg in case he hadn't had a chance to see it for himself.

Georg nodded. "Very good." He studied me for a long moment, making me fight the urge to squirm.

"What?" I asked, unable to withstand his inspection any longer.

"You've done well here, Bryn," he praised me with a soft smile. He nodded behind me towards the gates. "The warriors don't just respect your orders. They respect you. To earn that in just a few days is a testament to you."

I shrugged, not sure what to say. "We just did what we could."

"And showed them that you were willing to sacrifice yourself for them too." I winced at Rúna's words. "Yes, we caught that in the meeting this morning."

I groaned. "Great. It's not like we had any other options."

"But you were still there. Still fighting at the very front of the lines. The warriors see that and remember that, Bryn," Georg said. "The warriors I passed by when we were done were happy, and if they were on my path, they said something. But they didn't seek me out. They didn't joke and laugh with me like with you three. They are happy to follow you, Óskar and the others. They are *proud* to."

"I tried to do what I thought you would," I admitted quietly. "And if I'm being honest? I was terrified that we wouldn't be enough to get them through this. That we would fail them."

Georg ran a hand over his bald head. "That may be the case, but you left the fortress a warrior and stand before me a commander."

"What are your orders?" Rúna asked me with a grin.

I rolled my eyes. "We don't give each other orders. Not when it's just us. We're a team."

"That we are," Georg agreed with a nod. "There is nothing we can do until the scouts arrive."

We had the numbers to survive another push from the Skolli; I knew that without waiting for the healers' reports. But they could drag their attacks on for days if we didn't end it. And the scouts were our best bet at doing so.

"So now we wait," I agreed with a sigh.

GIL and I had collapsed into my bed, our bed now, exhausted from the fight. The sun was still high in the sky when we rose for the day. I pulled on my clothes with a wince, regretting my decision to go to sleep before seeing a healer. Sofie was no doubt waiting for me with a lecture.

I made my way to command with Gil by my side. Gier was already there, the door open to observe the gate from the room.

"I'm pretty sure he doesn't sleep at all," I whispered to Gil before taking a seat.

Gil chuckled as Hákon and Sofie entered, her hands already on her hips and ready to lay into me.

"You know better," she scolded me, her hands already landing on my skin, her healing bloodrite flowing into my body. "You need to be healed before you go to bed."

"There was nothing that couldn't be healed when I woke."

She smacked me on the shoulder before continuing her work.

Óskar, Fannar, and Luck entered, their heads bent together in laughter as Yugar trotted happily by their side.

"Open the gate!" A guard yelled out from atop the walls. I reached a hand towards my daggers. They wouldn't open the gate if there was a threat, but my nerves were shot from constant battle.

One of the scouts rode through, her short hair messy from the ride.

"We found them," the scout panted as she slid off her horse. A young boy ran up to her with a waterskin while another brought water for her horse.

I rose from my seat quickly, Gil by my side. The others quickly joined us.

I turned towards a group of children that often lingered near us in the city, excited by us and desperate to be helpful in the defence of their home. "Please get Jarl Einar and the other Verndari."

They scampered away with grins on their faces.

"You found them?" I repeated. The scout nodded. "And you can lead us back there?" I confirmed.

She grinned. "Absolutely, Jarl Brynja."

"Then let's end this," I said before turning towards Lúdvík, who had just joined us. "Round up the troops."

Lúdvík was already in motion. "On it, Lassie."

Within thirty minutes, fifty of the most trusted Royal Regiment warriors were gathered before us. Georg, Aron, and Rúna had arrived within moments of being summoned. Young girls ran amongst the gathered horses, tying torches to the saddles. I stood before everyone with Óskar beside me and the other Verndari mounted on their horses. Jarl Einar joined us and stood to the side of the gathered warriors.

"You have all fought valiantly," I said. "You have held this line for six nights and not allowed a single Skolli to breach the walls of Wolfmire."

Cheers went up from the gathered city folk as the warriors pounded their fists over their armoured chests.

"A bunch of warriors too stubborn to die." Óskar's words earned a laugh even as I rolled my eyes.

"We now know where the Skolli are hiding, and we will bring the fight to them. We will end this now," I said, cheers ringing again through the area. "Mount up."

As the warriors prepared to leave, Óskar and I approached Jarl Einar. "You need to stay here and lead the defence in case we are wrong," I told him, Luck pouting by his side. He knew that if Jarl Einar was staying, that meant he had to. We couldn't deplete the city of all of its warriors—it was too much of a risk.

"I understand," Jarl Einar nodded.

"We are leaving most of the Royal Regiment and healers here to support your forces."

Óskar's smile was as sharp as a razor blade. "Maybe make sure your forces help them this time, yeah?"

We didn't bother waiting for his response as we approached our horses. We mounted up and took our spot at the head of the train, directly behind the scout.

"Let's go," I told the scout. She led the way out of the gates with us just behind her. Once we were past the uneven battle-field, we kneed our mounts into a faster pace.

The scout led us through twisting game trails hidden amongst budding trees and into the mountains. The ground became steeper, the pathways narrowing. We had to slow down to keep the horses safe.

Eventually, the rocky pathway stopped at the opening of a cave.

"They're in there," the scout said quietly as she kept us a safe distance away from the mouth of the cave.

We dismounted, and Gil, Aron, and Georg immediately began to go to the cave to study the entrance. I joined them.

"Looks like the ground slopes down," Aron whispered from where he knelt just inside the cave entrance. "Just as we hoped."

The ground sloping down meant the Skolli would be below us, making burning them out much easier and safer.

"Time to light them up," I agreed quietly with a nod and signalled Rúna and Óskar. They started to weave through the warriors, and the sound of flint and steel filled the silence.

Eventually, each person held two lit torches and formed a rough line at the cave entrance.

One by one, they threw their torches down into the cave. The fire streamed through the air as they threw the torches into the darkness. A dim glow started inside the cave, growing with each torch that joined it.

Then we heard it. A sound, quiet, muffled by layers of rock.

Then another and another until the screams of Skolli rang throughout the area around us, and the smell of burning flesh filled the air. The fire burned its way through the monsters trapped inside their rocky tomb.

CHAPTER

THIRTY-SEVEN

BRYN

We stayed the night by the caves to ensure the Skolli had been killed. The first moments as dusk fell were the tensest, each minute feeling like an hour as we waited for the monsters to emerge. But nothing stirred as dusk settled into true night. The moon hung high in the sky as people began to relax. A strict guard rotation was stationed at the entrance to the cave. Still, the warriors not on duty breathed easier as the night continued.

By the time the sun began to rise in the east, the warriors cheered. Not a single Skolli had crawled out of the caves during the night.

It was over.

I laughed, my chest lighter than it had been in days. I turned to find Óskar by my side, the bright happiness in his eyes distracting me from the dark circles that had taken root under them. The same dark circles that I knew I had.

I threw myself at him, wrapping my arms around his neck. He spun me in a circle, his laugh joining mine.

"We did it," I grinned. "We made it."

"We made it," he agreed, finally putting me back on my feet.

He nodded behind me, and I turned to find the other Verndari. There was a softness in Gil's eyes as he watched us, and a proud smile on Georg's face. Aron nodded, grinning as Rúna stepped forward and hugged us both.

Georg turned to Óskar. "I have already told Bryn, but you did well here." Óskar eyes widened in surprise as Georg continued. "From everything I have heard, the battle would have been lost without you. It should have been lost even *with* you." He swallowed thickly. "But the fact that you stand in front of me, that Wolfmire wasn't sacked by the Skolli, is a testament to you. To both of you."

Óskar's fingers shook as he ran a hand over his head. He was always scared that he wouldn't be enough in a fight, that his bloodrite wouldn't be enough in a fight. To hear such praise from Georg was sure to warm him to his very core.

"Thank you," he finally said. "Does that mean I get an exemption from hand-to-hand sparring for a while as a reward?"

Georg laughed as he rested a hand on Óskar's shoulder and led us back to the horses. "We'll see."

I settled between Rúna and Aron, having been told that we didn't need to maintain our formation back to Wolfmire. I hadn't had a chance to spend much time with them since they reached us. Aron had immediately sought out Fannar and Luck to reassure himself that they were okay and Rúna had been withdrawn. Gil had suggested that I didn't push her, let her open up to me in her own time, and that he was on it. He was her rock until she was ready to open up to all of us and rely on us.

"I think my body has moulded myself around this saddle at this point," Aron grumbled.

"Is it better or worse than getting your sea legs?" I asked as we started heading back.

Aron studied me closely. "Did Luck tell you that story?"

"No, he seemed to be under the impression that you would hurt him if he did." Aron nodded, relieved, but tensed as I smirked. "He told us enough, though."

"Us?"

I focused my attention on the trail ahead of us. "Óskar, Fannar and I."

"Great," Aron groaned. "Just what I wanted, to be embarrassed in front of my little brother."

I smiled softly. "You should have seen Fannar's face as Luck shared what he did. He was excited to learn anything about his brother."

"Really?"

I nodded, my chest warming at the pure joy lighting Aron's eyes. "Yes, really." I was quiet for a moment. "He's always been my big brother, but I think he will enjoy having one now as well."

"I haven't been a brother for a long time. What if I mess it up?" Aron asked me, confiding his fears to me.

"You'll mess it up at times. Fannar and I fight sometimes— we did it the morning after the Skolli attacked our village when we were scared and grieving," I told him, Aron listening to me with wide eyes. "But you'll fix it. The bond between siblings is built to endure things like that. And honestly, now that he knows about you, I doubt Fannar will ever let you go. You're going to be stuck with him, with our family."

He smiled again, relief coating his features. "I'm okay with that."

Rúna was mostly silent during the majority of the ride. She occasionally chimed in with a joke or sly remark but mainly focused on the path before her.

"Are you okay?" I asked as we approached the gates to Wolfmire. I had been waiting for her to say something but worried she wouldn't.

"I think I've failed," she admitted, drawing both mine and Aron's attention. "I'm out of time."

I swallowed, understanding where her thoughts had taken her. "You haven't found any proof that Baldur is the traitor."

"Nothing." Rúna shook her head furiously. "And you know as well as I do that it is only a matter of time before he makes his move. Especially after this attack."

We dismounted and passed our horses to one of the many children who came forward to care for them. Hákon approached us with a grin, his gloved hands tucked into his pockets. "I see that you were successful."

A boy rode through the gates, his clothes dishevelled. He ran a hand over his close-cropped hair, and a cloud of dust flew from his hair. He strode directly up to Hákon and handed him a letter.

Gier jogged over to join us. "What does Ragna want?"

"I haven't opened it yet." Hákon paused and turned his attention from the letter to Gier. "How do you know it's from Ragna?"

"He is one of the people we've been training for the team." For the Striking Shadows.

Hákon slid his finger across the parchment, breaking the seal and unravelling it. He scanned the letter, his eyebrows scrunching.

"Did Baldur leave?" Rúna asked, clearly expecting Baldur to have left for the barrier just like Pétur had.

And we weren't there to stop him.

"No. Sigrún did."

I blinked once. Twice.

"What did you say?" Rúna's voice cracked. She shook her head as if to clear the thoughts from it. Gil stepped up close to her side to offer her comfort. "Baldur should have been the one to leave. He's cruel, and he's constantly working against us. Sigrún is quiet and—"

"Withdrawn. She has isolated herself from her family as a result of the arranged marriage she is being forced into," Gier said bluntly.

"You mentioned that she's disappeared before," I said softly, putting together the pieces Gier had laid out. "That Baldur has had to track her down."

Aron stepped forward. "But Sigrún and Pétur? Did they ever even speak to each other?"

"They did. We saw them together before Pétur left," Óskar told them all. "The way they looked at each other—I thought there may have been something between them, but I didn't think too much of it."

"Can we beat her to the barrier?" Georg asked before turning towards the messenger. "How long ago did you leave?"

The messenger didn't get a chance to answer as a loud crack rang out, echoing through the city and beyond. It bounced off the mountains, off the towers and walls before carrying on to the world beyond Wolfmire. I clapped my hands over my ears as what looked like a wall of sound barrelled towards us. It picked up dust as it travelled, shaking window shutters and sending parchments flying. It slammed into us, knocking me off my feet. I crashed into Hákon's side, sending us both careening into the side of a building. Aron and Óskar fell to the ground, one on top of the other, as Gil tried to keep himself and Rúna upright.

Hákon groaned beside me as I pushed away from him, my already bruised body smarting at the movement. He watched me wide-eyed as I rolled my shoulders and neck, making sure that nothing was injured in the crash.

Hákon swallowed. "Are you okay?"

"I think so," I assured him, hissing as I stretched out my arms. "I think it's just soreness, but I should really be asking you that question. I think you took the brunt of that."

"I know I'm fine," he said carefully, putting some distance between us, his eyes still carefully studying me.

I approached Aron and Óskar, pushing themselves into a seated position with a litany of curses. Aron had a cut on his temple, blood dripping down his skin. Hákon beat me to his side, his gloved hands already reaching out to heal him. I went up to Óskar instead and helped him to his feet. I couldn't see any noticeable injuries.

"I hit my knee on the pathway," Óskar cursed. "That fucking hurt." I knelt before him, ignoring my muscles' soreness, and reached for him. He swore as I pressed on his knee, but luckily, there wasn't anything to be too concerned about.

"I'll get you some bruise paste, but it's not broken," I told him.

Luck ran up to us, his eyes wild. Fannar wasn't far behind him, cradling his arm to his chest. Gil reached him before I could, hesitating momentarily before he gently laid his hands on his arm. Óskar and I slowly began to make our way over to them.

"Did you see where Georg ended up?" I asked him. I had lost sight of him when the shockwave hit.

"I'm right here," Georg grunted, joining us. "I went crashing through a doorway."

We reached Fannar, then. His shirt sleeve was torn, and the skin below it was deeply cut. Gil had already ripped the bottom of his own shirt off and pressed it to the cut to slow the bleeding.

"I need my supplies, or he needs a healer," I said. "It's probably better if he sees a healer."

Sofie rushed by me to Fannar and pushed Gil's hand out of the way. She laid her hands on Fannar's arm, the pink lightning of her bloodrite coursing under his skin. "Are any of the others hurt?" She asked, her eyes fixed on the cut slowly knitting itself together. Fannar was focused on Sofie, on the hair that had escaped her bun and the shoulder where her shirt had slipped down her arm from the force of the shockwave.

"Just bumps and bruises besides Fannar and Aron," I told her, drawing Fannar's attention. His eyes were wide as he craned to try and find Aron without dislodging Sofie's hands from him. "He'll be fine. It was just a cut, and Hákon is already healing him," I reassured him, allowing him to relax.

"What in the name of the gods was that?" Luck panted as he dragged a hand through his hair. "I've never seen anything like that. It was like a wave of air."

Georg sighed. "I'm not entirely sure. It reminded me of a shockwave or a backlash, but I don't know what would have caused something like that. Not to mention that awful sound that rang out before it."

That sound was the loudest thing I had ever heard, louder than the chaos of battle, louder than the bells at the fortress that we used to alert us to an attack.

My stomach rolled. "It was almost like it was a warning—an alarm."

"For what?" Luck asked, his brows furrowed.

"Sigrún left the fortress," Gil muttered under his breath, the colour draining from his face.

I wet my lips. "The shockwave was like something collapsed. Like it was torn down."

"*Fuck*," Rúna cursed, following the path of my thoughts.

"She reached the barrier," Georg said with a wince. "And the noise was the alarm that it had been taken down, the shockwave the backlash from its release."

Óskar let out a humourless chuckle. "I guess that answers your question from earlier, Georg. No, we aren't able to beat her to the barrier."

THIRTY-EIGHT

BRYN

L uck's family home was tucked on the bottom floor of one of the many towering buildings in Wolfmire. It had large windows, each with its own flower box and the scent of herbs throughout the space. Luck and Aron wrapped his mother, a short, older lady with grey hair and a slightly hunched back, in a warm hug.

The barrier was down. Sigrún was the traitor. But there was nothing we could do about it at this moment. We had thought we were going to die just a few nights before; we still bore cuts and bruises from days of battle. A moment to regroup, recharge, and relax was exactly what we needed before we had to face a barrier-less world.

Luck's mother led us into the home. The furniture felt a little big for the space, and the items were a little cluttered, but it was a warm, welcoming area. It was a lived-in home filled with love.

Aron wrapped an arm around Fannar's shoulders and led him to the woman. "This is my brother, Fannar."

"Blade brother or blood brother?" she asked as she set a tray of tea and cookies on the small table.

"Blood brother," Aron grinned.

She smiled softly. "I'm happy for you, my boy. Let's sit, and you can tell me all about yourself, Fannar."

They took a seat on one side of the room. Aron was just as enthralled with what Fannar was saying as Luck's mother was. As desperate to learn about his brother, just like I knew he felt about Aron. Gier and Georg settled at the kitchen table, Gier's familiar game board spread out in front of them.

Hákon pulled me to the side as the others settled on a pair of benches. "Are you okay?"

"I think I'm as okay as you are," I joked, knowing he had to be as sore and tired as I was.

"No—I meant—," he sighed before continuing. "Did you touch me when that shockwave went through?"

I stared blankly at him. "Hákon, I *crashed* into you. Of course, I touched you."

"Did you touch my skin?" He gestured to his neck and face with a gloved hand.

I thought back before shaking my head. "No."

His shoulders relaxed. "Good."

Hákon led the way towards the others, sitting on the arm of the bench that Óskar and Rúna shared. Luck and Gil shared the other, but instead of sitting on the arm of the bench, I slid into Gil's lap. He paused for a moment before wrapping an arm around me and pulling me back into his chest. Gil's hand rested on my waist, warming my skin through my clothes.

"Keep those hands where I can see them," Óskar teased as he leaned forward to run a hand down Yugar's side. Gil chuckled, the movement carrying into my back. "I don't know what's so funny about it. You're outnumbered by her brothers in this room with Fannar and I both here."

"Did I hear my name?" Fannar tore his attention from his conversation.

"I was just informing Gil that he should make sure that he keeps everything appropriate with both of her brothers in the room."

Fannar looked over at Gil and me and shook his head fondly, a smile on his face. "Oh yes, I agree."

"You forgot to include me. She has three brothers here," Aron added.

Rúna tilted her head. "How do you figure?"

"We're related," he said, gesturing between himself and Fannar. "And they are related." He pointed to Fannar and I. "So that makes her and I siblings as a result." His finger drifted between him and me, finishing the air triangle he had drawn between the three of us.

"I'm not quite sure that's how that works, but let's go with it," Rúna said as Luck's laugh rang through the room.

"I wish you luck, Gil." Luck patted his shoulder. "I think you are going to need it."

Gil's thumb brushed circles on me. "I think I have it under control. I know what I am doing."

"He does," I nodded in agreement.

"That's my girl," Rúna smirked as Óskar narrowed his eyes.

"I don't know if there is a double meaning behind your words, but I think I am happier without a confirmation," he said.

Gil pressed a kiss to my temple, his lips lingering. "I would like the confirmation." His voice was gravelly as his lips moved against my skin.

I twisted and pressed my lips to his briefly. "Later," I promised.

GIL LED the way into my room—our room—and I shut the door behind us. Gil shrugged out of his cloak and tossed it in the vague direction of his saddlebags. I followed his lead as Gil strode towards me. He placed his hands against the door on either side of my head.

"Was it as close as they said?" he asked me, his eyes darting between mine. Was I as close to dying as everyone had been saying? I had told him that first night, but to hear from everyone else how Fannar and I had stepped forward to die fighting side by side had to have made it quite clear just how dire things had been.

I shut my eyes for a moment before re-opening them. "Yes. But I was going to fight until the very end."

He pressed his lips to mine before resting his forehead against me. "I was worried we would not make it in time, but then you were there. Right in the centre of the line. You were bloody and bruised, but gods, were you magnificent, darling."

I kissed him. It was slow, but his control snapped when I wrapped my arms around his neck and pulled him closer to me. His body was flush with mine, pressing my spine against the wooden door.

"Do you know what nearly made me break that day before I took my spot in the line?" I asked him breathlessly. Gil shook his head, his green eyes locked with mine. "That I wouldn't have the chance to tell you that I love you before I died."

Gil's lips pressed to mine, a new sense of urgency behind

them. He pulled back just far enough to speak. "I love you too," he said quietly.

I giggled. "I didn't say it yet!"

"Close enough," he rasped. "You can tell me again later." His lips pressed to mine again; his mouth as familiar as my own.

My hands drifted down his body, then back up under his shirt. My fingers slid across his skin, following the dips and ridges of his muscles. Gil groaned, pressing even closer to me.

I gripped the bottom of his shirt and pulled it over his head, tossing it to the side. He returned the favour, my shirt quickly joining his on the floor.

Gil paused, his eyes snagging on each bruise I knew marred my skin. I pressed a kiss to the corner of his mouth. To his jaw. Down his throat as my fingers worked at his pants, pushing them down his legs. He stepped out, kicking them to the side. His hands found my cheeks, bringing my lips back to his.

His hands drifted down my body and under my legs, easily lifting me. I wrapped them around his waist as he pressed me back into the door.

"This isn't a post, but it'll do," I teased.

Gil huffed a laugh. "As much as I would love to, I am not about to fuck you against a door when those bruises serve to remind me just how sore you must be."

"I'm sure this will make me feel better," I told him before kissing him.

Gil pulled us away from the door and gently laid me on the bed a moment later. "I am going to save the door for a day when you are not covered in bruises."

He pulled my pants from my legs before his eyes drifted from the top of my head to my toes and back again.

Slowly.

He leaned forward and pressed a kiss to my black eye. Before he pressed a kiss to the one on my arm and the one on my ribs.

Gil's lips found every single bruise on my body and traced every red line before tracing them back up my body.

I pulled him down between my legs, too desperate, too excited for his drawn-out actions.

"Later," I muttered against his lips. "I need you now."

"I had a plan."

"You can do it later."

He huffed, a smile on his face. "As you wish." Gil pressed forward, pausing when we were flush against each other. "Better?" His voice was gravelly.

"Yes, but it would be even better if you moved," I said, rocking my hips and causing him to groan.

He moved slowly, carefully.

Too slow. Too careful.

I caught his ear between my teeth at the same moment I matched his thrust with my own. Causing his control to stutter.

Then snap.

He pounded into me, his hands, lips, and teeth everywhere. Adding some much more pleasurable bruises and marks to my collection. And I was adding my own to his body as I clutched at his back with my nails. No doubt scratching his skin and marking it.

My toes began to curl, pleasure tightening in my body until it finally broke. It flooded my body as Gil's name spilled from my lips. A few moments later, Gil stilled, his lips against my neck, brushing against my skin as he said my name over and over. Like a prayer—or a reminder. That I was there. That I was okay.

283

We shifted to lay facing each other, our hands and legs intertwined. A comfortable silence covered us like a blanket.

His fingers traced mindless shapes across my skin as I traced constellations across the numerous freckles on his body. Content, safe, for the first time in a week.

Filled with love rather than fear, surrounded by comfort rather than death.

Eventually, Gil propped himself on an elbow and brushed a curl behind my ear. "Can you confirm that I know what I am doing yet?"

I pretended to think for a moment, my finger tracing at his bottom lip. "I'm not sure. You may need to show me again."

Gil rolled onto his back, pulling me on top of him. I giggled; my heart lighter than it had been since we left the fortress.

Sofie hugged me tight, her hair falling out of its neat bun. Her outfit was wrinkled from the long hours she had put in to get the vast majority of our warriors ready for travel.

"Thank you for everything you did," I told her softly.

She scoffed. "You would have done the same thing for me. It's what friends do."

I pulled back to look at her. "I'll see you soon?"

"I'll make sure of it. Jarl Einar won't leave me behind when they head into battle. He'll need me in the healer tents."

I nodded. It seemed that every friend I made, every person I welcomed into my life, had a part to play in the war. Either on the front lines or in the healing tents in the war camps, they were all going to be facing the horrors alongside me.

It was both a comfort and a curse.

And a small, desperately pushed-down part inside of me

wondered how many of us would walk away from those battlefields.

And how many would have their final burning on its outskirts?

"I'll see you soon." I squeezed Sofie's hands and turned to Luck, who stood beside her. He had already said his goodbyes to the others while waiting for me.

He slung an arm over my shoulder and pulled me into a half hug. "You're a hell of a fighter, Bryn."

"Thank you, but I feel like I should point out that you can hold your own on the battlefield."

Luck released me with a shrug. "I had to show I could fight at a Verndari's side. Not just with you, but side by side."

"You did just that," I told him with a smile.

The last person waiting to say goodbye was Jarl Einar. Even though he had since pledged his support to me, I was still hesitant about him. He had still sent us out to die defending *his* city. I knew he had come out to aid us and kept our slaughter from happening. But the very fact he made us hold the line for *days* on our own in some sick test twisted my stomach.

He played a part in the death of every warrior who had given their lives protecting *his* city. *His* people. And I don't know if there is anything he could do to make me forget that fact.

"Jarl Einar," I said, barely tipping my head in respect.

"Jarl Brynja," he echoed, mirroring my motions. "We will be ready to move when you are."

"Good." I mounted my horse. "I'm sure that it will be sooner rather than later. Make sure you're prepared, and then get to the fortress. I have no doubt that I will be calling on you shortly."

Gil stepped forward. "None of this gods' damned last-moment bullshit either. You will be ready when she calls."

"I would watch how you speak to your comrade, boy," Einar said with raised eyebrows as Gil turned his back on him and mounted his horse.

"I yelled at you for simply being rude to him. You sent me out to die. I would say that his reaction is much tamer than mine would have been," I pointed out. "I'll be in touch."

Gil and I settled into our usual places at the head of the train of warriors and healers. When Georg and Aron finally led us out of the city, I reached to the side and gently squeezed Óskar's fingers.

And as we crossed the still blood-stained ground that we had held for days, he returned it.

We had faced death here and had accepted our end as we fought side by side.

But it did not win. Death did not get to claim us.

And I reminded myself of that fact as we started towards the fortress as we went to receive our first set of orders with the barrier dissolved.

We beat death once. We could do it again, no matter how bleak the outlook may be.

THIRTY-NINE

LEIFUR

I lingered at the edges of the room, watching my parents closely. They had divided the parchments and letters that the girl, Sígrún, had brought with her. The information would land on my desk shortly and be ready for my review. I needed to evaluate every decision that the new King Commander had made, where military players would be stationed, who his staunch supporters were, and who were sure to be the most prominent players on the battlefield.

It would only be a matter of time before the new King Commander would account for the fact that Sígrún would have knowledge of his plans and change them. But perhaps he wouldn't understand how much she knew; the girl had said her father overlooked her. Even if he adjusted his plans, it would take time to correct them all, and my parents would want me to take advantage of that.

Pétur had his insights when he arrived, his ranking of warriors, and his ideas about what would happen next. But enough time had passed that those would not be as useful to my parents' objectives as the information that Sígrún had brought.

She stood off to the side with my sister, her eyes darting from my parents to me and back to my sister before beginning the routine again. I could barely remember the fortress in Goldhelm; the centuries since I had seen it turned my memories to the briefest images. But I remember the light, the windows allowing sunlight to pour into the various rooms. And by the way that Sígrún's eyes caught on the heavily shadowed corners of the rooms she was noticing the total absence of it here. Not a single window existed, all of them long since filled to protect the Skolli and Ógn from the danger of the sun's rays.

Footsteps pounded in the hallway, growing ever closer to the room, gaining the girl's attention. The doors burst open to reveal Pétur, his eyes searching the room before landing on Sígrún.

She flew towards him, crashing into him with enough force to rock him back a step before his arms wrapped around her, holding her close to himself. His mouth was close to her ear as he whispered words that I couldn't hear.

They eventually separated, their fingers intertwining as they approached the thrones. It was only as they stood before the intimidating presence of my parents that I realized just how young Sígrún was. Easily hurt by her family's actions, easily enraptured by her love for Pétur, easily manipulated by my family.

Her naivety revealed itself as she seemed to realize exactly where she was and who sat before her.

Pétur sank into a deep bow before the thrones, urging Sígrún to do the same. He quickly learned the respect my parents demanded and what would happen if it wasn't shown to them.

"Pétur," Father acknowledged his attention still on the parchment he was reading. "Nice of you to finally join us." Pétur didn't move, holding his bow.

"I came as soon as I could, King Commander," Pétur said, his voice muffled by the stones beneath his feet.

Father finally looked up. "You may rise." Pétur stood from his bow. "Your girl did well. Not only has she freed us, but she has also provided us with some important information."

"I told you that she would not fail you."

Pétur had indeed told him that, had offered his neck to the executioner's axe to provide assurances that Sígrún would be able to accomplish her task. It may not have been as fast as my parents wanted, but it was done.

Had bet his own life on the fact when my parents were getting annoyed at how long it was taking.

"So, you did," Katrín practically purred as she studied her nails. "I am looking forward to having her with us."

Pétur swallowed, turning his attention back to my father. "How can we serve you now, King Commander?"

"You will wait until we are ready to send you in the field. It is still too early for us to assign you a task outside of our walls," Father said, already reaching for another parchment. "You are dismissed. Ludvík, Katrín, I have a job for you."

Pétur quickly led Sígrún from the room as my sister and I took their places before the thrones.

I HADN'T REALIZED that there was a heaviness to the air of our mountain fortress. Our mountain prison.

I hadn't realized that it was there until it was gone. It was easier to breathe, to move, to talk.

The barrier was gone. The bars to our prison were removed.

I walked through the fortress, my boots clicking on the stone floors. It was eery how empty this fortress was for how big it was. But if my parents had their way, it wouldn't remain empty for long. They planned to have it filled with their supporters and their warriors. Soon.

But until then, there were just the five of us: my parents, my sister, Pétur and I. Well, six now when I included the girl. Sigrún—the one that destroyed the barrier.

The one that was responsible for our freedom, for the ability for us to re-enter Drysden. The one that was putting my parents' plans in motion.

I pushed open the massive wooden doors and stepped out into the courtyard. Pétur and Sigrún sat together to one side, their heads bent together in conversation. The arm he had draped over her shoulders held her close as she tilted her head back into the sunshine.

Just as starved for the heat and light as I had been when we were locked away. Snow, wind, heat—it didn't matter. I had sat out in the courtyard on that bench and tried to soak in every drop of sunlight I could. As though if I absorbed enough, I would be able to carry it with me into the dark halls of the fortress. Eventually, I stopped visiting my bench in the court-yard, resigned to the life of darkness that lay in front of me. But with Pétur's arrival, hope sparked in me, and I allowed myself to return to the courtyard, my eyes requiring several trips to adjust to the brightness after years in the dark.

I strode across the courtyard, the places closest to the fortress meticulously maintained. My sister had developed a rather surprising green thumb, completely contrary to her bloodrite, allowing beautiful garden beds to bloom. And with the barrier down and our allies' arrival growing closer, our fortress's appearance mattered. But the closer I got to the barrier, the more overgrown it became; none of us had been willing to risk getting too close to it to impress our allies. When my parents had servants, willing or stolen, cleaning the fortress until it shone was sure to be at the top of their list.

I wondered how long it would take before the hallways were full of people, allies and servants. If my parents were to have their way, I was sure that it would be sooner rather than later.

As much as I had resented the barrier for keeping me locked away, I hadn't been able to bring myself to step beyond it since it had come crashing down. With it gone, I realized it had become a comfort in some sick way. And I had no idea what to expect of the Drysden that lay beyond it. We had been locked away for centuries, and I couldn't even picture how it might have changed.

There would certainly be new settlements. Had some of the villages that I had known blossomed into towns? Had the towns I loved visiting grown into cities and military hotspots?

My friends had long since passed. Would I recognize them in their descendants? That was if their lines hadn't been eliminated during the war.

I wasn't ready to face the changed world beyond the bars of my prison.

But I had no choice.

With the barrier down, our freedom regained, and our hand exposed to the outside world, my parents knew they couldn't hesitate. They had to start making moves before the new King Commander and his forces could respond to the barrier being broken.

They had to gather their supporters. They had to collect money, weapons, and supplies.

And then they would go to war.

"Are you ready?" Katrín asked as she trotted down the front steps and joined me. She was dressed for riding and travel like I was, her full saddlebags slung over her shoulder. We had no horses to ride; the ones that Pétur and Sígrún arrived on were forbidden from leaving the fortress. A last resort for my parents to escape should the enemy be foolish enough to attack them head-on.

"Ready," I told her, holding up a roll of parchment for a moment before tucking it carefully into my pocket. "I've got the list right here."

Our steps were synchronized as we strode towards the tall stones that were the marker of where the barrier had stood.

"Is the plan the same?" she asked.

"Yes. We will go to the nearest village and get a pair of horses. Then we will go to each person on this list to ensure we can count on them for support."

"And if they don't agree?"

I focused on the marker stones, now only a handful of feet away. A step away. "Then we will have to make them," I said.

Her grin was positively wicked.

Then I stepped over the line and into Drysden for the first time in centuries. Free.

ACKNOWLEDGMENTS

While writing a book can be intimidating, writing a sequel is its own beast. Daggers of Darkness was a challenge, a privilege, and a joy to write. I cannot thank the people that helped me shape it into the story it is today enough.

Samantha from Ravens Wing Editing Services has ensured that Daggers of Darkness is everything that I hoped for. Thank you for your encouragement and support—the reactions and feedback that you shared with me has made my story shine.

My incredible map maker, Rachael from Cartographybird, transported Drysden from my mind to the page with the most breathtaking map.

I may have squealed a little when I first saw the phenomenal cover that the team at MiblArt designed. It is a joy to work with you and it brings me so much excitement whenever I see your drawings of Bryn.

To my family, friends, and my dog (who was the inspiration for Yugar), thank you for your endless support and encouragement. Hearing your theories of the next books, or your reactions as you read, brings me so much joy.

And thank you, dear reader, for continuing to read Bryn's story. I hope that you have been enjoying her journey as much as I have enjoyed writing it. I cannot wait to share the next book with you.

ABOUT THE AUTHOR

Aspen Sherwood is a self-published author from Southwestern Ontario who loves all things fantasy and romance. As a 20-something herself, she loves writing about 20 year olds who are exploring their worlds and discovering themselves just like she is. When Aspen is not writing she can be found cheering on the Toronto Maple Leafs or the Toronto Blue Jays.

Follow Aspen Sherwood on TikTok (@aspen.sherwood), Instagram (@aspensherwood) on Facebook (Aspen Sherwood), or by joining her email list on her website (www.aspensherwood.com).